The
CURSE
of the
RAVENS

REBECCA LISLE

Also by Rebecca Lisle

The Curse of the Toads

Acknowledgements

With thanks to Jason Bennett, Sam Harvey, Karen Jarvis, Jenni Mills, Pam Moolman and Anthea Nicholson – fellow students on the MA Creative Writing course, Bath Spa University, 2005/6.

ISBN 978 0 340 89448 4

Typeset in Goudy Old Style by Avon DataSet Ltd,
Bidford-on-Avon, Warwickshire

Printed in the UK by CPI Bookmarque, Croydon, CR0 4TD

The paper and board used in this paperback by Hodder Children's Books
are natural recyclable products made from wood grown in
sustainable forests. The manufacturing processes conform to the
environmental regulations of the country of origin.

Hodder Children's Books
A division of Hachette Children's Books
338 Euston Road
London NW1 3BH

For Angus McLaren

1

September 1682

In the Dead of Night

'Doctor Flyte! No!'

Reuben struck out wildly but instead of the flesh and bone he'd expected, he hit the wooden bedposts. He opened his eyes. He saw the familiar thick, red fabric of his bed-curtains. He wasn't surrounded by menacing tall trees and caught by brambles. He wasn't fighting Flyte. He pulled the curtains aside; there was his bedroom, sliced through with white moonlight. He was home.

He put his hand to his chest where his heart knocked and pounded like galloping hooves. He could hear his blood swooshing through his head like a gale in the treetops.

He slipped from the warm bed and stood, just breathing, savouring the quiet. No Doctor Flyte, he told himself. Flyte was a dream. He smelled beeswax from the scrubbed and polished boards. Much better than the vinegary odour he thought he'd smelled on Flyte. How powerful a dream could be!

Reuben went to the window and knelt on the cushions. He stared out through the diamond-shaped panes of glass. Glory jumped up beside him: moonlight made the tips of her fur golden. Reuben stroked her head.

'No Doctor Flyte,' he whispered.

But every single day, Reuben saw him somewhere. The old chimney pot leaning at a drunken angle was Flyte's tall hat. The shadow cast by the crumbling wall of the cowshed became Flyte's hunched shoulder. Once a maggot-eaten leaf took on the hawk-like profile of the dreaded man. When wooden wheels squeaked as they trundled past the house; when he heard the jangle of brass and leather on a harness; when he smelled the leathery, yeasty smell of the inside of a wagon, then Flyte was close by again.

Outside, the tall elm trees hardly moved. There wasn't a breath of wind.

Flyte's dead and he can't get me. He's lying at the bottom of Cal's Cauldron.

But there *was* something stirring outside. Glory erupted into a volley of shrill barks making Reuben jump. Goosebumps rippled across his skin. 'Shh! Shh!'

Reuben thought he saw something darker than the darkest shadow flit between the trees.

But it couldn't have been Flyte – a fox maybe. Flyte was dead.

Reuben crawled back between the lavender-scented linen sheets. Glory snuggled under his chin. They both slept.

2

Doctor Brittlebank and
Hetty and Wycke House

Up until a few months ago, Reuben had lived with his grandmother, Sarah Mearbeck; but she had been accused of being a witch and hanged. Reuben was thrown out of his home and kidnapped by 'Doctor' Flyte and his accomplice, Baggs. They intended to kill Reuben by throwing him down Cal's Cauldron. But it was Flyte who fell to his death in the deep pit.

Now Reuben lived with his cousin, Doctor Brittlebank.

Reuben was helping the doctor in his study. He had packed dried specimens of fish and frogs into boxes. He'd collected and put in order the doctor's papers about breathing and blood flow. Now he was laying glass phials of coloured liquid in boxes of straw and sawdust for travelling. They were going to pay a visit to Lord and Lady Marley.

'I fear there is a touch of madness in the Marley blood,' Doctor Brittlebank said. He took his spectacles off and polished them on his cravat.

'Madness?'

'Yes. I find madness and excessive quantities of money often go hand in hand . . . Lord Marley owned half a county once and gambled it away. He is squandering his wife's fortune too. Lady Marley is not happy; aristocrats cannot afford to marry for love. I suppose she was attracted by his title.'

'In my village the boys marry the girls because they're pretty or good at milking,' Reuben said, 'and that makes them fall in love, I think.'

'I did love my wife,' Doctor Brittlebank said with a shake of his head. 'She'd had schooling. Her Greek was better than mine. She had an excellent brain. It was the child-bearing that killed her. A woman's lot is hard.'

'My grandmother was clever, too,' Reuben told him. 'She had ideas.'

'So I understand,' said the doctor. 'Did her no good, either,' he added. He picked up a pile of papers and carried them across the room. 'The truth is— Oh, Glory!'

The spaniel was under his feet. The doctor tripped, slipped on the polished floor and banged into the doorframe.

5

'Heavens above! That dog!' He straightened his wig and glasses. 'Get her out of my way! Out!'

Laughing, Reuben scooped the dog up in his arms and ran to the kitchen.

Hetty, the maid, was sitting on a stool at the back door, shelling peas. 'I heard the shouts. What've you done now, Ruby?' she said.

'Nothing. The doctor's all of a tizz, because of our trip.'

Reuben sat down on the stone step. Glory scampered out into the back yard and began worrying the chickens.

'Oh, look at her!' said Hetty. 'That dog of yours is proper larky! We'll have no eggs if she scares those birds. Help me pod these peas, and no eating them. All the food you eat! You got hollow legs, is that it?'

'I hardly eat a thing,' said Reuben. He popped a pea into his mouth.

'Seems to me you do. I'm the one that prepares it all, aren't I? I'm the one that digs the carrots. I make the bread. I churn the butter. I bake the pies . . .'

'I'm sorry, Hetty.'

'And then I have to do it all the way *she* says.' Hetty jabbed her thumb towards the housekeeper's room. 'Her. Mistress Susan.'

After a moment, Reuben peeped up and saw Hetty was smiling again.

'I knew it were a bad idea getting that dog from Cobb Johnson. I said she'd be under my feet and all over the place, piddling and shitting and Lord knows what. And she is.'

'But isn't she sweet, Hetty? Her fur is like silk. She has the longest ears ever. You think she's pretty, don't you? Look at the curly bits on her legs.'

'Well, all I know is, she were the runt of the litter, and acts daft,' Hetty said. 'I suppose she's young yet and needs to find herself, like you.' She nudged Reuben playfully.

'I'm learning. I shall be a doctor like Doctor Brittlebank one day. You'll see.'

Hetty flapped a pea pod across the back of Reuben's hand. 'Not if you don't learn to shell peas without eating them!'

Reuben peeped up at Hetty. Her round face was blocked from his view by her white linen headpiece. Hetty could see what he was up to without looking; the way a mother chicken kept an eye on all her chicks while pecking at the ground.

'Don't you go looking at me like that,' Hetty said. 'I'm a plain, plump thing.'

'I don't think you're plain!'

'I'm twenty-three!' she wailed. 'I'm getting fat and old just sitting and waiting for a man to come and marry me!'

'I'll marry you, Hetty . . .'

'Can't wait *that* long!'

'I'm eleven. That's quite big. We could sit together peeling potatoes and cooking soups. I'd like that, Hetty.'

'Hmm. Dare say you would.' She sounded gruff, but she was grinning. 'Don't suppose no one shall marry me.'

'You shouldn't hide yourself so, then,' said Reuben. 'No one will find you under that big cap and all your aprons and pea pods!'

Hetty blushed and bent her head over the bowl. Her cheeks and forehead were scarred from a bad dose of smallpox. Her teeth were grey; others were missing.

'I'm a sight,' she whispered.

'The best sight,' said Reuben, leaning against her.

'Ah, get away with you . . .'

That afternoon, Cobb Johnson's son, Matt came in his wagon to take them to Lord Marley's estate.

Reuben and the doctor sat opposite each other on the upholstered leather seats behind the driver.

'Take care!' cried Mistress Susan.

'Mind and don't get a chill!' said Hetty, dabbing her eyes. 'Eat plenty.'

Reuben had Glory tucked in beside him. He

laughed as the dog's ears lifted upright in the stream of air. Glory looked like a fox. She barked when she saw a bird, barked when she saw a cow, barked at the wind, the trees – everything.

'She's such a silly little thing sometimes.' Reuben gripped Glory's collar. 'She'd be away if I didn't hold her.'

'My wife, dear departed, had a silly little dog,' said Doctor Brittlebank. 'Called her Mercy. She yapped. She peed on the bed. She growled when I put my arm round her – round my wife, I mean.' He chuckled. 'She loved that horrible little beast.' He lifted his tiny spectacles to wipe his eyes. 'Oh, don't mind me,' cried Doctor Brittlebank, seeing a look of alarm in Reuben's face. 'I'm getting old and sentimental, that's all.'

They reached Marley Hall in the afternoon. They had to stop at the tiny octagonal gatehouse for the gate to be opened. An old man hobbled out to unlatch it. He nodded at them, but did not speak. His boots were worn down and patched; his shirt was dirty. As he swung the gate closed behind them, they heard him hawk loudly and spit.

'Surly fellow!' said Doctor Brittlebank, sitting a little more upright. 'I shall inform Lord Marley.'

As they drove off, Reuben glanced back. An old woman with white hair was staring at them through a tiny open window. He smiled at her, but she didn't return his smile. She stared hard at him with her pebble eyes until he had to look away.

The long drive down to the house was lined with graceful elm trees. On the surrounding slopes, copses of oaks and sweet chestnut trees grew, casting long shadows over the grass. Cows and sheep looked up from their grazing as the wagon rolled by. A woman gathering flowers turned and stared at them.

Marley Hall was a low building made of honey-coloured stone. Reuben gazed at it in awe; so many rooms, so many windows, and chimneys and acres of sloping roof. Lord Marley must be very rich.

Matt Johnson steered the wagon up to the front porch and stopped. They all got down; their feet crunched noisily on the gravel.

Reuben looked more closely at Marley Hall. Weeds grew in cracks in the walls, moss padded the roof and some of the thick glass was cracked or missing from the windows. A broken rake lay in the path. A half-empty tankard of ale had been left on the wall. The lavender bushes beside the front door needed trimming, the roses needed dead-heading.

Reuben pulled his collar up around his ears. This place sent cold shivers trickling down his back.

3

Lord Marley's Odd Ways

Matt and Reuben took the bags from the back of the wagon and set them down on the path. Glory scampered off across the lawn. Doctor Brittlebank stood with his hands on his hips, looking about. 'Well, this is some welcome,' he muttered. He slipped his wig to one side and scratched his head. 'I did expect his Lordship to—'

Dogs barked from somewhere inside the Hall. Glory ran to Reuben and begged to be lifted up.

'Baby,' he whispered at her. 'Little baby.' He gathered her into his arms and stroked her head and ears to comfort her.

The invisible dogs went on barking, but no one appeared.

'Is no one here?' said Doctor Brittlebank, gazing up at the windows. 'I shall knock again.' But before he could reach the brass knocker, a young servant appeared.

'Evening, gentlemen,' he said, grinning. 'The

name's George.' He straightened his green jacket, pulled up his wrinkled stockings and tucked them into his knee-length breeches. 'Sorry to keep you waiting.' He did not look sorry. 'Lord Marley is most particular that everything is in order. This way, this way. Your man can find a drink and bite to eat if he takes himself round to the kitchen – thataway.'

Matt Johnson bid them farewell and disappeared in the direction George pointed.

George led Doctor Brittlebank and Reuben into the house. The hallway was gloomy. A wide wooden staircase led to a gallery above. Reuben heard dogs barking and scratching to get free. The noise grew louder and more frantic.

Reuben squeezed Glory tight.

'Wait here,' George said. 'I'll go and inform his Lordship of your arrival.' He slipped away through a door below the stairs.

Doctor Brittlebank peered round the hallway. 'Fine place, isn't it?'

There was dark wooden panelling. The floor was paved with uneven grey stones and strewn with dirty reeds. Dust, balls of dog hair and leaves nestled in the corners. The clock did not work. The furniture looked greasy and unpolished.

Reuben nodded.

Somewhere a door opened. Claws scratched and

slipped on the floor. The barking sounded closer. Suddenly the door beside them was flung open and two enormous, long-legged greyhounds burst into the hall.

The sleek black dogs bounced towards them, barking. Reuben thought they would attack, but they slithered to a halt, scuffing up the reeds on the floor, and stopped just inches away from them. The dogs growled. Their bodies were a mass of rigid, taut, bulging muscle. Lips curled back over sharp yellow teeth.

Doctor Brittlebank and Reuben backed into a corner. The dogs followed them slowly, each delicate step accompanied by a deep-throated, warning snarl.

Doctor Brittlebank coughed. 'Don't worry, Reuben, they mean no harm . . .'

'Caspar! Portia! Down!' A loud, commanding voice rang out. The dogs stopped growling immediately.

A finely dressed man appeared. He had to be Lord Marley, he was so very grand.

'Caspar! Portia! Down! *Friends!* Down!'

The two dogs stopped growling. They slunk about looking embarrassed. They wagged their whip-like tails and were now so friendly they leaned against Reuben and nearly knocked him over.

'Good dogs,' said Reuben. One greyhound sniffed

at Glory Be and nudged her with its long snout. 'Good dog. It's all right, Glory.'

Lord Marley was an odd-looking man. He was around thirty-five years old, Reuben surmised, with eyes like marbles, unblinking and bulging. His shoulders were narrow. His hips were wide. So much frilly lace billowed around him he looked like a mug of frothing butter beer. His tan leather boots were the longest Reuben had ever seen, with gold buckles and blue ribbon. His wig was elaborate and grand, falling in ringlets over his shoulders.

'Lord Marley!' Doctor Brittlebank bowed. 'Delighted to meet you again, sir.'

Lord Marley ignored him. 'God's teeth, what's that?' he roared, pointing at Glory Be.

'This? It's Glory Be,' said Reuben.

'Glory Be? What's a Glory Be in the name of God?'

'A dog, sir. She's a spaniel. Hetty, our maid, she tripped over her all the time and shouted "Glory Be!" at her. So that's her name.'

Lord Marley's eyes goggled till Reuben thought they would pop. Then he burst out laughing and clapped his hands. 'Spaniels! Spaniels! D'you know King Charles has decreed his spaniels can go anywhere they wish? Anywhere! They go with him into the Houses of Parliament. What d'you say to that? Give me a greyhound any day,' went on Lord Marley. 'Spaniels get trod on. Or eaten. Well, well, welcome, Doctor Brittlebank. Master Brittlebank. Delighted to have you here. We shall have a grand time!'

Gesticulating wildly, he ushered them out of the hall. 'Come and see my study.' He tottered on his high-heeled satin shoes. 'Come and see my treasures. Dogs! Come!'

Reuben tried to catch Doctor Brittlebank's eye, but the doctor avoided looking at him. He removed his spectacles several times, polished them, put them back on. Reuben knew he was as nervous as himself. He followed them down a long, low-ceilinged corridor. The walls were crammed with ancient leather books that were damp and rotting and gave off a smell of decay.

'May the boy come too?' asked Doctor Brittlebank.

'Boy? He's out of skirts, is he not? Had his curls cut off? He can read and write, can he not? How old is he?' Lord Marley snapped.

'He's, er . . . How old *are* you, Reuben?'

'Around about eleven, I believe,' said Reuben.

'There! A man! He must join us.'

'Very well.' Aside, Doctor Brittlebank whispered to Reuben: 'He is a little changed since last I saw him,

Reuben, but take heart. He has many wonderful instruments and specimens. We shall learn while we're here, shan't we? Don't mind him, eh?'

'My chamber of horrors!' declared Lord Marley, flinging open a wide door and standing back for them to go in. 'Enter!'

Reuben gazed around in astonishment. His eyes darted from one strange exhibit to another, never daring to linger too long on one thing in case he missed another.

From the low ceiling hung two stuffed baby crocodiles. They had frozen smiles and evil glittering eyes which stared back at Reuben as he craned his neck to look at them. There were cages full of brightly coloured stuffed birds. There was a skeleton of some strange sea creature, with paddles for arms and no legs. A mermaid, perhaps? A great tusk, ten feet long and dangerously sharp, hung on five large hooks above the window. There was a large stuffed owl, a stuffed hen and a piglet in a cabinet.

Shelves covered most of the walls. There were books and glass jars full of mummified creatures. Reuben went closer and stared at the floating things. A baby lamb with two heads. Baby piglets with smiling snouts. A cluster of curled up little pink balls, which turned out, when he got nearer, to be baby hedgehogs with soft spines. Their eyes were tightly closed, their minuscule feet tucked beneath their chins. Reuben could have looked at them for hours. In other jars were fragments of things that he guessed came from inside the body, lungs perhaps, or livers, and horrible grey tubes and floating skin and tissue. A jar of eyes, jellied balls, looking in every direction and straight at Reuben. A tiny human baby, not ready to be born, arms and legs folded up close, floated like a waxy ghost in its fluid-filled jar.

Reuben backed away quickly, tripped over a low stool and would have fallen if Doctor Brittlebank hadn't caught his arm.

'You are admiring my latest acquisition, boy?' said Lord Marley. 'Isn't it a dear? A darling little foetus?'

Reuben nodded.

'I think perhaps the boy should go for a wander while we talk,' said the doctor. 'Go on, Reuben. Go out and let Glory have a walk.'

Reuben hesitated for a second, then nodded and went. He would never dream of disobeying, but he didn't like to leave Doctor Brittlebank on his own with this peculiar man.

The front door was open. Reuben crept out quietly into the late afternoon sunshine. He headed west across the meadow, which was full of flowers. He made for some distant trees, hoping not to meet anyone. Butterflies, bees and moths lifted from the grass, clouding around him as he walked. The pollen was heavy in the air. Scents of roses and honeysuckle, clover and daisies bombarded him.

He thought immediately of his grandmother.

Squinting into the sunshine he could almost make out her tiny figure by the next gate, her straw bonnet, her white-and-blue striped shirt and her wooden basket on her arm. She was bending over to examine a rare flower or strange mushroom. Any moment now she would look up and see him and wave and call . . .

But she wasn't there. The light changed and she was gone.

Reuben shook the picture from his head. 'Come on, Glory! Come on, girl! This way! Glory!'

Glory took no heed. She was off, leaping in the long grass, pouncing on anything that moved. Her tail waved like a flag. 'You are such an undignified dog,' Reuben told her. He followed her down a little bank and under some alder trees. He glanced back towards Marley Hall, but they had dropped out of sight from it. 'Come here. Come back!'

Glory bounded away beside a shallow brook. She yapped shrilly at something she'd caught the scent of.

Reuben followed.

On the other side of the stream he spied a building. A ruin shadowed by beech trees and hemmed in by hazel bushes. The walls were covered in brambles and a sheet of shining, fluttering ivy. Many of the blush-pink bricks had fallen and the walls were crumbling, but a fine arched window and a tall tower still remained. It must have been some sort of church or chapel.

Reuben went closer. A bridge, made of two giant slabs of stone, crossed the water. The grass and nettles were trodden down. People came here, then. Why?

'Glory?' he called, but she had disappeared across the stream. Reuben knew he'd have to go and get her.

He stood very still. How quiet it was. No birds sang. The wind stilled. Reuben swallowed and stepped across the bridge.

He followed the path. It curved around behind the crumbling tower to a gate set in a low wall surrounding a tiny yard. The yard was littered with rubbish. A path crossed the grassy cobbles to a split door, like a stable door only smaller, the top half hanging open. Perhaps it's a place for donkeys, Reuben thought, or pigs, or sheep? Something lived here, but he couldn't smell pigs or sheep. He sniffed. He could smell something bad. Very bad. A cess pit? Definitely human waste and rotting things. He pinched his nose with his finger and thumb, then unlatched the gate and went into the yard.

'Glory! Glory!'

He followed the line of trodden-down plants towards the shed. There were bones and broken eggshells lying around. The smell of decay grew stronger.

He reached the half-door.

'Hello?' he called softly.

He leaned into the room beyond. It was very dark. He let his eyes grow accustomed to the dim light. Needle-thin shafts of golden light pierced the blackness.

A chain rattled.

Something moved.

Reuben's heart lurched in his chest. He was frozen to the spot.

He saw a small white shape, like a bone, emerge slowly from a pile of filthy rags.

He spun on his heel and ran for his life.

He ran like the wind, without looking left or right. He ran listening for feet pounding behind him. He ran as if his feet were on fire and a band of demons were on his tail.

He only stopped when he tripped over a root and fell flat on his face.

Glory Be appeared as if by magic. She flopped beside him, nibbling his ears and licking his face.

'Stop it! Leave off, you silly creature! Leave me be!'

He rolled over and stared at the clouds scudding by. He let his chest settle, his breathing go quiet.

Oh, my Lord! What was that?

Glory lay beside him. She looked as if she were laughing, her tongue lolled and her eyes were full of fun. She stretched out her legs and settled her belly on to the cool earth. When he looked at her she lurched at his face and licked him.

'Stop, stop,' he said gently. 'Can't you see I don't want to play.' He wrapped his arms round her and held her fast. 'What was that? Demon? Fairy? Ghost? What could it be?'

Reuben looked back down towards the river. You couldn't see the little tower. It was completely hidden by the trees. Whatever was in there was safe from prying eyes. Why? Why hide? What was it?

'Come on, Glory. Come on.' They made their way back towards Marley Hall.

There was a rough path that meandered across the meadow and round to the back of the Hall. The path meant that someone knew about the thing in the ruin. They went there. They visited it.

There was a group of yew trees between the fields and Marley Hall. As Reuben went past, he noticed dark oblong shapes in the grass. They looked like gravestones, Reuben thought. Nobody was watching him, so he went to look.

They *were* gravestones, about seven of them, lying flat on the grass as if they'd toppled over.

Reuben walked around the stones. Maybe there are others at the ruined chapel too, he thought. He knelt down beside the smallest stone and read the words chiselled into it: *Marley. Here lies the remains of an infant child born and died August 21 1674.*

A baby. Poor thing, it had not been long in the world. Reuben felt suddenly sad. He got up and ran.

He skirted round the side of the house quickly. He glimpsed a paved courtyard with a pump and a well. A mangy ginger cat sat on a discarded jacket in the sunshine. Women were at work in the kitchen. He spied the gleam of copper pans. He could smell food cooking too. But something told him this kitchen would not be like Hetty's warm, comforting kitchen at Wycke House.

He didn't stop.

4

Hetty has a Visitor

Wycke House was very quiet without Doctor Brittlebank and Reuben. Hetty missed them.

'Stop moping, girl,' said Susan Tippett, the housekeeper. 'It's a fine time to do the linen. With the doctor out of the way you can wash it all, every scrap. We can eat cold meat and bread while you use the fire to boil up the water. We don't need hot food, do we, Hetty?'

'No, Mistress Susan.' Hetty shook her head. It was all right for little Mistress Susan Tippett, she was no wider than a stalk of barley and never appeared to enjoy her food anyway. When she did eat she got indigestion and the gripes.

Hetty was glad it was warm. The washing would dry quickly. I don't rightly *need* hot potatoes or hot gravy for that matter, she told herself. Though just thinking about them was making her mouth water. I'll get Cobb in to help lift the heavy wet things when he comes by. He said he would be calling with a fresh barrel of mead.

Mistress Susan and Hetty cleaned and washed all day. Hetty boiled up the water in the big copper for the laundry and got hot and red-cheeked in the process. She wondered what Reuben was doing.

When Cobb came at last to deliver the cask of mead, Hetty was glad to sit with him outside in the cool. They tested the mead, checking it had travelled well.

'There are some advantages to having the master away!' Cobb nudged his pewter mug against Hetty's.

'I suppose so. Mistress Susan's cleaning the doctor's study right now,' she told him. ''Tis full of dead creatures and stuffed bats and all manner of things. If I didn't know Doctor Brittlebank was a good honest doctor – remember how he lanced that pustule on my shoulder? – I'd think he were in league with the Devil, I would.'

'Aye,' agreed Cobb. 'When Widow Anne put the evil eye on my ram and made him sick, Brittlebank took the curse off. Gave it a fancy name, of course, the way he likes to do, while we all knew it were that old woman and her crossed-eyes, but there. It worked.'

'He's a fine man,' agreed Hetty. 'Glory be! I miss them both, I do.'

Cobb helped her with lifting and moving the

wet linen and, after another mug of his fine mead, went home.

Hetty walked down the narrow path between the beds of cabbages, carrots, potatoes and beans, to the washing line strung up between two apple trees. The bed sheets and the doctor's second-best shirts hung there, flapping in the warm wind. Little Reuben's shirts lay on the mounds of lavender, hopefully getting scented and ridding themselves of the smell of dog. Hetty examined her washing critically; had she put enough lye in the water to get them truly clean? Had the water been hot enough? Was the sun strong enough to bleach out those stains? Yes, it looked perfect. She smiled to herself.

It was quiet, with such a soft wind blowing and the sun so hot. Hetty glanced back towards the house to check if Mistress Susan was watching, then, believing herself to be safe, lifted her face to the sun. She stayed there, her hands raised as if reaching for the linen, letting the warmth bathe her cheeks, willing it to take away her blemishes.

Make me pretty, make me pretty as a—

'Good afternoon, miss.'

Hetty shrieked, dropped her arms. She blushed wildly at being caught out so.

The sun was blinding her, but she could make out

a tall figure wearing a large flat, round hat, black as black against the brilliant sunlight.

'Did I surprise you, missy? I didn't mean to.' His voice was slow, not cultured, but neither was it as rough as it might be. A chapman selling books and poems? A pedlar with ribbons?

Hetty stepped to one side and shielded her eyes. She saw the man wore preacher's black clothes – wide-brimmed hat, long coat buttoned from knee to neck with a white band at the collar. He held a Bible in his hand. Hetty relaxed . . . until his face came into focus – a beak-like nose, one eyelid drooping, scars on his cheeks. She took a step backwards.

'Oh, sir, you did give me a shock. I—'

'What a shame you hide those lovely brown eyes beneath that headcloth,' he went on as Hetty turned away. 'They are beautiful eyes, little missy, softer than honey. And did anyone ever tell you that you had the perkiest nose this side of Bristow?'

'Sir! Please!' Hetty stared down at her shoes peeping from beneath her skirt. 'Please. Don't. I'm a good girl.'

'Of course you are. What's your name?'

'I don't think I—'

'Is it Hetty, my dear? Are you Hetty the doctor's maid, is that it?'

Hetty nodded, eyes still cast down. Her heart was

fluttering like a bird caught in a trap. She'd never been spoken to like this. It was making her knees weak. *Their* preacher, Reverend Worlidge, he didn't talk like this. She might faint. And the preacher was so close, he didn't smell so good up close. Rancid sweat, and old food and – what was it, vinegar?

'Tell me, honey eyes, tell me, is the doctor gone to Bristow?'

'No, sir.'

There was a pause. Hetty didn't think her news was a surprise to the stranger; she felt more as if he was slowly absorbing the information like water sinking into dry soil. A few seconds later he said: 'Ah, that's right, he did say it was north. To Shretton, then? Or was it . . . ? My memory is poor.'

'Lord Marley's, sir.'

'Of Marley Hall?'

'Aye, that's where he's gone and I'm sorry he's not here for you to meet with him.' She peeped out at him. But seeing the stony expression in the preacher's dark eyes, she quickly looked down again. 'Do you want to come up to the house and speak to the housekeeper?' She glanced towards the house, half wishing she'd see Mistress Susan at the door, even if Mistress Susan was angry. But there was no one.

'I do not, Hetty. I do not. Not when I have you, pretty little sparrow, to talk to.'

'Sir . . . I—'

'Did he take the boy with him to this Marley Hall?'

'Reuben? Oh, yes sir, they went together. They'll be gone for several days, a week, maybe. He didn't say for certain.'

'Still, Hetty, what do I care, hmm?' He moved closer. 'Why should I mind when I've got you all to myself, and it's you I want to see.'

'Me?' She stepped back nervously. 'Me, sir? I'm just the maid; I shouldn't even be talking to you. As God's my witness . . . If Mistress Susan catches me, she'll be so very cross with me. She's only tiny but she's built of iron . . .'

'Then we won't let her catch you. Come here, come here behind this linen and let me whisper in your ear . . .'

But that was too much for Hetty. She fled. She raced up the path holding her skirts up to her dimpled knees and flung herself into the house.

She was panting as she closed the door behind her. She leaned against the solid wood, listening.

The stranger was playing on a tin whistle. The tune floated up from the vegetable garden; a high-pitched, thin-sounding noise. It was a simple melody, going up and down the scales again and again, but it was eerie. It made Hetty think of graveyards and mother's crying for their dead children. She shivered like a cat caught in the rain and ran further into the house, shutting each door firmly behind her, hands clasped over her ears so she shouldn't hear any more of it.

The preacher slipped his whistle into his jacket pocket. He looked up at Wycke House, swore, spat, then turned and walked away.

If Hetty had been watching him, she would have seen that he had a most distinctive walk. He dragged his left foot as if it were heavier than the other, or didn't quite belong to the rest of his body. He was lopsided, one shoulder higher than the other. His ears didn't match either, one was torn off, leaving nothing but a tiny fragment, like a potato peeling.

He limped off along the road in the direction of Marley Hall.

Smiling.

5

Lady Marley

Reuben found Doctor Brittlebank sitting in a room off the hall. It was a big chamber, with three large windows and heavy tapestries hanging on the walls. The tapestries were so dirty it was impossible to make out the pictures.

The two large greyhounds jumped up as Reuben came in. They bounded over to greet him, circling and whining, whipping Reuben's legs with their tails.

Lord Marley clicked his fingers. The dogs quickly lay down again at Lord Marley's feet. Reuben thought they were the best behaved and finest dogs that he had ever seen.

'Ah, Reuben, lad, you're back,' said Doctor Brittlebank. He looked tired, a little glum. He glanced across at Lord Marley. 'We've had a remarkable afternoon. Yes, sir, remarkable.'

'I am pleased for you,' said Reuben. He put Glory on to the doctor's lap to cheer him up.

'Praise be to God,' said Lord Marley, suddenly

looking heavenwards. He focused his protruding, boiled-egg eyes on Reuben. 'My wife, my Lady Marley, has expressed a desire to see you, young man,' he said. His pale eyebrows danced. 'She's in her room. She likes to call it the library. She reads, you know. Books. Books. Books. Catherine will take you to see her.'

Reuben nodded politely although did not want to part from the doctor so soon.

'We have just a few more matters to discuss, I believe,' said Doctor Brittlebank. 'We'll join you presently.'

'Dinner is served at five before the hour of seven precisely,' Lord Marley piped. 'Carp. Oysters. Pheasant and peacock.'

'Very well,' said Reuben. He went out throwing a beseeching look at the doctor, who pretended not to notice.

Catherine was waiting in the hall. She was young with brilliant blue eyes and fair hair escaping from her cap. Reuben supposed she was pretty, but he didn't like her haughty look or malicious smile. Hetty was much nicer.

'I've to take you to mistress,' Catherine said bluntly. 'C'mon.'

Reuben followed her. The hem of the maid's striped skirt was muddy and her blue apron was blotched with bloodstains and gravy spills. Her arms were grubby, even the back of her neck was ingrained with grime.

Catherine stopped outside Lady Marley's room. 'She's a cat, that one,' she whispered. 'Mind she don't scratch you! In, and watch how you go!'

She knocked loudly on the door then hurried away.

'Come in,' a voice called softly.

Reuben pushed open the door gently and went in. The room was not well lit. He couldn't see her at first, then made out a small person sitting in a tall, thin brocade chair beside the fire. The chair had its back to the door.

Reuben advanced gingerly over the creaking wooden floor and soft Turkish rugs.

'Good afternoon, Lady Marley,' he said.

She was pale, as if she had been rubbed and scrubbed against the washing board like Hetty's petticoats and all her colour had leached away. She was still young, but her hair was sparse and her pink scalp showed through. She had eyes of the palest grey, with hardly any lashes. Her lips were the same wan colour as her chalky cheeks. She stared at him.

'Are you the doctor's boy?' she asked quietly.

'Yes, ma'am. My lady.'

The library was very hot. A wide stone fireplace

stretched across one entire wall and a fierce fire burned in it. There were dusty-looking tapestries and leather hangings on the walls. Crooked shelves contained a multitude of leather-bound books.

'Here, here, beside me,' she said in a tiny voice, holding out her hand.

He went nearer, stepping carefully on the rug. It was patterned with birds, tangling leaves and faded flowers. It seemed a shame to tread on it.

Lady Marley studied him.

Reuben did not dare look her in the face, so he let his eyes wander over her rich costume. She wore a gown of faded pale blue with grey sprigs on it. Patches of the fabric glimmered like the tissue of butterfly wings. The front was open to reveal a lead-coloured quilted petticoat. The bodice was slashed to show the soft yellow silk below, and tied with ribbons. Her costume could have been either very out of date, or very modern. Reuben had no idea which.

'Well, boy,' Lady Marley said, 'tell me this. Since woman is responsible for Eve's sin, what chance does she have to redeem herself?'

Reuben blinked. 'Eve's sin? You mean Eve in the Bible?'

'Yes. She sinned, did she not, to eat the apple?'

'Yes, ma'am, she did.'

'And then she must pay for it and there is only one way for her to redeem herself. I tell you, only one way. By child-bearing!' She slammed her small fist down on the arm of her chair. 'My punishment is to be barren, possess a dry and miscarrying womb. I am aching, Reuben, aching. Every month I beg God, I pray that my emptiness will be filled . . .'

Reuben swallowed dryly and locked his fingers together behind his back. He stared at his feet.

Lady Marley picked up the book lying on a little round table beside her. '*The Ladies' Companion* by William Sermon. Do you know this work?'

'No, ma'am . . . Perhaps my grandmother did. She knew a lot about women and babies and medicines. She could read, even though she was only poor and not a gentlewoman at all.'

'A common woman has no use for reading,' said Lady Marley. 'It will have done her ill. Better to have done her husband's bidding and bear him children.'

'Well—'

'Do not interrupt me, Reuben. I have tried Mister Sermon's remedies. White ginger in the powdered form, for example. I have bathed myself in water in which Ale-hoof, oats and pease straw have been boiled together for a potion. I have drunk mares' milk. Sage juice. I have worn the cool Holland-drawers so recommended. To no avail.

Naught. I am still barren . . .' She held out her hands, palms upward. 'Empty. Like a bowl that should be full of fruit.'

'I'm sorry . . .'

Grandmother had treated women like her. And others. The pregnant girls, who didn't want their babies. It happened all the time. It was a shame you couldn't just swap them around so those that wanted the babies got them.

'Don't be sorry for me, Reuben, it is not for you to pity me . . . My husband isn't sorry. He—'

The door opened and Lord Marley and Doctor Brittlebank came in. Glory scampered over to Reuben and danced around his feet happily.

'Your medicine, dearest,' said Lord Marley. He placed a tiny glass of green liquid beside his wife.

'Is Lady Marley not well?' asked Doctor Brittlebank.

'It is nothing,' said Lord Marley. 'A special remedy for her condition. It is made up for me by my apothecary.'

Lord Marley leaned down and whispered in his wife's ear. Reuben and Doctor Brittlebank moved nearer the windows.

'Doctor – there you are at last!' Reuben said in a low voice. 'I have hardly seen you. I wish we could go home, back to Stonebridge and Hetty and Mistress

Susan. These rich folk baffle me.'

The doctor pointed towards the cows grazing in the fields outside, as if they were fascinating. 'Shhh. We're not accustomed to their ways. I find them not exactly easy either, but my Lord Marley has such magnificent things, Reuben! He has all the latest pamphlets from London. He's a member of the Royal Society, you know? He's going to take me to meet Mister Newton, the greatest scientist in the whole of England. I can bear anything for that!'

'So we won't be staying here?'

'*You* will stay here, I'm afraid.'

Reuben could never question the doctor's decision, but he was disappointed. And he'd been looking forward to telling Doctor Brittlebank about the monster shackled in the shed. He wouldn't be able to share that discovery. He wouldn't even tell him now.

At exactly five minutes before seven, they went into a further room where a long oak table was laid with six places. Crystal glasses sparkled in the candlelight, silver knives gleamed. The plates were thin porcelain. Reuben had never seen anything like them. He dreaded eating – he would break something, surely.

Six glasses? Six places? Who else is coming? Reuben wondered. What shall I say to them? I don't know how to talk like a gentleman. I must try very hard. I am so ignorant of real life and books and learning. And all these candles burning! Such expense. Granny and I used to wait until dark before we lit even one.

Lord Marley sat at the head of the table, a spare place on either side of him. Lady Marley sat at the other end with Reuben on one side of her, Doctor Brittlebank on the other. Glory Be had followed him into the room. Reuben shooed her under the table by his feet.

'Are you acquainted with the fork?' asked Lady Marley, waving a metal implement at Reuben.

'No, ma'am.'

'It is this instrument here. You spear the food with it and convey it to your mouth. We have found this contrivance most useful.'

Reuben used a knife to eat everything. He put it down quickly and took up the fork. It had two long prongs and a handle made of bone. Doctor Brittlebank hastily put down his knife too. He gripped his fork fiercely, staring at it as if he thought it was about to jump up and stab him.

An old woman brought in some roast meats. She was almost bent double by the weight of the dishes. George came in carrying an oval platter of fish and oysters. Catherine brought in a plate with a pheasant, dressed with its own colourful feathers. Another servant poured out tankards of ale. George came back with sauces, potatoes and cabbage. When they had brought the food, the servants stood discreetly around the room, waiting and watching.

Reuben glanced at the two empty seats.

'Caspar! Portia!' Lord Marley clapped his hands smartly and the two greyhounds bounded over to him. 'Up! Chairs!'

The dogs leaped up on to the two empty chairs. They sat up as tall as the humans. They watched Lord Marley intently. Saliva fell in long strands from their open mouths on to the shiny tabletop.

Doctor Brittlebank's eyebrows shot up and his spectacles fell on to his plate. He caught them, polished them, coughed, and took a sip of his wine.

George stepped forward and tied napkins around the dogs' necks. Catherine – without a glimmer of a smile – put porcelain plates in front of them. Lord Marley put food on the dogs' plates. The dogs ignored it. They stared at him, waiting. After a full minute had passed, Lord Marley clicked his fingers. At the signal both dogs attacked the food and gobbled up their dinners. They licked the plates until they were spotless.

Lord Marley laughed and patted them.

'Good dogs! Good dogs!'

He snapped his fingers and they jumped down gracefully and slinked away under the table to join little Glory.

'Come on, Doctor, eat!' Lord Marley cried. 'Are you not hungry, man?'

Doctor Brittlebank appeared to be paralysed with amazement.

'I do think it would be pleasanter if the dogs wore jackets and breeches, don't you agree, Doctor Brittlebank?' said Lady Marley.

Doctor Brittlebank spluttered and mopped his face with his napkin. 'Certainly, of course, yes,' he said. 'My goodness, the fire is powerful hot, isn't it? And the weather so mild for September. Do you hunt, Lord Marley?' He speared some pheasant meat with his fork and managed to get it to his mouth without dropping it. He winked at Reuben, who was watching him.

'I love hunting, sir!' said Lord Marley. His mouth was full and some of its contents sprayed out as he spoke. 'I have birds on the estate you know, pheasants and doves and pigeons too.'

'That sounds—'

'Clip their wings, you see, and they can't fly away from me, can they?'

'But then you don't shoot those, do you?' asked Reuben.

'Certainly I do, young sir. Why else would I go to the bother and expense of clipping their wings?'

Lady Marley folded the lace back from her wrist, took an oyster from the plate and leaned across to Reuben with it in her hand. 'Open your mouth and let me slip this in,' she said.

Reluctantly, Reuben did as he was told and the slimy cold meat slithered on to his tongue. He had never had oyster before. It was like a mouthful of snot and he gagged.

'No chewing,' she said. 'Let it slip straight down. That's the way!'

Reuben reached for his ale and somehow swallowed the thing without being sick. His eyes watered.

'Tasty? Good. You will be staying here with me, then, boy?' she said. She peered at him with her strange pale eyes. 'I will find your company amusing, no doubt. I would like to spend more time with children but I have no child of my own, no nephews or nieces who visit . . . You are a handsome lad. We shall have a quiet time together. Do you play rummy?' Before Reuben could answer, she turned to Doctor Brittlebank. 'Don't let that husband of mine kill you, will you? He's a dangerous man. He once raced his carriage over a wooden gateway, you know, having placed a bet he could clear it. He could not.'

Lord Marley hooted with laughter and slapped the table so the glasses jumped.

'What other perils do I face with your husband, Lady Marley?' asked Doctor Brittlebank.

'Who knows, Doctor? You are dabbling in the mysteries of sorcery and – what else?'

'Science, Lady Marley, I prom—'

'Science and sorcery are one and the same,' said Lady Marley. 'You are delving into things about which you know nothing – God's things. It is God alone who understands the workings of the body, the soul, the heart. Not man. Man has no right to these wonders.'

There was a moment's silence.

'We are only trying to understand a little of God's beauty, my lady,' said Doctor Brittlebank. 'To advance man's thinking and appreciation of God's work.'

'Humph!' said Lady Marley. 'My advice would be to spend more time reading the Bible, Doctor, and not go wasting your time, as my husband does, with *ideas*.'

'Doctor Brittlebank makes people better,' said Reuben, proudly. 'He's a good physician.'

'I dare say he is,' said Lady Marley. 'But can he make a barren woman fertile? Can he prevent newly born babes from slipping back into God's embrace? Can he—'

'Lady Marley is a little overwrought,' said Lord

Marley, getting up and putting his hand on her bare shoulder – so firmly that her flesh grew white beneath his fingers. 'Drink some brandy,' he ordered. 'There is nothing wrong with her except her melancholia, Doctor. She is possessed of water and earth, the heavy elements, and they are dragging her down.'

Reuben felt Doctor Brittlebank choosing his words carefully.

'Well, Lord Marley,' he said, 'the cure for the melancholic is to avoid root vegetables as they came from the earth. I would advise plenty of milk, eggs and a brisk walk each day around the estate for Lady Marley.'

Lord Marley clapped his hands. 'There! The doctor has proposed a new remedy,' he said. 'We must encourage the lighter humours in her, fire and air, as they naturally rise and make one happy, eh Doctor?'

'Quite.'

'Might I give up the green infusion you bring me?' asked Lady Marley.

'Not yet, my dear, not yet,' said Lord Marley. 'Doctor, do you not think Lady Marley might stop reading about women and their conditions, too?'

'My feelings are that a little reading is a good thing,' said Doctor Brittlebank.

'Her soul and body are at work against each other, one side is reason and the other passion,' said Lord Marley, dryly. 'This is causing the problem.'

Lady Marley scowled. 'A child would put me right,' she said bitterly. 'A child would mend my melancholia and rid me of these fevers and passions!'

'Have you forgotten that you had one, my lady,' said Lord Marley, harshly. 'You gave birth to my son and heir. He died. It is your fault there are no more children, madam, yours!'

6

The Preacher in Pursuit

Six-year-old Gilbert Bootling trudged down the path from Marley Hall back to Little Hollow. The sun was sinking, the shadows were long and black, like Devil's fingers, ready to snatch . . .

He stared down at the path, at his small black boots bobbing in and out of view, trying not to think about gypsies and goblins and all the twilight things that might be lurking in the surrounding woods.

George, the pig-faced servant at the great house, had given him strong wine to drink. It had made words slip about all loose and silly on his tongue and his head grow big and heavy like a pumpkin. It had been amusing; now he regretted it.

Gilbert had been on a special mission. He had carried a brew, made by his mother, to Lady Marley. The potion was made especially for her Ladyship with snakeweed, fern and gladwin. Gilbert had watched his mother make the medicine; it had smelled gaggy bad! Powerful stuff, it was. Brown-coloured and sludgy. Something to do with babies and birthing. He wasn't to tell a soul, specially not the master of the house, Lord Marley. He had to deliver it right into her Ladyship's hands. And he had. She'd smiled at him and given him a penny. She took a multitude of medicines, green ones, yellow ones. Powders too. He'd seen them. But his ma's smelled the worst; he was certain it would work.

Now he had to walk all the way back home and oh, it was gloomy and lonely on this stretch of road . . .

'Boy!'

Gilbert jumped. He looked around fearfully and saw no one.

'Lord help me!' he shrieked. 'I never did nothing wrong!'

'Boy!' The voice was louder and closer.

Little Gilbert fell down sobbing. 'I done what were asked. I never did mean to drink that rich wine, but the mister made me do it. I swear.'

'Stop snivelling and look at me.'

Gilbert looked up and saw a man dressed all in black, with a large wide hat pulled down low over his face.

'Sir? Sorry, sir, sorry . . .'

'Do you have anything to drink, boy? I feel like a cat's kittened in my mouth . . . Where do you come from?'

'No drink, sir.' The boy pointed back up the path. 'I've come from the Hall, sir, from Marley Hall. 'Tis 'bout three miles up that way.'

'I know where Marley Hall is, you noddle head.'

'Yes, sir, of course you do, sir. Are you going that way?' Gilbert desperately hoped the gentleman wasn't going towards Little Hollow. He could never walk all that way with this black crow beside him.

'I am. I'm looking for someone. Believe he might be there.'

'There's lots of folks up at the Hall. Lots and lots,' said Gilbert enthusiastically. 'Sure, I'll wager he is there, him that you're looking for.'

The crow-man nodded. 'I'm weary, but I'll walk on. Three miles?'

'Yes sir,' said Gilbert.

'Tell me, did you see a boy up at Marley Hall? Ugly little toad of a boy. He'd be about twice your age with brown hair, brown eyes. Surly, expression.'

'A boy? Well, sir, I did see a boy, and he had a real pretty little dog with him. A spaniel it was. It had golden curls and a tail like a flag . . .'

'Damn the dog! What about the boy?'

'The boy, sir?' Weren't all boys the same, give or take a bruise or a hole in their breeches? 'He was with a doctor man from far away – from Bridgestone or somewheres . . .'

'*Bridgestone?* Do you mean Stonebridge? Are you a fool, boy?'

Gilbert shook his head violently.

The preacher looked back the way Gilbert had come. The light fell on his face and Gilbert saw clearly his cold dark eyes, his twisted features, his scars. Where would a decent man come by such scars?

'I must go,' said Gilbert, scrabbling up the bank beside the path. 'Mother'll be . . .'

'Yes, yes, you scabby little runt. Off you go. Run home to mamma. And mind the fairies don't get you!' He laughed.

Gilbert ran.

He did not look back. But if he had looked back he would have seen the man in black hobbling along the road towards Marley Hall. And if he'd looked very carefully, he would have seen a knife blade glinting in his hand.

7

The Ruins and the Ruined

Reuben stood at the front of the house next morning, watching the carriage toiling away up the long drive. Inside it were Doctor Brittlebank and Lord Marley.

Reuben had managed not to show his unease while the doctor was getting ready to leave. But now he felt himself sinking inwards, like a cake fresh out of the oven.

He knelt down beside Glory. 'Don't worry, Glory,' he said, smoothing her fur. 'The doctor's coming back soon.'

He set off aimlessly. It was good to walk. What a strange, sad place Marley Hall was. The grass, the trees . . . even the stones of the house, seemed melancholy.

At the side of the Hall a group of labourers idled on the grass chatting, drinking cider and laughing. They nodded to him as he went by. Still, he felt there was something hostile in the way they watched him.

He forced himself to whistle jauntily and swing his arms, but was sure he hadn't fooled them. They knew he was lonely and confused and had nowhere to go.

He found himself following the path of flattened grass over the meadow towards the ruins. Glory skipped and pranced and ran in circles around him. Reuben looked about, but nobody was watching him. Nobody cares, he thought, I can go where I want. Do what I want.

When Reuben saw the rose-coloured walls of the old chapel rising up out of the trees, he slowed to a snail's pace. The place was eerie, but then ruins always made him feel uneasy. They might be hundreds of years old, maybe more, and real people had lived here and laughed here and touched these very stones, walked on this ground. The folk that had lived here might have seen Queen Bess. Queen Bess could have even lodged in Marley Hall. And now they were all gone to dust . . . But it was the thought of the living thing now inhabiting the place that made him tremble.

He came quietly to the courtyard and leaned his hands on the crumbling wall. The stones were warm from the sun. Valerian invaded gaps in the wall, pushing the stones apart. Bindweed curled and twisted around the gateposts, showering white trumpet flowers. Reuben tried to smell the flowers, but all he could smell was garbage and rotting food. He almost retched. The stench was worse today, like something had died.

Reuben put his hand up to his mouth and nose. He was breathing fast, his heart was hammering in his chest.

Go back, go back, he told himself. But he went on.

'Hello?' he called. His voice cracked. 'Hello.'

There was no reply. High above him, the trees waved in the wind, creaking softly, sighing and swishing. A large shaggy-necked raven called down at him bleakly, a loud cry, like something breaking. It must be nesting in the tower. It glared down at him with its dark eye. Reuben couldn't suppress a shiver.

One for sorrow.

He pushed open the gate and crossed the yard towards the low building. Marrow skin, carrot tops and other rubbish was strewn about. Glory skittered at his side. The top half of the door was open, as it had been before. The dog scratched at the wood. She whimpered softly and wagged her tail.

'What is it?' Reuben called quietly. 'Who's there, Glory?'

Reuben stood as close to the doorway as he dared and looked in.

The interior was so dark it was like staring into

a curtain of black velvet. He called out softly again. 'Hello!'

He saw a pile of rags and blankets on the straw. A dented pewter mug. And a chain! *A chain!* I thought I'd heard one clinking! So it is some wild, mad person they keep here!

He knelt down and rubbed Glory's head. 'It's all right,' he whispered to her. 'It's all right.'

Once he was breathing properly again, once he'd stilled his racing heart, he stood up and braved himself to lean right over the half-door, willing his eyes to penetrate the blackness.

The rags had gone.

He leaned in further, looking from side to side.

A sudden clink of metal, a shifting movement and something loomed up from below: a white round face, just inches from his.

'Ahhh!' he screamed.

Reuben jumped as if he'd been scalded. He turned and ran. He raced down the track, leaped over the stream without need of the bridge and ran all the way back to the open meadow.

My God, that is something terrible and unworldly . . .

What is *that in there? In God's name, that is unholy. Oh, Lord! Lord!*

He had seen a tiny human face. But a face that was

all wrong. Monstrous! Not just the face of some idiot – much worse.

Reuben tried to calm his thoughts. Not all folk are the same, he told himself. Because my grandmother was old and wrinkled, because she had whiskers on her chin and muttered under her breath, she was called a witch. Jethro Carter had a withered arm – he was sane enough otherwise. Might that thing in there be just odd? Different?

But then why is it chained?

Reuben stood beneath an oak tree in the dappled shade with the insects buzzing and whining around him. Gradually his heartbeat settled, and the coldness that had gripped his innards began to melt.

I'm just a coward, he told himself. It can't be dangerous, it's too small to be dangerous. And Glory wasn't frightened, though Glory probably hasn't got the brains to be scared . . .

Glory? Where was she?

There was no sign of her. She had not followed him. He called and called, but there was no answering bark.

I'll have to go back then.

No, I'll just wait a while and see if she comes.

No, I'll go back.

I can't.

He waited and waited and Glory didn't come.

Very well, he *would* go back there. He wasn't scared, was he?

He got to the bridge and he stopped.

What if it *isn't* chained up? he thought. It moved to the door didn't it? What if it bites? Or *is* some sort of demon? Why would anyone put it here unless it was dangerous?

Perhaps he would go back without her.

Glory began barking.

'Glory! Glory! Come!'

She didn't come. Glory was still in there, maybe trapped, maybe captured by that thing.

Reuben moved. He went stealthily towards the courtyard. Glory was sitting beside the shed. She was wagging her tail and gazing up at the open door.

'Glory!'

She looked at him over her shoulder and wagged her tail more forcefully.

'You silly thing! Bad dog!' He pushed open the gate. 'Come here! Come!' But Glory turned back to the door and jumped up, scratching against the wood.

'When I get my hands on you . . .' Reuben tried to sound fierce as he inched across the yard towards her. 'Bad dog!'

He stopped. Something shuffled on the other side of the door. He heard it snuffling. He heard it rubbing against the wall. Reuben stood completely still, eyes focused on the black square of the half-open door, his heart thudding.

Suddenly, oh, God! It was there. It was at the door.

He couldn't see its face, it had put a hat on. It must have got something to stand on, it was taller than before; a tiny scarecrow, covered in ragged clothes. There were scraps of threadbare fabric and bits of sacking around its shoulders and arms.

It was only a little child. A boy, he was sure, six or seven years old.

Reuben breathed again. He tried to see its face beneath the brim of his hat. It was just a boy.

'Fish,' said the child. His voice was muffled. He was staring down at Glory.

'No, that's a dog,' said Reuben. 'Dog.'

The child looked up briefly.

Beneath the dirt and snot and scabs, the boy's face was extraordinary. Looking at it sent a tremor up Reuben's spine. His face was flat as a plate. The forehead was wide, enormous. The eyes, which were too large, too round and set wide apart, slanted downwards, as if they were sliding off his face. His upper lip was bowed and plump, though the mouth itself was very small, so was the nose. It hurt Reuben to look at it; it was an unnatural face and yet it filled him with a tender feeling.

'Caf'rin?' said the child, extending his arm. His hand was hidden beneath a bandage of filthy cloth. He kept his face turned away. 'Caf'rin? Food?'

Leper! Of course! That's why he is wrapped up, thought Reuben. Hidden away by law, not allowed to mix. His fingers and toes all eaten away and rotting. Those sores on his lips . . . That gagging smell . . .

Contagious!

'Caf'rin,' said the boy. 'F'end.'

The boy looked up and his giant eyes pinned Reuben there. Reuben opened his mouth but no words came. He tried to move away, but he was rooted to the ground.

'F'end?'

Reuben nodded. Perhaps he didn't have leprosy. He had no rotting flesh on his face. He didn't seem ill. Perhaps he was just an idiot with a clitchy face.

Reuben picked up Glory. 'Friend,' he said.

The boy smiled. It was a wonderful smile. Reuben had never, never seen a smile like it.

'Do'.'

Reuben smiled back. He nodded. 'Yes. My *dog*. She's called Glory Be.'

The child reached out. His hands were hidden beneath strips of dirty rag. Reuben snatched Glory back. He couldn't help thinking of rotting flesh and exposed bones.

'Lory! Lory! Lory!' the boy cried. His eyes filled with tears. His strange fish-lips pouted and trembled. Reuben hugged Glory even tighter and backed away. He looked round wildly. Someone would hear!

'Hush! Hush!' he begged. 'Stop!'

Suddenly the raven swooped down.

'*Kronk, kronk,*' it called hoarsely, alighting on the ground.

The boy stopped crying. He watched the bird as it strutted arrogantly across the yard and picked up a discarded morsel. It opened its great wings, rose up and skimmed over Reuben's head like a passing cloud. They both watched it go.

'Ravens are so cocky,' said Reuben.

'Riv'n,' said the boy. '*Ronk, ronk!*' Then he started yelling. Only it wasn't just yelling, it had a pattern, a rhythm. The oddmedodd thing was singing, and Reuben knew the song. He recited the words:

'*There were three ravens sat on a tree,*

Down a down, hey down, hey down . . .

'My grandmother sang that to me! How do you know it?' He felt almost angry that this strange child should sing his song, his and his grandmother's song.

'Mary,' said the boy. 'Singed. Riv'ns.' He looked up at the bird hopping through the branches. 'Watch I.'

Reuben looked up at the bird too. He watched it

slip into the tower. Where was its mate? What was it doing there? A raven would attack an injured or weak animal if it got a chance. It could be waiting – he shivered – waiting for the boy to die.

What a grim place for a little child to live.

'Dog! Dog!' yelled the boy. He leaned over the door and pointed at Glory. He banged the wooden door rhythmically. 'Dog! Dog!'

'Shush! Stop it! What's the matter with you? Who do you belong to, anyways?' Reuben asked, suddenly irritated with the boy. 'Why are you here in this old hovel? What's the matter with your arms?'

The boy snatched his arms back behind the door. He folded his hands into his armpits and tucked his chin down, hiding his face.

'Fish,' he muttered. All the light had gone from his face. He got down from whatever he'd been standing on, and backed away. 'Fish.'

'What?'

'Fish.' He retreated into the dark of his gloomy shed. 'Fish. Fish. Fish.'

There was a rustle in the bushes. The raven lifted from its perch calling out loudly, desolately, and flew off through the canopy of leaves.

Someone was coming.

8

Catherine

Reuben scooped up Glory and hopped over the wall into the surrounding shrubbery. He hid behind an elm tree. He had a good view of the ramshackle place from here. Glory wriggled in his arms but for once had the sense not to bark.

It was one of the maids from the Hall. Catherine. *Caf'rin?*

The maid's skirt was smeared with oil and soot. Her hair hung round her face in greasy strands. In one hand she held a basket of food. In the other she was carrying a wooden bucket that sloshed out water as she walked. Her plump, pretty face was screwed up.

'Gabriel? Gabe?' she called. 'Oh, look at me skirt now! Soaked. Got your food here.' She kicked open the gate and let it slam back against the wall. She marched up to the door.

'Show yerself!' Catherine put the basket and bucket down. She unbolted the door top and bottom. 'Gabe! Come here!'

The boy shuffled into view.

'What's the matter with you?' said Catherine. 'Got food here. Poultry today, you lucky doddle head. Pheasants. God knows what. They had such a guzzle up at the house. Fat pigs. Did that Mary ever bring you the like?'

'Dog? Dog?' said the boy. ''Oof! 'Oof!'

'What you talking about? Dog, is it? No dogs here, or is it you fancy eating roast beagle pup? They bay worse than you, you mad bat. Oh, look at the mess you're in! How did Mary ever...? Didn't I tell you, Gabriel! You poor motherless idiot! Get out of the way, there, and I'll come in.' She pushed at the door and barged in, nearly knocking him over.

Reuben could still hear her when she was inside.

'Spilled the water and your bucket. What a mess. The stink! No better than an animal, that's the truth!' There was the sound of slapping followed by the boy's whimpers. 'Stop blathering! Move away there! How am I 'spected to do this and all else in the house? Bloody Mary! It's her fault! Oh, my Lord, you lousy boy, you stink to the heavens!'

Catherine emerged again – a look of disgust on her face – carrying a heavy bucket of slops, which she emptied out over the wall. She swept some of the dirty reeds and remnants of food out, then took in the basket. 'Don't give it to them bloody birds, neither,' she scolded him. 'It's for you, you caw-baby.'

She backed out and locked the door. 'What did I do wrong to get landed with a mad doddy-poll like you? 'S'not fair, 'tis not. And don't jiffle with that sore on your gob, either, or it'll get worse. I'm telling you now.'

Catherine carried some dirty things away in the basket with her. She swirled her skirts and headed back towards the house. Reuben heard her singing as she crossed the stream.

The boy reappeared immediately. He got up on his perch and flung his arms over the half-door. Somehow he knew Reuben hadn't abandoned him.

'Dog! Lory! Lory!'

Reuben climbed back over the wall. The boy smiled broadly. He reached out for Glory, flapping his arms impatiently. Reuben picked the spaniel up and held her close to the boy.

'Is your name Gabriel?' Reuben asked.

The boy nodded. 'Angel,' he said. 'Angel Gabel.'

'Angel? Are you? Why do they keep you locked up here, Gabriel? Are you mad?'

The boy shook his head. 'Fish.'

Reuben stared at him. Why did he keep saying that?

'Does Catherine bring the food to you?'

The child wasn't looking at him. He rocked back and forth. 'Mad boy. I mad.' He nodded. 'Mad.' He was still staring at Glory. 'Mary gone. Mary good.'

'What happened to her? Was she your mother?'

The boy shook his head. He rattled the door suddenly. 'Get out. Gabe out! Dog. Dog!' He was jumping up and down. He bashed against the door. 'Out! Out!'

'Hush! Be quiet, you fool!' Reuben looked round anxiously. 'Someone will hear us!' Reuben shook his finger at him. 'Don't you understand? I can't let you out. I can't!'

'Out!'

'All right. Stop!'

Gabriel went quiet and still. His mouth dropped open and hung there. He eyed the dog. 'Lory.' He nodded. 'Lory.'

'Now listen, I'll just open the door a little way then you can pat Glory properly. Stand back now.'

Reuben struggled with the bolts; his fingers felt boneless. The door swung open and Reuben held up his fists, ready to fight.

The boy wasn't going to fight. He didn't even look at Reuben. He threw himself down beside Glory and rubbed his funny flat face against her fur. He put his swaddled arms round her and hugged her.

He wasn't chained. Reuben saw the iron anklet

lying on the straw inside. Perhaps Catherine had undone it. He tried to see further into the shed. The room was big. It seemed to go back a long way, right into the bottom of the chapel tower. The smell was bad, rotting food and shit and worse.

'Lory! Lory!'

'*Glory*,' Reuben said.

Did the boy have leprosy? Pox? Why was he so dirty and smelly? He was worse than a pig.

'Lory, Lory, Lory,' Gabriel cooed. He rolled on his back and let Glory lick his face.

A coldness sneaked meanly round Reuben's heart. 'Why don't you take the stuff off your hands?' He asked stiffly. 'You could feel her properly, touch her fur.'

The boy shook his head. He tucked his arms round himself and rolled about. Something caught the boy's attention. He suddenly reached out, just like he might have reached for a bright toy. But it was not a toy. It was the shining berries of the deadly nightshade. Belladonna.

'Don't touch that!' Reuben yelled.

Gabriel stopped. Reuben leaped towards him and broke off the stem of purple berries before Gabriel could touch them. The berries were almost as big and round as cherries. He shook them at Gabriel.

'Poisonous! This stuff is deadly, you fool!'

He made to throw them down – then stopped. Gabriel might find them. He stuffed them into his pocket. Anyway, Doctor Brittlebank would be pleased with those when he got back, he thought. The doctor made a poultice from deadly nightshade for skin ulcers, as his grandmother had done.

'I've got to go,' said Reuben. 'Me and Glory. They'll be looking for us back at the Hall.' He took a few steps away from the door. 'I have to get back.'

'Back,' said Gabriel. 'C'm back. Mary gone. Mary gone. C'm back. Boy back!'

'I will. I will. I'll come back tomorrow, shall I? I promise. With Glory.'

The boy's face split into a vast, dribbling grin, like an orange that had burst against the floor. 'Dog. Dog. Swear't!' He was jumping up and down.

'I promise. I swear it.' Reuben licked his finger and made a cross with it over his chest. 'Swear. Now you must go back in there.'

Gabriel glanced back into the dark room. His shoulders fell. His chin drooped. He gave Reuben a quick, keen look then shuffled inside. Reuben shot the bolt home. Then he went. He knew the boy's eyes were following him. And above him, he was aware of the raven, flying rhythmically and powerfully through the sky. The raven was watching him too.

He broke into a run, faster and faster through the trees.

Glory Be thought it was a game, some sort of challenge. She put her head down low and streaked past him easily, ears and tail streaming behind her.

The sun and wind on his cheeks had never felt so fresh and so good. I pray no one ever locks me up! I'd die. I'd die locked away in the dark like an animal. Never!

Poor Gabriel. Who is he? Why is he there? Catherine knows . . . Why don't they wash him? He's so small and ugly. What's wrong with him? Thank the Lord I'm free!

As he got closer to Marley Hall, he heard pipe music and he slowed down and listened. It sounded like a cheap tin whistle, the notes were thin and hollow. He liked pipe music, but this was mournful. Somehow it brought to mind the cold, grey morning they had hanged his grandmother.

For a moment he wondered who was playing it. Then he lost interest. He had other things on his mind.

9

Stinking Motherwort

Lady Marley had been asking for Reuben. Reuben had barely time to take off his jacket before a servant found him and sent him to her room.

'Where have you been, boy?'

'Just out walking with my dog,' said Reuben. 'She loves it here.'

'I dare say she does. I expect you do also. I have been asking for you this last hour. I informed Doctor Brittlebank that I was happy to have you here to keep me company. He thought you might read to me. Or play cards with me. And yet you spend all your time in the woods like a gypsy.'

'I am very sorry, Lady Marley.' He was sorry. She looked small and lonely and sickly. He wiped his grimy hands over the seat of his breeches.

'Well, you are here at last.' She sighed. 'Before you come and sit with me, I want you to find George, and tell him to bring me in some lavender. Something taints the air this morning. And then hurry back to me. I wish to speak with you.'

'Yes, ma'am.' He hesitated. 'Is George the one with the upturned nose?'

'That is George.'

Reuben found George sitting on a stone bench at the front of the house. He was swinging his legs and crunching on an apple. An old man was leaning on a rake beside him, chatting. A very small pile of weeds lay by his feet.

George indeed had a nose like a pig and small dark eyes. 'Hello, lad!' he called. 'What's the hurry?'

'Lady Marley sent me. She wishes for lavender. Something doesn't smell nice in the house, she says.'

'Well, we're not in it, are we Smithy, so it can't be us,' said George with a grin. 'Right-ho. Lavender for the mistress. I must leap to her command.' He took another bite of his apple and turned his face up towards the sun.

'And George?' Reuben asked.

'Yes, boy?'

'Who's Mary?'

George and the old man exchanged an amused look.

'Who told you about Mary?'

'I just heard her name spoken,' said Reuben. 'Just wondered.'

'She's gone missing,' said old Smithy. He grinned,

showing three brown peg teeth. 'Disappeared these two weeks or so.'

'Truth is, young lad, she got a pudding in the oven, you know?' said George, winking.

'On the nest. Expecting! A *babby!*' said the old man.

'Oh.'

'And she weren't married.'

'And rumour was, it were Lord Marley's byblow,' added the old man.

'Oh,' said Reuben, again. 'But—'

'Mistress sent her packing once her bump were showing. She were staying up at Mistress Foster's at the big gate, but then she left. 'Tis about two weeks we ain't heard from her. Our Catherine's right put out about it, since they were friends and all.'

'She were fair on the peepers,' said old Smithy, rolling his eyes. With his hands he outlined an exaggerated shape of a big-breasted woman. He laughed. 'Lady Marley were jealous, that's truth of the matter. Mary was all cream skin and freckles; long red hair and green eyes. Loverly! I'd've gladly . . .' He made a rude gesture.

'That's enough, that's enough,' said George. 'Not in front of the innocent young lad, here.'

'It's all right,' said Reuben. 'I understand. So she's gone away because she was going to have a baby. Oh, well . . . Don't forget that lavender, George. I must get back. Thank you!'

Reuben ran.

Lord Marley wanted a baby. Why did he throw Mary out? Lady Marley wants a baby. They could have had Mary's if she didn't want it. Grown folk are so stupid.

Lady Marley was waiting for him when Reuben got back. The sun had broken up the cloud. Now it streamed through the opaque window glass, giving everything the appearance of being underwater.

Why couldn't she have a baby? What was it, Reuben wondered, that makes some ladies like a pea pod, all ready to swell up and pop babes out, one after the other with no trouble at all and others so dry and remaining so flat?

'Sit down, Reuben,' Lady Marley said. 'There, where I can see you. I'm looking through this volume of Culpeper's Herbal. Culpeper is very learned.'

'My grandmother said his book was full of good advice and recipes for medicines.'

'It is. I am of the earth,' said Lady Marley. 'The cold, damp earth . . . Do you know the herb called stinking motherwort?'

'I do,' said Reuben. 'My grandmother showed it to me. It has small round leaves with a little pointed end and it grows on dunghills and it smells like a dunghill too. Or rotten fish, or something worse.'

'Mister Culpeper commends it as a medicine for the womb. Do you think I have heat of the womb?' She scrutinized him with her pale, diluted eyes. 'He says it is one of the greatest causes of hard labour in childbirth. I had a long, hard labour to deliver my dead child.'

Reuben shook his head and shrugged and nodded, hoping one would be the correct response.

She fixed him with her stare. 'Can you find me some?'

'I will try, your Ladyship. If you wish it.'

'I do. I take a multitude of potions and brews, infusions and distillations. Some, I believe, do me no good at all, like that green concoction my lord makes me take . . .' She leaned back in her chair wearily. 'It is quiet here without Lord Marley, is it not?'

'Yes.'

'And the dogs. Don't you miss them, with their loud voices and bad manners?'

'Yes, your Ladyship.'

She closed her eyes. Reuben thought she wished to sleep, and got up to go.

'No, stay.' Lady Marley smoothed the folds of her dress slowly. 'Reuben, you're a nice-looking boy, but you require better clothes. What do you say to some lace instead of that coarse linen? Some fine stockings instead of those thick cumbersome things you wear? Breeches of deerskin? Soft black shoes with silver buckles? Or red ribbons, perhaps? Why Reuben, you'd make a fine lord's son. I'd have you. It's an idea that's taking root. I'd take you as my own. That might be what God wishes: that I should give you a home here. I strive to follow God's will and I believe that could be it.'

'Lady Marley!'

'I know. I know. Such a great honour for you, to be brought up above your position in life, to have a title, property and land. But it wouldn't be the first occasion a commoner has risen in this way, Reuben. God only knows how many times a healthy peasant baby has replaced the mistress's sickly, dying one . . .'

'Please—'

'Listen, Reuben. Doctor Brittlebank told me all about your past and how you are alone in the world apart from him. I can change that. I can! I shall pray for it. It's what you want, isn't it?' Her pale cheeks were flushed. 'Come here.'

Reuben knelt beside her chair. Lady Marley gripped his shoulder with her small hand.

'There has been much slackness in this house and not enough prayer. Let us pray.'

Reuben felt his body grow heavy, as if lead ran in

his blood. He bowed his head and waited for the prayer to be over. At last Lady Marley stopped speaking.

'May I ask you something, please,' he said.

'Yes, boy, of course.'

'Doctor Brittlebank will hardly believe the honour you are thinking of bestowing on me,' he said carefully. 'It is so generous . . . Do you think he will agree to it?'

'He will. It is my wish, Reuben and he must agree.'

Reuben's heart sank. 'When do you expect them to return?' Soon, soon, he urged inwardly.

She smiled at him. 'Are you fond of the doctor? My husband and the doctor will stay in Felton for several days. Their host is captivating, apparently. I'm so pleased my husband is away. Though I mistrust all this talk of science . . . He can be so, so . . . difficult.'

Reuben swallowed, breathed out, tried to act as if nothing was wrong. 'I see,' he said. 'May I go now, Lady Marley?' Please, please let me go, he added silently.

'Yes, you may.'

As Reuben got up, he staggered. The dark panelled walls closed in on him. The place was turning into a prison. The smells of the dank reeds on the floor and the rich food smells from the kitchen caught in his throat. He almost tripped and put his hand on a chair back to steady himself. He felt the layer upon layer of grease and wax on the ancient furniture. Somehow he got himself to the door.

'Oh, Reuben,' Lady Marley called him back. 'There is someone come to the house. A stranger. A stranger who plays the pipe. Talking with the maids also. I heard him. Ring that bell, I wish to know who it is.'

Reuben had heard voices too. The noise was coming from the servants' area. He rang the handbell on the round table beside her. It took several minutes before George appeared, breathing fast, grinning and tucking his shirt into his breeches. He managed to wipe the smile off his face before Lady Marley saw it.

He bowed. 'Your Ladyship requires something?'

'Who is come?' she asked.

'Your Ladyship?'

'I said, who is come? There is a stranger in my house and I demand to know who is come!'

Reuben was surprised and rather impressed by the pitch of her voice. It didn't look as if her tiny body could produce it, and so effortlessly too.

'It is a travelling man,' said George. 'He is a preacher of some Puritan sort, I fancy, going by his starky manner. Very learned and rather handicapped. He's talking to Catherine and old Patience in the kitchen, my lady.'

Lady Marley turned aside. 'I wish to see him. Send him to me.'

'Very well, my lady.'

George whisked out of the door, making a comical face at Reuben as he slipped out.

Reuben wanted to leave but Lady Marley held up her hand and stopped him.

'Wait,' she said. 'You must learn to wait for my wishes to be carried out, Reuben. You are a little impulsive. I may need you. Wait until we know who is here.'

Reuben sank like a stone on to the chair.

They heard George's softly shod feet running down the stone-flagged corridor and a heavy door slamming, followed by giggling and hushed voices. Lady Marley opened her book and went on reading. A while later, there were whispers outside and Catherine appeared. She smoothed down her skirt and tucked her untidy hair into her bonnet as she came in.

'Your Ladyship. 'Tis a preacher man that's called. A Mister Smith. Do you truly wish to admit him into your chamber?'

'Yes. But send George back in also, to chaperone. And bring me some port wine.'

'Yes, my lady.' Catherine slipped out again.

'Very well, you may leave me now, Reuben.

But don't go far. You are a comfort. I may need you.'

Reuben went.

He heard voices approaching from the kitchen area so he ran out to the front. If he could have run all the way back to Stonebridge he would have done so, but he had to wait for Doctor Brittlebank to return. Instead of running, Reuben made his way to the fruit bushes. The doctor would never let Lady Marley keep him, would he? He hoped there were raspberries still. The taste of a raspberry would carry him back to Wycke House.

10

Starky Mister Smith

When Reuben had exhausted the raspberry bushes and then the gooseberry bushes, he made his way back to the study.

There was a tall-backed chair just outside Lady Marley's room where he would sit and wait to be called. Glory sat at his feet, her chin resting on his knee. She wagged her tail at him, eager to get back outside.

For the hundredth time Reuben wished the doctor were there. He wondered where he was at that very moment. What was he doing? Not wasting time thinking about Reuben, certainly.

Suddenly Reuben heard a deep voice through the wall. He jerked upright. His heart stopped. He stared straight ahead with sightless eyes.

He knew that voice! Surely it was . . .

No. It was the preacher! Of course it was! Reuben collapsed like an empty sack. Nothing to fear. The *preacher's* voice had sounded similar to Flyte's, that was all.

Flyte!

Reuben put a hand over his racing heart. Why does it go so fast when I'm frightened? he wondered fleetingly. That's something I shall find out when I'm a doctor.

Am I going to be haunted by Flyte for the rest of my life? I hope not. He stroked Glory's head. Thank goodness you're here with me, Glory. You'll keep me from going mad, won't you?

A little later there was a rustle behind the door, it opened, and George stuck his head out. 'You're to come in, Reuben,' he said. Then in a whisper: 'Try and cheer them up, can't you? It's like a funeral in here.'

Reuben went in.

The visitor had his back to the door. At first Reuben only saw the preacher's black clothes. He noted that the man was crooked and he stooped. He saw he was holding a wide-brimmed hat and a Bible. But even then, though none of this was familiar, something about him made Reuben hesitate, fearful . . .

The preacher turned.

Flyte! It *was* Flyte.

It was his nightmare come to life. That great curved nose! That drooping, red-rimmed left eye! If nothing else, ever, Reuben would recognize that hideous eye. It was Flyte. A dead man risen again!

It was Flyte, but he was changed. He dragged his foot as he walked. There were deep scars across his cheek, and one ear was torn so badly only a shred was left hanging.

He must have had a terrible accident . . .

Reuben shuddered. An accident – such as falling down an old mining shaft?

Reuben could hardly breathe; an iron band was buckled round his chest. His fists were clenched, ready to fight, his legs wanted to run, but nothing was happening. He had turned to marble.

I am finished! I am dead!

'You're not about to pass out are you, Reuben, lad?' asked George, stepping towards him.

'Do sit down, Reuben, if you feel sickly,' said Lady Marley. 'George, go and get us some drinks. Cakes too. See if there are any almond cakes.'

George whisked away.

Flyte had merely glanced at Reuben as he came in. But in that second Reuben had felt the man's malice like the thrust of a knife.

'Is this young man a relative, Lady Marley?' said Flyte, raising an eyebrow. 'I should like to be introduced to him.'

Clever, clever, thought Reuben. Flyte the trickster at work again.

'No. A visitor,' said Lady Marley. 'His name is Reuben Brittlebank. Come and say how do you do, Reuben.' She turned back to Flyte. 'I'm afraid, Mister Smith, that he has not been brought up with polite gentry.'

Reuben did not move. *Mister Smith? Mister Smith?*

'I have no son of my own,' said Lady Marley, 'and I like this peasant boy . . . despite his manners. Well, stay there then, Reuben, if you will. You must be ill, I believe.'

'I might be able to help him,' said Flyte. 'I am well acquainted with the skills of the apothecary. But firstly you, my lady. You were describing your spiritual condition . . . This interruption has broken our train of thought.' He reached over and took Lady Marley's small hand. 'May I?'

Her hand lay in his great paw like a crumpled leaf. Gently, he cupped it with his other hand and held it enclosed. In a flash Reuben was reminded of Flyte at the fairs. Quack! Charlatan! Liar!

A weakness, like a great tiredness, came over Reuben. He yawned and staggered. He tripped over his own feet and fell into the chair behind him. His hands clutched at the brocade-covered arms. He let out a little cry.

Lady Marley threw him an angry glance.

'Reuben! Be still!'

A sweat had broken out all over Reuben's body, his clothes felt glued to his skin. Escape! I must get out! Let me out!

But he was stuck to the seat, so frightened he felt if he were to move something would give inside him and he'd shatter into a thousand shards.

Flyte spoke quietly to Lady Marley. His voice was hoarse and gravelly now. Reuben pictured Flyte at the bottom of Cal's Cauldron, shouting and calling for help. Perhaps for days and days . . .

Reuben had been this man's slave and prisoner before. Now it felt as though he were again. He had no power to speak, move, think – his will had vanished. He tried to shake his head, to move, but only a muscle twitched in his cheek.

Lady Marley and Flyte went on talking.

'I have the worst affliction known to any wife.' Lady Marley smoothed the silk of her skirt. 'I'm barren, Mister Smith.'

'Let us pray!' The preacher tapped his long fingers on the front of the Bible. He put the book on Lady Marley's knee, set her hand upon the book, and his upon that. He stared up at the ceiling.

'God's Providence has brought me here to you God-fearing folk. Who shall turn from the ways of the Lord? We must follow the chosen path. The Lord purchased me with His blood. He shall purchase you also. It is God's will that all women do bear the burden of Eve's guilt and so labour to produce children. If you love Him, He will bestow His love on you. Another child will come to your empty womb. Mark me. God is with you!'

Reuben shut his eyes. Words. Flyte was so good with words. I must not heed him, he thought. Lady Marley must not also.

But Lady Marley seemed entranced. She fixed her shining eyes on Flyte and smiled at him.

Pray don't let her Ladyship believe this nonsense, please!

'Mister Smith, you speak very fine,' said Lady Marley at last, 'but – is it of any use to me? Mister Culpeper here,' she tapped the book, 'at least offers me hope with his herbal remedies.'

'All is predestined, that is God's will,' said Flyte. 'All are not created in equal condition.'

'I know that,' snapped Lady Marley. 'You are very much lower than me, take care to remember that, preacher!'

Reuben saw Flyte flinch, but quickly recover. He crossed his hands over his chest. Fierce red and white jagged scars snaked over his hands. Reuben had last seen those hands clawing at the edge of Cal's Cauldron, scrabbling on the rock, digging into the earth . . .

'God's will be done,' said the preacher. 'Eternal life is ordained for some, eternal damnation for others.'

'I'm perfectly sure I shall go to Heaven,' said Lady Marley, lifting her chin. 'I say my prayers morning and night. I read the Bible. My staff read the Bible. Lord Marley needs an heir. God surely wishes this also.'

'Through prayer and contemplation, His will shall be done. But there are things we can do also. Lady Marley, there are ways . . . I have had success before with ladies in just such a condition . . .'

'You have? Tell me!'

'I speak directly to the Lord our God . . .' He paused as he knelt down beside her. 'Through my direct communication with Him, I have knowledge of a certain – potion.'

'Potion? What manner of potion do you speak of?' She leaned closer to him, her pale cheeks flushed with expectation.

'God showed the making of it to me. He took me to the deepest woods, down a deep pit, like a *cauldron* carved into the ground . . .' He glanced up at Reuben and winked slowly. 'I found a plant there, never before seen by mankind. A small herb. Each leaf shaped to mirror the female form. And white flowers, Lady Marley, shining like moonlight, white and silver. As you know, the moon governs the female cycle.'

'Oh.' Lady Marley laid her small hand over her flat belly as if she could already feel the benefits of the herb working inside her 'And would you . . . ? Could you . . . ?'

'I am fearsome tired and hungry,' said Flyte, getting up slowly from the floor and rubbing his back. 'I've walked all the day long and as you can see, I am afflicted. I have calcifications of the joints, fibulations and fixifications of my scapula, sclerosis of my ankles. The result of recent injuries. But I will do all I can when I am rested. God must have set my feet on this path to you. To be your salvation.'

Lady Marley rang her bell for a servant. Catherine came.

'What happened to George and our cakes?'

'Don't know, m'lady.'

'Well, lay an extra place at the table for Mister Smith this evening. He is staying for supper. And make up a bed for him.'

'Yes, m'lady.'

'Go with Catherine and she will show you where you can wash yourself. You look well travelled,' said Lady Marley. 'You may return when you are done.'

The preacher bowed. As he went out of the room

he smiled at Reuben. The smile reminded Reuben of the crocodile in Lord Marley's study.

The moment they were alone, Reuben rushed to Lady Marley's side and snatched up her hand. It was limp and cold.

'Mistress, please listen! He lies! That Mister Smith is no Mister Smith! He lies!'

'What are you saying, boy?' She snatched back her hand and pushed him away. 'How dare you approach me in this manner? Leave me be!'

'No, please! I must tell you. He's an imposter! He isn't who he says he is. He isn't a preacher! He was the man who—'

But Lady Marley held up her hands in front of her face.

'Silence. You don't understand, Reuben. You cannot understand a need like mine. I must have a child. I must! What use am I if I don't?' Her voice sank to the tiniest of whispers. 'Reuben, if I don't produce an heir, my Lord Marley means to dispose of me. He does. I know it.'

'Lady Marley! No, that's . . . What are you saying?'

'He must have an heir, you understand? He is mad for an heir. If I don't produce one soon, I will be too old and dry . . . I believe Mister Smith can help me fall pregnant. I must trust him. I must!' She clutched his arm and spat out the last words at him. 'I don't care what he is! I just need a child!'

'But—'

'Now go.' She leaned back in her chair. 'Perhaps you've imagined Mister Smith to be someone other than he is. It's easy to do so when the light is poor. You are tired. Alone. Confused . . .'

'I am not confused, Lady Marley, truly I am not.' Reuben cast about for a way to convince her. 'I swear to you that man is not a preacher. He's a fraud. A trickster. Please, please believe me. Doctor Brittlebank would know him. He would tell you the truth.'

'Ah, but the good Doctor Brittlebank is not here, is he, Reuben? When he returns we will see what he has to say. In the meantime, you will rest here with me, won't you? You will keep me company and help me with my quest? Do you know, Reuben, with you by my side, I feel already stronger.' She patted his shoulder. 'You are a good boy. You'll help me, won't you?'

'Of course I will, my lady, but—'

'Reuben, don't question my wishes.'

'But my lady, that man is—'

'I will not hear another word!'

Reuben nodded weakly.

'Good. Now leave me for a while. Go on.'

Reuben ran like the wind up to his bedchamber.

He slammed shut the door and locked it. He flung himself on to the window seat and leaned his hot brow against the windowpane. If only the doctor was here, if only . . .

Glory jumped up beside him and licked his cheek.

Oh, Glory, what am I to do? He stroked her head and fondled her velvety ears.

Flyte. Flyte! How is he alive? It's not possible. Did he know I was here?

He did.

I know it.

Flyte has tracked me down. He's found me and he means to kill me.

11

Flyte's Three Reasons

I was so certain he was dead, thought Reuben. I felt so sure. I *wanted* him dead! Yes, I am guilty for not helping him out of Cal's Cauldron. Now I will pay for it.

Flyte will kill me!

He began to pace up and down. Glory scampered beside him, nipping playfully at his heels.

If only Lady Marley would believe me! But she won't. I'll stay locked in here until Doctor Brittlebank comes back. But he will be days! Lady Marley won't let me lock myself in the room for days and days . . . What shall I do? I cannot stay here! I cannot!

I will run away. Now! Yes!

He wrapped a scarf around his neck and pulled on his warm jacket. He slapped his thigh to call Glory and went out quietly to the landing. He peered over the banister. It was silent below. He ran quickly down the steps. Catherine came running along the hall at the same moment. She swung on to the bottom step and galloped up the stairs. They almost collided.

'Reuben! There you are! What's the hurry? Her Ladyship wants yer,' she said. She wiped her greasy lips on her apron. 'Mutton's oozing fat, mind.'

'I was on my way out . . . Glory needs—'

'Here, ain't that preacher a fine talker? I could listen to him all night. He's chock-full of words.'

'He seems to be,' agreed Reuben, cautiously. 'Where is he now?'

'He were out in the yard playing his pipe. Can't you hear him?'

Now that Reuben listened, he could hear, very faintly, the tinny sound of the whistle streaming through the house like a thin baby wailing. Then it stopped abruptly.

'Mistress is right struck on him, ain't she? George says he's going to get her pregnant. We had a laugh. We was all wondering how exactly!' She bit the corner of her apron and chewed on it. 'Begging your pardon, and all, but, well, Heaven knows, that husband of hers can't seem to do it – well not with her, anyways. Mad as a March hare, he is. You know what I mean, I'm sure.'

'Lord Marley is a bit unusual,' said Reuben, trying to step past Catherine. 'But—'

'Unusual? Oh, is that how you name it? Mad's the

name we give it. Just waiting for him to be taken away, we are. The Hall will crumble. It's all going, you mark my words.'

Reuben suddenly saw the roofs of Marley Hall fold inwards, scattering tiles across the lawn. Ivy rampaged over the walls. The inner walls tumbled, the porch collapsed. It would happen.

'Thank you, Catherine. Do you know what Lady Marley wants from me?'

'I don't. But she was right keen you went to her.'

Reuben felt momentarily safe knowing that Flyte was outdoors. He hurried to Lady Marley's room and sat Glory down at the door to keep watch.

'Stay,' he whispered. 'On guard! If you see *him*, bark like the larky thing you are. Loud, mind!' He ruffled her fur and patted her head. 'I won't be long.' He knocked gently on the door and went in.

Lady Marley was not there.

But Flyte was.

Alone.

He was standing beside a cabinet, peering inside at its contents. Hearing the door open, he turned quickly and replaced a silver jug on a shelf. He smiled graciously – until he saw it was Reuben.

Reuben felt his insides plummet.

So many times Reuben had imagined coming up against Flyte: in the dark woods, in a cave, at the house . . . Each time Reuben had been so fierce, so brave. He'd always won.

Seeing Flyte now turned Reuben's blood to ice water in his veins, caused a sour sickness in his throat and a churning in his bowels. The air between them was sharp and hard.

For three seconds Flyte stood there as still as a log. Then he rushed at Reuben.

Reuben didn't have time to move.

Flyte was like a dog suddenly loosed from its lead. His face was twisted, his jaws rigid and teeth bared. He flung himself at Reuben. Reuben dodged, but Flyte, growling, caught him and threw him to the ground. Reuben felt Flyte's bony knees in his back, pinning him to the floor. He was pressed into the rug, hairs and crumbs caught on his lips. His nose was squashed flat.

'Look at me!' hissed Flyte.

Reuben closed his eyes: he will kill me, he will kill me . . .

'Look at me!'

Reuben slowly twisted up to look at Flyte. Flyte's face was inches from his own. Reuben saw the blood vessels on his yellow eyeballs. The long grizzly hairs in his eyebrows. He smelled his foul dog's breath. Smelled the vinegar on his coat. He retched dryly.

'Look at this!' Flyte jabbed his forefinger at

the husky flake of his torn ear. He stabbed at his scarred cheek. 'Here!' He pushed his hunched shoulder towards Reuben. 'And this leg!' He kicked Reuben. 'Crippled. Maimed. I hurtled against the walls, Reuben. Smashed! Wallop! Here!' He slapped his head. 'Here.' He thumped his shoulder. 'And here!' His leg. 'That's three I owe you, Reuben. Three.'

'It wasn't my—'

Flyte dug his knees harder into Reuben's back.

'Not your fault? Whose was it then? The fairies? You didn't save me. You let me drop. It's thanks to Baggs that I live.'

'Baggs?' Reuben twisted round trying to see Flyte's eyes. Was Flyte lying? 'Baggs saved you?'

Flyte nodded.

'Where is he?'

'Maybe you should take a trip to the woods near Stonebridge, Reuben. Maybe you should walk the path to Cal's Cauldron. Stop. Look down . . .'

'What d'you mean?'

Flyte laughed. 'Baggs came looking for me. His conscience got the better of him. Yours didn't!' Reuben wriggled but Flyte only leaned on him harder. 'Baggs came down on a rope to help me out . . . But only one man left Cal's Cauldron that day . . .'

'You let him die?'

'Maybe I did. Maybe I didn't. Meanwhile, Reuben, it's *you* I've come for. It's time to pay your dues, lad.'

Flyte had hold of both Reuben's arms behind his back and now he began to pull Reuben's right arm, forcing it up towards his neck.

'One,' Flyte said, jerking the arm.

Reuben yelped.

'Hush, hush, Reuben. This is nothing, nothing yet.' Flyte yanked his arm again. Harder. 'Two.'

'Please!' His elbow burned.

'Three.'

'Ow! Please! No!'

Reuben's shoulder was on fire. He heard the bones grating together, the awful sound travelling through his blood and flesh; he felt his ligaments straining like taut catgut.

Tears pricked his eyes. Oh, God save me, save me! It hurts!

Flyte filled Reuben's senses; his nose was clogged with his vinegar and sour milk smell, his gravelly voice grated in his ears, his weight on his back was squashing him. Even with his eyes closed he could see Flyte.

I shall die . . . He will kill me, just like this . . .

Suddenly Reuben felt a great lightness as Flyte stood up and released his hold. He heard himself coughing and choking. He sucked in air in spasms, gasping, retching.

I'm still alive. Lady Marley? Why doesn't she come? Oh, my God! Or George? George! Flyte will kill me! But he couldn't speak out loud. He found himself rolling into a bundle on the floor, cradling his arm, whimpering.

'Was I too rough?'

Reuben heard Flyte's voice from a long way off.

'Was I? There, boy, there. Don't take on so.'

Reuben looked up at Flyte through half-closed eyes. The pain in his elbow and shoulder was terrible.

'Please accept my apologies, young sir. Let me help you up.'

Dazed, Reuben reached for the proffered hand. Flyte grabbed Reuben's little finger in his fist and twisted it sharply.

'Aagh!'

It was as though a red-hot needle was driven right up through his finger, hand and arm.

'Aagh!'

Flyte wrenched the finger harder.

Reuben dropped to his knees, his body bending like a bow. No words came out, just a stream of half-words, half-cries. Flyte twisted further and further. Reuben was bent double, contorted like a hairpin. He tried to bend away, to escape, to go with the pain, but Flyte was pushing his finger further and further . . .

'No!'

It's going to break. It'll break. Oh, my Lord!

The pain was everything. Red and black swirling shapes skidded before his eyes. The pain shouted in his head. It burned his nerves. It bubbled his blood.

'No! Please! No! I can't—'

Crack!

The noise was like a dry twig snapping.

Flyte let go. 'Oh, fancy,' he said mildly.

Reuben collapsed on the floor.

'An accident,' said Flyte. 'I don't know my own strength, do I?'

'Oh, my finger! My finger!'

The pain was unlike anything ever before. It filled Reuben entirely. It seared and throbbed and pulsed in waves from his finger, up his wrist and into his shoulder. He felt his body heaving with sobs. His mouth hung open wetly. He blinked tears.

He stared down at his twisted finger. It stuck out at a right angle, like a joke.

'It's important you know I am serious, Reuben,' said Flyte. He walked towards the table and straightened a book. 'I am deadly serious.'

Reuben made some rough, broken reply.

'Did you hear me? I say I'm deadly serious.'

'Yes,' sobbed Reuben. 'I know it.'

'Good.'

'I could kill you now.' Flyte slid a knife out from his coat and showed it to Reuben. 'See. I am ready.' He twisted the blade back and forth then quickly slipped it back beneath the folds of fabric. 'But the folk here would know it was me. And it would be too quick. I've been planning this these last months. Fortuitous that my – errand – should bring me close to you. I have such a horrible, slow and tortuous death planned for you, Reuben. I won't be cheated out of it.'

The door opened and Lady Marley came in.

'Ah, Lady Marley, what a pleasure.' Flyte stood in front of Reuben so Lady Marley didn't see him immediately. 'You look very beautiful, my lady, if I might be permitted to say so.'

Reuben heard Flyte's voice as if it was part of another time and place. Lights buzzed and burst inside his head. His finger throbbed.

'What is Reuben doing on the floor? What's going on?' said Lady Marley. 'Reuben, you must be ailing as I thought. There is scarlet fever in the village.'

'My finger,' Reuben groaned. 'My finger, Lady Marley, I—'

'He tripped over the chair,' said Flyte. 'I fear he

might have broken his finger. I am a practised bone-setter, perhaps I could . . .'

Reuben shook his head violently. The sudden movement sent a fresh wave of pain undulating through his hand.

'My finger,' he whimpered.

Flyte went over to Reuben and pulled him to his feet.

'There. Be silent now. An aristocrat would never show pain.'

'Now, Reuben, dear,' said Lady Marley, 'see how real gentlemen behave? There is a great deal for you to learn. But he is coming along, Mister Smith. He improves. Come and sit beside me, Reuben.'

Reuben felt his mouth open to say something, but what could he say? It was no use looking to Lady Marley for comfort. She was smiling at Flyte.

'If I might be excused?' Reuben managed to say.

'Nonsense. I want you with me. Here, drink some liquor, that will make you better.'

Reuben managed to reach the chair beside her and sit down.

'I think you will also benefit from listening to Mister Smith. He has a considerable knowledge, Reuben,' Lady Marley said.

Reuben drank a whole glass of wine in one swallow.

'Show me your hand, dear boy.'

Reuben lifted his hand up very slowly.

'I see it. Do you know, Reuben, that it is dislocated? I expect you thought it was broken, but I have had experience of this myself,' said Lady Marley. 'My elbow often slips out of place and I have to call Doctor Goodwin to come and put it back in. Let me send for him.'

Reuben could not speak. He nodded. He rested his injured hand on his lap. It hurt. But if he could get past the hurt then he could run. Get out. Get away from Flyte. How was it to be done? How can I go, he thought, with this pain?

He drank another glass of ruby-red wine very quickly.

Flyte was standing beside Reuben. Reuben felt him looming over him like the gallows.

'As I said, Lady Marley,' said Flyte, 'I have studied as a bone-setter and an apothecary. Please let me help the boy. I would like to.'

'No!'

'Reuben, don't be so ungrateful,' said Lady Marley. 'Of course you may, Mister Smith.'

'I shall do it myself!' cried Reuben.

He jumped up. He *would* do it himself! Anything rather than let Flyte touch him.

Reuben grabbed his little finger with his right

hand and pulled. It was extraordinary how he could *feel* the wrongness of the joint. The ends of the bones were scraping against each other instead of nestling softly. It just needed a yank outward, a push across, and the end of the bone would slip back into the socket. He could feel it.

The pain was white and silver lines searing across his head. Reuben bit down hard on his lip. He would not give in to the pain. He would not.

Reuben closed his eyes. He pulled the finger hard. In his mind's eye he saw what he needed to do and did it.

12

Belladonna

Reuben sat down again heavily.

'Will you faint?' asked Lady Marley. She gave him another glass of wine.

'No. No, I am not going to faint.' He could speak. He could speak and sound normal. 'That is better. Much better, thank you.'

The knuckle below his little finger was swelling and beginning to turn blue. The throbbing pain was bad, but oh, it was so much better. He tried a weak smile. 'Thank you, my lady.'

His thoughts were elsewhere. He saw himself running. His legs pumping, hair flying as he pelted down the driveway and disappeared into the trees – to Doctor Brittlebank. I will go so fast, Flyte will never catch me.

He looked out of the window. The sun was streaming down from a purple-blue sky. A man was hammering a post beside the gate with a large wooden mallet. Two others leaned comfortably against it, one puffing on a clay pipe, the other scratching his head. It was all as it should be. *They* did not have anything to fear from Flyte.

A small maid was picking herbs from a patch beside the wall and gathering them in her apron.

Herbs.

Grandmother.

What sort of herbs was the girl collecting? Herbs. Potions . . . Sleeping draughts . . . Deathly drinks . . .

Reuben looked up and met Flyte's eyes. He knows exactly what I am thinking, Reuben thought. He cradled his aching, painful finger. Damn you, Flyte. He sees inside me. He knows my shame and my plans . . . But I must outwit him! I must get away!

What excuse could he make to get out of the room? How could he stop Flyte from following?

'Perhaps Reuben should leave us now and we can talk about your proposed cure, Mister Smith?' said Lady Marley.

Flyte glared at Reuben. He turned to Lady Marley with a smile.

'God speaks to me, your lady. He hath purchased me with His blood. He let His heart run out in one deep gaping wound for me! Let me share that glory with you. Let me save you!' He got down on his knees and dragged Reuben down beside Lady Marley's chair with him.

'I don't require saving, I simply require a child,' said Lady Marley. 'That's what you promised me, Mister Smith. There's much to discuss. Reuben, please leave us now.'

'Yes, your Ladyship.' Reuben attempted to get up.

'I would that he stayed,' snapped Mister Smith. He squeezed Reuben's arm tighter.

'I think you forget your station, Mister Smith . . . but you are right. Reuben, stay. I do find your presence soothing. I want to talk about that plant with the moon leaves, Mister Smith . . . Get up. Come, sit by there.' She pointed to the chair opposite her.

Reuben heard Flyte mutter something under his breath. Slowly he unwound his fingers from Reuben's arm like a snake releasing its prey. Reuben could feel the pressure points left by his bony fingers, like toothmarks after a bite.

So close! So nearly away! Reuben sat down again, trembling. Lady Marley had no idea what a disservice she had just done him.

There was a knock at the door and George came in. He brought more red wine, a jug of ale, cakes and a bowl of dark cherries.

Reuben's pulse quickened: the belladonna berries and those glossy cherries were almost identical. And he had them still.

Reuben felt in his right pocket. Some of the berries had detached themselves from their stalks. He rolled them between his fingers.

Poison.

'Reuben, pour me another glass of wine,' said Lady Marley. 'Pass Mister Smith the fruit.'

Yes. Yes!

Reuben poured the wine. As he picked up the bowl of cherries, he slipped five belladonna berries on to the edge of the dish.

What chance Flyte would chose them? He must! He must!

Reuben turned back to Flyte and offered the fruit. The Belladonna berries looked hardly any different, a little smaller perhaps. Flyte was talking so intently with Lady Marley that he reached for the cherries without looking. His fingers scrabbled over the berries and gathered a handful. He took two or even three of the bogus fruit along with some real cherries and put them all in his mouth.

Reuben was frightened. This was a dangerous game. He bit his lip. Would Flyte realize the trick? Would his tongue feel the different texture and taste?

'I am honoured to be of service to your Ladyship,' Flyte said. He popped some pips out of his mouth into his palm. 'I will go straight out this afternoon and search for the moon herb. I will take Reuben.

Hey, Reuben?' He slipped two more purple cherries into his mouth. Reuben was too scared to watch whether they were his berries or not. 'What do you say, boy? Will you come with me?'

Reuben did not dare look at Flyte. He knew that the fruit of the Belladonna plant was quite sweet at first and then mawkish.

He nodded. Waiting.

Flyte made a face. 'Those cherries are sour,' he said. He took another gulp of his wine. 'Give me a cake, Reuben, to take away the taste.'

It was done. It was done and Flyte knew nothing about it.

Reuben picked up the small dish of cakes. His hand was shaking. His cheeks were burning. His mouth was dry. He was guilty. Guilty. But what else could he do? It was him or me, he told himself. I have no choice.

Reuben carried the dish of fruit back to the table. He removed the two remaining belladonna berries and slipped them in his pocket. If Flyte had eaten even three berries he would be ill. More and he would probably die. Reuben wished he could have forced Flyte to eat handfuls of them. Hundreds of them . . .

The poison worked quickly.

Soon Flyte began to shiver. 'I am mighty hot, Lady

102

Marley,' he said. 'Would you mind if I went out for some fresh air?'

'Please do, Mister Smith. Your cheeks are red. Indeed now I see you look quite feverish. Are you well?' She held her handkerchief up to her nose.

'I am. Might the boy come with me?' Flyte grabbed Reuben's arm. Reuben winced; any movement of his left arm set his hurt finger jangling painfully.

Reuben could have tried to resist him, but he wanted to see what would happen to Flyte. He needed to know.

Reuben walked with Flyte out into the hall. He walked on the balls of his feet, ready to spring, to leap and run.

'What is it, Reuben? A hex? What did you do to me?' hissed Flyte. He was leaning heavily on Reuben's shoulder. 'I know you did this, witch's boy. You did it! Devil child!'

'I do not know what you mean.' Reuben stared ahead blankly. Flyte would see his guilt if he could see Reuben's eyes.

They reached the front door. Glory bounded up to Reuben, wagging her tail, pleased to see her master after such a long while. George was there, smoking a pipe. He put it down quickly when he saw them and rushed over to help Reuben with the preacher.

'What's amiss with him?'

'I don't know,' Reuben said. 'Perhaps he had too much wine.'

'Hold your gulsh, boy!' cried Flyte. He staggered and swayed. 'That witch's brat is trying to kill me! I don't give a tomcat's balls what you say, that's a maggot boy!' Flyte lunged at Reuben, who shrank out of the way. 'Poison down the mine shaft. Don't tell me what, Baggs! Toad's arse!'

He collapsed on the ground.

George grinned and winked at Reuben.

'Fine words from a preacher, eh?'

'He's confused,' said Reuben. 'With the fever.'

Flyte lay stretched out on the stone flags in the doorway. His cheeks were fiery red. His eyes looked very black; his pupils were massive. He shivered but when Reuben touched his skin, it was hot.

'Baggs! Bind your head! Poison!' Flyte rolled over and was sick.

'Scarlet fever, maybe,' said George, stepping away from Flyte. 'That's what it could be. We must get him to bed and keep him apart. There's fever in the village. Preacher must have come that way by here. I'll go tell the women and get old Smithy to help carry him in. Keep away, Reuben. Keep away!'

13

Glory Keeps Her Promise

Reuben ran. He gulped at the fresh air, filling his lungs as if he were filling them for the first or the last time. Running pained his finger. He pushed his left arm into his waistcoat so it wouldn't be jogged so much.

Reuben ran along beside the wall of the house. Large dusty bushes and swathes of grey-leafed lavender kept him out of sight.

There was nobody near the gateway. The labourers had gone. He stood up and gazed down the drive, longing to run that way, out across the fields, over the river and back to Stonebridge. He held out his arm towards where he imagined Wycke House to be, trying to touch it. He wanted it. He wanted Hetty. But Wycke House would be the first place Flyte would look for him. He had to go to Felton, to the doctor.

Reuben ran and leaped over the wall. He knocked his bad hand against the wall as he jumped. The sudden pain was like a burning sting. Like ten wasps had spiked him. He sat very still, cradling his swollen hand until the pulsing pain subsided. As he crouched there, he listened and watched. All was still and quiet.

No one was following him yet.

Nothing.

Not even Glory.

'God damn that dog!' He peeped over the wall. There she was. She was running hell for leather towards the ruins.

The ruins! Gabriel! He had forgotten Gabriel. Oh, Glory, you silly dog! Cobb said you were no good; he was right. Gabriel's the same as you too, isn't he? The runt of the litter. Not wanted. Maybe that's why he likes you.

Damn! Damn, he thought. Gabriel trusted me. He had that sort of face too, like a daisy, all open and trusting – and bees walk all over daisies . . . Ah, but surely he doesn't have feelings. He's not human in truth . . . But he trusted me . . . And who else could he trust around here? And Reuben had sworn, and crossed his heart . . .

Reuben stared across the meadow as Glory disappeared into the distance. He would not leave Glory. And after all, she was keeping her promise. He would have to.

It would be a day, at least a day, before Flyte was well enough to travel.

He hoped.

Reuben raced across the meadow and down the narrow track that led to the ruins.

It always felt as if the sun had gone behind a cloud when he reached that spot. The tall swaying trees blocked out the light. The high crumbling walls and tower seemed to waver as if about to fall.

The raven called: '*kronk kronk*'. It was perched on a high, narrow ledge of the tower. It bobbed its head as if in greeting.

'*One for sorrow,*
Two for mirth,
Three, a wedding,
Four, a birth . . .'

The words the children in his village said when they saw a crow or a raven.

And there is sorrow here, he thought. Lady Marley would like four birds to herald a birth. And I'd like two!

'Glory! Glory!'

There she was! Waiting by the open gate. She wagged her tail and ran to greet him, but before he could catch hold of her collar, she rushed back to the stable door.

And there was Gabriel. He was leaning out waving

his arms, cooing and crowing at Glory. He broke into a continuous stream of sounds, then, 'Dog! Dog! C'mon!'

Reuben meant to smile. He'd imagined he would perhaps touch the boy kindly while he explained about going away. But he couldn't.

Today the sun was shining right on to Gabriel's face.

Gabriel's open mouth was ringed with caked food and dry saliva. His nose was clogged with snot, and shiny streaks of dry snot smeared his dirty cheeks like slug trails. His scalp showed red bare patches. The smell of him wiped out all others. Reuben put his hand over his mouth and almost retched.

'Dog. Dog!'

'Yes. Dog. I promised, didn't I?' Reuben forced out the words. 'I said I would come and I did. I meant to bring you food, but, oh, I forgot.'

'Out!'

'I'm in a hurry. There isn't time!'

'Out!' Gabriel started banging the door with his bandaged fists.

Reuben felt so panicked, he agreed quickly. 'Very well. Hush now. Why should you be locked up like a pig, anyway?'

Reuben pulled back the bolts and Gabriel fell on to the grass. Glory pounced on him. She licked his face.

'Glory! Can't you see what a dolt he is? He smells like a dung heap and his teeth are rotten!' Reuben sighed and folded his arms, winced at the pain in his hand. He tapped his foot.

'I have to go,' he said. 'Gabriel! Do you hear me? I have to go. We're on our way to Felton, to see Doctor Brittlebank. I just came to say goodbye because we're going away. Forever. I brought Glory for you to see for one last time. Understand?'

Gabriel looked up at him. His face crumpled, tears spilled down his cheeks. 'No!'

'I'm sorry. We have to go now. I can't explain, but we do have to go.'

'No,' Gabriel whimpered. ''Lone. Gabe 'lone. Mary gone.'

'I'm sorry. I am sorry. It's not my fault. I have to go.'

The boy scrambled to his feet and lunged. Reuben pushed him away fiercely. He'd forgotten his finger; he jarred it and set it throbbing with fresh spasms of hot pain. Reuben felt furious. He hated Flyte; Gabriel too – the feel of his louse-infested clothes. He didn't want to lay a finger on his flesh. Gabriel fell back into the shed and Reuben quickly closed the door. The boy lay sobbing.

'I'm sorry, Gabriel.' He didn't look at the boy. 'I am sorry.'

Reuben yanked a bit of string from a nail by the door and slipped it into Glory's collar for a leash. He ran to the gate and slammed it shut. He dashed over the bridge, across the meadow and circled Marley Hall, keeping beneath the cover of the trees.

No one must see me. No one must know which way I have gone.

It took a long while, but at last he was standing in a copse of trees on a hill behind the house. He looked down at the Hall. It looked so small from here, was it really full of all those rooms and people?

How was Flyte? Would he die? Reuben doubted it. Two or three berries would not kill. I've got this day and night, he thought, and that is all. Then he'll be on my trail. I must hurry.

Keeping on the edge of the trees, Reuben walked until he came to a lane. Wearily, he turned on to it, heading north towards Felton. To the doctor.

It felt like there was only Glory Be and Reuben in the world. The fields were turning golden. The trees were tipped with red and yellow. A flock of starlings twittered noisily from their roost in an ash tree. The sun gave him a long September shadow.

He glanced over his shoulder down the road. Nobody.

He quickened his pace. And although he was worried about Flyte, no matter how hard Reuben tried to dislodge it, Gabriel's face was what he kept seeing. It sailed in front of his eyes like a daytime moon. That peculiar, sad face.

14

The Cockerel-Fighter

Reuben could not walk more than ten paces without a furtive glance behind him.

Would Lady Marley send someone after him? Would he hear a creaking, clanking cart? Would it be someone galloping on a horse?

And Flyte? How was he? Vomiting and feeling very ill, Reuben hoped. Flyte would not die – he hadn't taken enough poison. But, say, just say that he ate enough belladonna to kill him, Reuben thought. Who will know it was me? No one. I will have killed him first, that's all . . . before he got to kill me.

Glory loved being out in the fields. Reuben hoped she would notice if Flyte were creeping up on them, but doubted she would. She spent her time and energy on things that he could only guess at. Glory pounced on the dullest patches of grass. She bristled at suspicious stones and jumped at shadows. She would probably wag her tail at Flyte if he appeared.

Towards the end of the day, Reuben sat down on a

grassy bank away from the path and rested. There was the little geranium known as herb robert growing there. He mashed some of its leaves, rubbing them between his palms, and made a green mush. This he smeared over his swollen finger joint, wrapping two large wormwood leaves round it to hold it down. Same way as you'd do it, Granny, he thought, with a smile. The pain lessened.

He was feeling light-headed and weary. He ate some blackberries from the mass of brambles beside him. Stretched between the thorny bushes he saw a large spider's web. A fat spider was winding a line around a hoverfly. The fly and the web shivered nervously. If only I could catch dinner like that, he thought. A brown speckled butterfly came down and rested for a moment on his knee. It fanned its wings thoughtfully, oblivious to where it was perched. When the butterfly took off, Reuben got up. He was cold now, suddenly. The sun was almost gone from the sky. He had to find a place to rest for the night. Somewhere out of the way where he and Glory could be well hidden.

As he stood up, a building came into view. He had not seen it before, tucked away amongst some trees across the shallow valley.

Reuben went towards it. The thought of being out alone in the damp and the dark was suddenly hard to bear. A shed or a stable, a pigsty, anything would be better.

The building turned out to be a low, thickly thatched cottage with two tiny windows either side of the door. The chimney smoked thickly and Reuben pictured a big fire and warm food. At a right angle to the cottage was a long, low stone barn. A wall surrounded the yard and a sprawling sycamore tree sheltered it.

Reuben had almost reached the place when there was a terrible scream. He stopped dead. The noise made his ears burn and his scalp leap. What was it? The awful shriek rang out again. What could it be? He grabbed Glory's collar and together they crept closer.

He stopped beside the rough stone wall, crouched down and peeped over.

He saw a small man running across the yard. He was bespattered head to foot with mud. Tucked under his arm was a fine golden cockerel. Chasing him, with its neck outstretched, was a fierce-looking black cockerel. The bloodcurdling row came from these two birds.

The man stopped at the base of the steep dunghill on the far side of the yard. He turned and checked the black cockerel with blazing eyes was behind him, then he raced up the hill, shouting and hollering.

'Yahoo! Yahoo! Yahoodawallera!'

The golden bird in his grasp screeched and cock-a-doodled. Its scaly orange feet kicked and pushed against him.

The black cockerel followed. It flapped its wings. It shook its glossy feathers and snapped its beak, screamed and shrieked.

'Come on you beauty!' cried the little man. He raced to the top of the dunghill. 'Come and get us!'

Just as the black cockerel had strutted up to the top of the dung pile, just as it was inches from them, the man turned and faced it.

'Yahoowha!' he yelled, thrusting the golden bird into its face.

The black cockerel, incensed at the taunting, launched itself in the air, wings out, beak snapping, claws thrashing. The screams and squawks from both of them were terrible. Reuben covered his ears.

'Whoa! Good work! Yahoo!' The man rushed down the dung heap again with the black cockerel right behind him. He slipped on the wet rotting stuff, sat down and slithered all the way back down on to the cobbles, and jumped up, grinning and dancing around.

A cock-master! That's what he was. Training his birds for fighting in the pit. For as long as he could remember, Reuben had longed to go to see a cock fight.

He stood up and waved. 'Good evening, sir!'

Reuben took the man by surprise; his grip on the golden bird lessened and he only just managed to hang on to it as it tried to squeeze free.

The black cockerel skittered sideways and squawked crossly. Confused, it jumped up in the air, changed direction and made a sudden rush at Reuben.

Glory, thinking her master was under threat, leaped over the wall, barking.

'Glory!'

'Ho, Blackie! Here!' The man raced after the cockerel, but the bird was faster. It was frightened. The cock flapped and squawked and ran in circles.

'He's lost the fun of it! He's away! After him, young man!'

Reuben jumped over the wall and gave chase. So did Glory.

The black cockerel ran for a dark hole beneath the window.

'No!' yelled the man.

The cockerel bobbed down and disappeared into the hole.

'Ah, now that's done it!' said the man, slapping his thigh. 'Blackie, you devil! Knew I should've blocked that gap up!' He turned to look at Reuben. 'Who's you and what you doing in my yard? You've lost me my bird. You're not trying to cobble my cockerels are you?' He sounded cross, but his eyes and mouth were smiling.

'No, I assure you . . . I am sorry. Can you not get him back?'

The man stuck out his bottom lip. 'Last time he went in there it took me days to coax him out. Though he wants the food, he wants to be free. Little devil. Curse on the cockerel population. When will you learn, Wilmot, you duffer!'

'Wilmot?'

'That's me.'

'I could get him,' said Reuben, looking towards the hole. It was where a stone had come loose and the cobbles were dug up. 'I'm small. I could reach in, I think. But shall I tie up Glory first? She's scaring him.'

'Good idea, my friend.' Wilmot found some thin rope for Reuben and they fixed Glory to the iron ring in the wall normally used for tethering horses. 'Now, could you get him for me, d'you suppose? Would you do that?'

'It was our fault,' said Reuben. 'I would like to try.'

'True it was your appearance that did it, but Blackie's mighty vicious even with his spurs wrapped up, which they are, thank the Lord.'

'What about his beak? It looks very sharp.'

'As an iron nail,' agreed Wilmot, proudly. 'But I've

thick gloves. It would be a right good favour you'd be doing me, if you got him out.'

Reuben slipped his small hands into the thick leather gauntlets without too much pain to his hurt finger. He lay down on his stomach in front of the hole. The cobbles dug into his bony ribs and the smells down on the ground made his eyes water.

Reuben peered in. He could see the bird's bright eyes staring back at him, and little else. Reuben did not like their expression. A weird rumbling, clucking sound, like a warning growl, was bubbling up from inside the small bird.

Reuben sat up. 'A worm?' he suggested. 'Would that entice him a little?'

Wilmot chuckled. 'Worms is favourite. Good idea.' He stroked the golden bird's head. 'Worms is favourite, isn't it, my beauty?'

The dunghill was seething with worms and it took Reuben no time at all to find one. Soon he was back lying on the ground at the entrance of the hole and dangling the writhing worm from his gloved hand.

Blackie did not know he was being tricked. He came straight for it, beak snapping, eyes flashing. As soon as the bird was close enough, Reuben slipped his other hand round behind it and scooped it out. The cockerel was furious; it flapped its wings and tried to go back. Reuben had to flatten it on the ground then drag it out. He hoped he wouldn't damage it. He was glad its claws were strapped.

Blackie came out snapping, crowing and slashing with his feet.

Reuben tucked the bird's wings down and put his arm around it, holding it the way Wilmot was holding the golden bird. It was a fine feeling, like holding a cabbage made of feathers. Blackie went on snapping and growling and squawking.

'There! What a bird! What a beauty, eh?' cried Wilmot. 'That's a grand job, young man. Thanking you so much.'

'What shall I do with—'

'Ah, this way. To the barn! Don't you go letting go now!' Wilmot pulled open the large barn door and ushered Reuben inside. 'That's right. Pens are here.'

Reuben followed obediently.

It was very dark inside. The barn smelled of barley and hay and dust and mice. And birds. Reuben could make out six wooden cages about three feet by four feet down the wall. Each had a slatted wooden front that slid up and down. Inside each there was clean straw and wooden dishes for food and water. Three of the crates already had cockerels in them. They started crowing quietly and jabbing their heads from side to side.

'Listen how they talk,' said Wilmot. 'See, they know you're a stranger, is what they're saying.'

'They live like kings,' said Reuben.

'Aye, they do.'

A rope dangled beside each pen. Wilmot pulled it. The front panel slid up so he could put the cockerel inside. 'Here we are. In you go. Now it's just Blackie and we're done.'

He took the black cockerel gently from Reuben. The bird stopped struggling in his master's arms, put his head back and looked up at Wilmot with his yellow eyes as if he were just about to speak.

'It is a beautiful bird,' said Reuben. 'So glossy. Those long feathers on its wings are magnificent. Do they take much looking after?'

'They do. Cockerels have got filth and grease and glut in 'em. They need scouring out with powders. And then I've to run the chase – what you witnessed – that heats them up so's they don't get pursy . . .'

'*Pursy?*'

'Short of breath. I've to feed them special, too – wheat meal, eggs an' all.'

'Better than some folk eat!' said Reuben.

'That's for sure.' Wilmot stroked Blackie's back. 'What a beauty. What a prize! Then I— Ah, now, I'm not giving away all my secrets to you, young man. You could be a spy.'

'I promise I'm not.'

'No, nor do you look one.'

'But don't tell me if you don't want to.'

'Then I won't,' said Wilmot, after a moment's hesitation. 'But you can watch this, see, my last ritual, only don't tell a soul.' And Wilmot began to lick the cockerel's head and eyes, working all over the bird's feathery head with his tongue. Blackie went very still, closed his eyes and made soft muffled clucking sounds. 'Makes the scouring work, you see,' said Wilmot. 'Cleanses his head and body right wonderfully. Best fighters in the region, my beauties.'

When Blackie was safely stowed in his pen they went back into the yard. Wilmot turned to Reuben and stuck out his hand. Reuben took it and they shook hands firmly.

'Wilmot's pleased to make your acquaintance!'

'My name's Reuben,' said Reuben.

'Reckon you need food and water and a pen yourself?' said Wilmot, nodding and winking at Reuben.

'I do, sir.'

'Come along in then and bring your little dog. 'Tis almost dark, ain't it?'

Reuben followed Wilmot in through the low, wide doorway. There was only one large room in the cottage and it also smelled of birds.

Wilmot lit two candles and set them down. The long table was cluttered with papers and feathers and candle wax and apple cores. Apart from that large item of furniture, there was one good chair and one stool. Wilmot's bed was pushed into the corner by the great fireplace. Over the fire hung a round black pot. Something was cooking in it that smelled very tasty.

Reuben sat on the stool and smiled round at everything: it was much more homely than Marley Hall. Wilmot gave him some mead to drink. He cut a slice of ham, handed it to Reuben off the spike of the knife, and tossed Glory some fatty scraps. They ate the stew from wooden dishes and wiped them clean with their fingers.

'I could do with a woman around here, and no mistake,' said Wilmot, looking round. 'Can't get it clean. Can't get the bad smells out. And though I do love my birds, I'd prefer to love a plump young girl, that's the truth.'

Reuben thought of Hetty. She'd put this place straight in no time at all. 'I know a young lady that would answer your requirements,' he said, grinning.

'Do you, now? Then maybe you could arrange a meeting? Eh? Is she kind, and good with poultry?'

Reuben pictured Hetty out in the yard strangling

the hens for dinner with one deft twist of their necks. Best not tell Wilmot about that particular skill of hers. 'Very good,' he said.

'Well, then, you get her to meet with Wilmot, why don't you?'

'When I can . . .' said Reuben. Quite suddenly he remembered why it was that he was there. He shivered.

'Don't be thinking I'm rude and over-curious, but what brings you and your dog here?' said Wilmot. He leaned back in his chair. 'I will help you if'n I can.'

Reuben hesitated. 'The truth is,' he said, after a while, 'there is a man after me. He's dressed as a preacher – white neckerchief, long black coat and all, but he is no preacher. He's someone I used to know. He hates me and he means to do me ill.'

'Why's he after you?' Wilmot's eyes were round as marbles. He bit noisily into an apple. 'What've you done?'

'It's a long story,' said Reuben, stroking Glory, who had settled down at his feet. 'He holds it against me for the loss of his business, which was quackery and so unlawful. He holds it against me that he was run out of town and made an outcast. And he holds it against me that he had an accident. He fell down a deep old mining shaft in the woods near Stonebridge and was injured badly. But, Wilmot, he would have pushed me down that hole if he could and it was an accident that he fell!'

'My, my, this is all mighty complicated for a cock-master,' said Wilmot, shaking his head.

'Trust me, Wilmot, he's a bad man and if he catches up with me, I believe – I know – he will kill me.'

'Bless me!' said Wilmot, slugging down more mead. 'Poor lad. Well, you're safe here. Birds will set up a hullabaloo if a stranger comes by. Better'n dogs they are. So rest easy and tomorrow you can start on your way.'

'Thank you, Wilmot. That's kind of you. Thank you.' Reuben did not tell him about the belladonna berries he had given Flyte. Whenever he thought about what he'd done, Reuben felt his cheeks burn. If Flyte died – surely he wouldn't – Reuben would be a murderer!

'Don't need thanks,' said Wilmot. 'You're a young lad in need and you helped me with Blackie. 'Sides, I do get lonesome. Cockerels ain't the chatty type.'

Reuben slept that night on the floor on a pile of old clothes and blankets that smelled of wet animal. The floor was hard and despite his day's walking, Reuben couldn't settle. His finger ached. His head was whirling with thoughts. The cockerels started crowing gently and persistently before daybreak.

Reuben lay staring into the room, thinking about Lady Marley and Flyte; what was going on back at the Hall now that he'd left, and how he could reach Doctor Brittlebank quickly. Glory lay beside him, untroubled by everything, her eyelids fluttering and toes twitching as she raced and chased in her sleep.

Wilmot woke at daybreak and went out to see to his birds and to feed his horse and let it out into the field. When he returned he stoked up the fire and fed Reuben some ale and oatcakes.

'I'm fighting my birds in less than a week,' he told Reuben. 'Shall you stay, young man, and see them win? Make a wager and get some money?'

'I'd like to very much,' Reuben said, truthfully, 'but I have to move on. If this man – Flyte – if he finds me . . . I have to get to the doctor, he's the only one who can help me because he knows Flyte, knows he's no preacher. And he knows *me*.'

'Right you are. I understand. Not a worry, young man. He won't find you through any words of mine. Just you know that there is room here at Wilmot's should you ever need it.'

But Reuben lingered. Reuben told Wilmot about Hetty and Wycke House and how kind Doctor Brittlebank was and how clever. He told him how he planned to be a physician himself and make folk better.

On the doorstep, Wilmot shook Reuben's hand solemnly. Reuben clung to Wilmot's small, rough hand, suddenly afraid to let go. 'I – I would stay if I could. It would be a pleasure. It would be—'

He stopped.

'What d'you hear?' Wilmot cocked his head like a bird.

'Oh, no!' Reuben knelt down and clasped Glory tightly. 'Did you hear? Did you hear?' His voice trembled.

Wilmot frowned. He stood very still. ''Tis music!' he said, breaking into a smile. 'A flute is it? Piping? I love a tune. It's just a traveller, boy, that's all—'

'No, no! It's him. *Flyte!*'

Reuben picked up Glory and spun round. Fields, trees, the house and barn . . . Where could he go? He felt both on fire and icy cold. His legs were heavy and yet he wanted to spring on them and go leaping away over the ground like a hare.

'Oh, oh, oh,' was all he could say.

'The man that's after you?' Wilmot's round face was suddenly serious.

'Yes. Oh, Wilmot, please! Help me. I never thought he'd be this quick. He was ill . . .'

'Shh. Wilmot said he'd help you and he will. Music's far off, it travels faster than a man, be sure of that. Now, no hiding nook in the house. The barn!

I've just the place . . . Dog too. Here, come on. Cockerels shall hide you.'

They went into the barn. The birds broke out chattering and squawking, scratching and pecking the ground nervously. Blackie pointed his beak up to the roof and crowed as if he wanted to rouse the entire county.

'Fearful noisy ain't they? Scares away most. Here, into this pen, Reuben, quick as you can. Cockerel called Billy lived here. Lost 'im in May. Throat torn out by Golden Boy of Rob Hampton. Cheatin' brute. There, in you go. This pen's bigger than the rest, got a bit at the back, d'you see? If someone looked real well they'd find you, but I'm hoping I can put them off so they won't get a chance.'

Reuben crawled through the smelly straw. The back of the pen wasn't where he expected it to be – it extended further beneath an overhanging ledge. He squeezed under it.

'Now pull this over, see.' Wilmot gave him a bit of wood like a lid. It was made from three planks nailed together roughly. It fitted across the back of the pen exactly. 'I must hide a bird on occasion, I admit to it,' said Wilmot. 'Can be a dirty business this cock fighting: stealing, sabotage . . . that's the truth.'

Reuben slipped his trembling fingers into the spaces between the planks and pulled it into place.

His heart was pounding. Now he was hidden behind a false wall. There was no room to move. He and Glory formed a tight knot.

Reuben's eyes watered and his nose itched. The straw stank.

'Sorry 'bout the smell,' whispered Wilmot. 'Weren't expecting visitors. Mind that dog don't bark.'

Glory didn't mind the squash. She liked it. She snuggled down in Reuben's lap and pushed her nose into his armpit.

Reuben heard Wilmot shuffling up the straw in the pen on the other side of the false wall. Then he heard Wilmot drop the slatted panel down and lock it with the peg.

'Good luck!' Wilmot called.

Reuben heard him walk back across the barn, heard the great barn door squeaking on its hinges as it was drawn shut.

It went quiet.

Flyte. Flyte!

He was near. He was coming to get him.

How did he recover from that dose of deadly nightshade so quickly? Reuben thought. He must have insides of iron. Dear Lord, I promise I'll be more careful after this. I'll hide all day and walk at night. I'll creep and crawl and never speak to a soul. I promise I'll read the Bible and say my prayers. Wilmot! Don't give me away! Don't believe what that man tells you. It's lies.

Reuben buried his face in Glory's fur. Dear God! Please God!

Reuben heard the sound of horses' hooves tramping over the yard. The jingle of a metal harness. A sharp knocking on the cottage door. The door opening with a scraping sound as it grazed the uneven stone floor.

Then silence.

15

Wilmot Almost Helps Too Much

There were two men on the doorstep. One was the preacher and the other a big, square man with a broken nose and thin red hair.

'Excuse me,' said Flyte, removing his hat. 'Excuse me for disturbing you so early. Were you at prayer?'

'Er . . . well, not so as you'd notice,' said Wilmot, looking from one visitor to the other quickly and not liking what he saw.

'My name is Mister Smith. And this is Mister Scarfe,' Flyte said. 'We will tie up our horses here by the door.'

Wilmot nodded.

Flyte pushed his way smoothly into the cottage. The other man followed. 'I am looking for a boy.' Flyte stood tall and still, he was like a black streak of soot in the sunny room. 'Do you have a boy?'

Wilmot shrank beneath Flyte's look. He retreated to the fireplace and poked at the embers. His cheeks glowed as red as the logs. Reuben had not exaggerated

Flyte's unpleasantness, thought Wilmot. Mister Scarfe looked mean and nasty too, but in an ordinary bad way. There was something bleaker and crueller in Flyte than he had ever come across before.

'The name's Wilmot, sirs. Cold for the time of year, ain't it? Do come in.' He could not get nearer to the fire now, without falling in it. 'All travelling persons are welcome here.'

'I did not come to discuss the weather, Mister Wilmot. I'm looking for a boy,' said Flyte. 'Brown hair and brown eyes. Chin's too sharp, perhaps, and shows his waywardness. Wears a dark blue jacket. He is a plain child with no redeeming features. No scars, no marks . . . not like me!' He tilted his face into the shaft of sunlight.

Wilmot shuddered. The preacher was certainly a mess; his hands and face covered with raised white lines and puckered skin. His shoulders were crooked. His left eyelid hung open; Wilmot did not like that, it was too much like seeing into the man's insides.

'So answer me, please, have you seen a boy around the place?' Flyte was looking round as he spoke. 'He's a dangerous, lying fellow and . . .' He stopped and pointed. 'Ah, now! I fear for your safety, Mister Wilmot, seeing as I do, those *two* tankards on your table . . .'

Wilmot stared at the table. There was his pewter tankard and beside it, Reuben's. Two plates. Two knives.

'I . . .'

'You had a visitor?'

'I . . . Well, this lad did come by last evening. He seemed harmless enough . . .' Wilmot stopped and drew breath. This was his house. He'd surely dealt with the likes of these two before. The cock pits were full of rough types. 'What was you wanting him for exactly?' He stepped forward, frowned and stuck out his chin.

'He is my sister's son. My nephew,' said Flyte. 'He's my blood, you understand, Mister Wilmot, blood ties are strong. God has given me the task of bringing him back to my sister. The poor woman wants him returned, despite what he's done . . .'

'What did you say he has done?'

'I didn't say. And you wouldn't sleep at night if I told you. He's a bad boy. Evil ways. He's all my sister Susanna has in the world, Mister Wilmot, otherwise I'd say, "Give him up, Susanna, give him up".'

'Would you?'

'I would. I couldn't sleep a wink with him in the same house as me.'

'Could you not?' said Wilmot. 'I'm a kindly man, preacher, and easily taken in. I felt sorry for the boy.

Liked the little spaniel dog too. Gave the boy a drop of ale and a slinch of ham.'

'I could do with something to wet my whistle,' said Scarfe.

'I wish mightily that you had not fed the boy.' Flyte's voice was heavy and slow. 'He does not deserve charity.'

'As I said, I'm an easy touch,' said Wilmot, forcing himself to smile. 'And this were last night, see. I said, "Stay, stay and I'll cook us an egg and break some bread with you in the morn", but he wanted to go.'

'He did?'

'He did. And I didn't want the lad hanging around – I thought he were a bit shifty, too, truth be told. I sent him off. Gave him an apple and a lump of cheese and sent him on his way. I saw him go.' Wilmot turned back and nudged a stick in the fire. 'I saw him off.'

Flyte nodded slowly.

'Then you won't mind if we have a look around your place? It occurs to me that you have many hiding places here. The sneakerly fellow might still be here, yet.'

'Well, I am sure he is not. There is nowhere for the boy to be hid. There's only my chickens and cockerels. My horse.'

'You refuse us?'

'I have no reason to refuse you, except that he is not here, and you'd be wasting your time.'

'Mister Wilmot.' Flyte folded his arms and glowered at him. 'Perhaps I should explain. Mister Scarfe here, works for the Marley estate.'

'That's it. There. I am employed by my Lord Marley,' said Scarfe. 'Lord Marley employs me to rid his estate of scum; those that don't pay their rent, those that disobey, those suspected of bigamy or fornication, those that harbour thieves and cheats . . .'

'Exactly,' said Flyte.

Wilmot swallowed. 'Lord Marley's estate?'

The big man rubbed his big hands together. 'If Lord Marley found you'd got this boy, this Reuben person on your place, you'd be out on your ear,' he said heavily. 'There. I've done it before. I'll do it again. It's me job. Cockerels and all livestock confiscated, too. I like cock fights meself. Always fancied keeping some fighting birds. There.'

His meaning was plain.

Wilmot could have managed with straightforward bullying, but to lose his cottage? To be put out with nothing! When he was a boy, the closest his family had come to having a home was a lean-to shed with a leaking roof. He glanced round at the pot of geraniums on the windowsill, the truckle bed he'd fashioned himself, his Windsor chair. He pictured Reuben out in the pen.

'I have nothing to hide,' he said. 'I've told you. You take a look around. The cockerels, mind, they're fierce critters. You must not mind the noise.'

Wilmot led Flyte and Scarfe around the cottage and its outbuildings. Somehow he had to stop them from looking too closely into that empty pen. He should have put Blackie in there! Blackie'd see them off. Why hadn't he thought of that? You fool, Wilmot! he told himself.

'This here's the pigsty,' said Wilmot. He opened the door to the low building and stood back. 'Pilton, that were my pig, he's gone to market last week. I mind I haven't cleaned it yet.'

Wilmot rubbed his hands over the top of the wall. He toyed with the loose fragments of stone chippings. 'Why don't you go in?'

Flyte held his nose and looked into the dark little shed. There was more manure than anything else and no place to hide. Wilmot showed them his wood store and his chicken hut. The empty stable. Finally they came to the barn where the cockerels were.

''Course I'd know if he was in here,' said Wilmot. 'Wouldn't I? Since the birds would have made a row.'

As they opened the door, the cockerels began clucking and crowing.

'Hush, hush my beauties,' said Wilmot. ''Tis only me.'

Quickly, Wilmot flicked a couple of the tiny stones from his fist at Blackie. His aim was good and they found their mark, striking the black cockerel's head and back. It jumped up screeching and crowing furiously. The other birds started squawking in sympathy.

The two men had not noticed Wilmot's sleight of hand.

'The birds pay you no heed, Mister Wilmot,' said Flyte, raising his voice above the racket.

'I did warn you,' shouted Wilmot. 'They are like guard dogs – better. There's no way a boy could be hid here.'

Wilmot stopped in front of Blackie's pen, willing the other two to join him.

Blackie turned his fierce yellow eyes on them, stretched himself to full height and crowed loudly and piercingly.

'What d'you think, Mister Scarfe?' Wilmot cried. 'A fine bird, isn't he, Mister Smith? He's won a great many fights.'

'As a man of the cloth, I do not hold with betting and gambling,' said Flyte.

'You're missing a treat, then,' Mister Scarfe said loudly. 'They do make a great din, though, like you said.'

'Blackie's the best fighter I've got,' said Wilmot. 'Fine bird. See that brilliant plumage. That fine wattle? Beautiful, don't you agree? Next week it'll be out with me shears and I'll cut his main off, close to his neck, right from back of head down to shoulders, though' tis shame to lose that colour. And I shall scrape smooth his spurs and sharpen—'

'In truth I am not as interested in cock fighting as you seem to imagine,' said Flyte. 'I'm searching for the boy.'

'Ah, yes, the boy,' said Wilmot.

At the back of the empty crate, Reuben crouched like a toad. His trembling was making the straw crackle beneath him; but the noise the birds were making would hide it. Through the tiny chink in the planks he caught a glimpse of Flyte's lower half, the hem of his long black coat and buckled black shoes. He saw Mister Scarfe's legs go by, bulging calf muscles in tight brown stockings. He could not see Wilmot.

'There's no cockerel in there,' said Mister Scarfe. He stopped at Reuben's pen and kicked the wood lightly. A shiver ran through Reuben; he felt like the hoverfly trembling in the spider's web. Glory lifted her nose and sniffed. Her ears went up. Reuben squeezed her muzzle gently but firmly. Shhh!

'True. Nor no room for a lad, neither,' said Wilmot. 'I beg you sir, do not kick it. They're not so strong and—'

'I think it would be an ideal spot to hide in,' said Flyte. 'Don't you, Scarfe? Beneath the straw there?'

Reuben squeezed his eyes shut as he heard the peg yanked from its lock and the door hoisted up on the rope. He stopped breathing.

Scarfe took up a stick and jabbed it into the straw.

'Nowt,' said Scarfe.

'What a smell!' Wilmot said. He squatted down and peered into the pen. 'Was my Billy's place – he died of some foul pox. All his feathers dropped out and he went blind, you should have seen the mess he was in. That's why it's empty. Didn't want another bird to get it. Why don't you have a closer look, preacher? Mr Scarfe?'

Reuben kept as still as a rock. Why was Wilmot insisting so? Let them go on. Let them go!

But Flyte had turned away. 'I'm sick enough as it is without catching bird pox.'

The two men turned to the bags of flour and sacks of corn and barley that were stacked against the walls of the barn. They pulled them out and searched behind them. They prodded everything. Scarfe climbed up into the empty hayloft and searched that too.

'He's not here,' said Scarfe. 'No, he is not.'

'I see that,' said Flyte. 'He *was* here though.'

'Aye, he were, but like I said, I fed him and sent him on his way,' said Wilmot. 'Last night. Said he had to hurry.'

'And where did he hurry to?' Flyte turned his cold eyes on Wilmot.

'Oh, he never told me,' said Wilmot, with a little laugh. 'He just said he were heading out east. Said it were the place anyone'd least expect to find him. Does that make sense to you?'

'It might,' said Flyte, darkly. 'Or it might not.'

'You could search down the bottom of the hill in the trees, there,' went on Wilmot. 'There's caves in there. Or maybe he stopped in the barns at Holme Farm – that's just a mile or so south from here. Or then you could—'

Flyte held up his hand to stop him. 'Enough. We've wasted enough time here with you.'

They returned to the cottage and Wilmot poured out the dregs of ale from a barrel for them. He was glad to see that it came out of the spout cloudy and dull.

The sky was grey and overcast. Wilmot led the men outside. Flyte stood in the yard beside his horse.

He gazed down across the strips of field to the river. 'Show me exactly the way the boy went,' he said.

Wilmot pointed eastwards, up towards a copse of beech trees.

'That way. You'll soon catch him even though he was gone last night, you're a gangrel fellow with them long legs, even without your nag you'd—'

'Be quiet. You are altogether too helpful.' Flyte smiled. He fingered the leather pouch that hung at his neck.

'What's that?' Wilmot couldn't help but ask.

'My amulet. My talisman. A lucky toadstone,' said Flyte. 'If I had not had this about my person I would surely be dead by now. I will find Reuben for sure. Wherever he is.'

16

Someone Else is Following Reuben

'Sorry to leave you so long, lad.'

Wilmot yanked out the false wooden wall and Reuben rolled out. Their eyes met and they grinned. 'I didn't trust them,' said Wilmot. 'Thought they might double back and catch us out.'

'You have reason to suspect them.' Reuben flexed his legs and arms. 'I'm glad to be out of there.' He rubbed his damaged finger joint. It was as purple as a plum, but the swelling was going down.

They went out of the barn cautiously, in case there was any chance that Flyte and Scarfe were around, then into the cottage.

'A drink of water, then I will go,' said Reuben. 'I must go.'

He did not want to leave. The way ahead seemed suddenly too long and too lonesome.

Wilmot handed him a leather tankard of water from the bucket. 'You know, Reuben, I did not like that Mister Flyte of yours, that Mister Smith as he calls himself. His eyes, eh? Crueller than our Blackie's. Eyes like that cockerel that took out our Billy, that's what I was thinking.' He shook his head. 'But why'd he play that ruddy flute, that's what I would know. He didn't need to. He'd've caught you without that warning.'

Reuben shrugged. 'I believe he would.' He shook Wilmot's hand fiercely. 'Oh, Wilmot! Thank you so much. So much! I'd be . . . well, I believe I'd be dead, without you! Thank you. Thank you.'

'Hey, lad, give my arm a rest there!' Wilmot chuckled. He patted Reuben's shoulder. 'I did what had to be done, and enjoyed it too. He won't get you, that Flyte man. Boy like you can run fast and you'll need run fast from that feller.'

Reuben sighed. 'So . . . that is the way to Felton?' He pointed across the valley to where he could just make out a narrow path crossing the fields and leading up towards a ridged hill in the distance.

'Aye, that's the way. Other side of Hamford Hill. About a day and a half walking straight. But like I said before, Reuben, I've to go to Easton Pacey tonight. That's on the way. Will you not stay and take a ride with me?'

'I – I can't!' said Reuben. 'I'd like to, but my feet are twitchy to get started! Flyte might come back. Time moves on. I must find Doctor Brittlebank.'

Wilmot thrust a chunk of bread into Reuben's hand and gave him a friendly shove. 'Go on then. Get a move on or I'll chase you like I do my cockerels!'

Reuben went.

He looked back several times towards Wilmot's cottage and was glad that Wilmot stayed by the gate, waving cheerily.

When he was no longer in sight, Reuben's spirits sank. He walked slowly down the hill, along a hedge of hazel and blackthorn on the edge of a field of pale yellow stubble. He could hear a river down below.

I could have stayed. I could have stayed with Wilmot and become a cock-master too, he thought. Doctor Brittlebank's so fine and educated, he wouldn't mind not having me. He'd be better without me. No, but I love the doctor! I do wish we'd never left Wycke House. Moving on. I'm moving on again. Like after Grandmother died. It's all happening again. I thought I was settled with Doctor Brittlebank and everything was so snug, but I've to move on. I don't want to walk and walk and be alone and wonder what's coming up behind me. I wish I were back at Wycke House . . .

Glory stopped suddenly with her nose up in the air, ears pricked. She barked.

'Glory? What is it?' Reuben looked around, back up the hill, towards the woods on the eastern side, but saw nothing. 'What is it?' He crouched down, expectant and worried.

Glory bounded off towards the water.

'Glory! Come back!'

She streaked across the wheat field towards the bridge. Her tail was windmilling with excitement. What had she seen? Fox? Hare?

Reuben ran. He followed her to the river. She had stopped beside the bridge, sniffing at a heap of old clothes and dirty rags there. She circled it, yapping.

Reuben walked towards her very slowly . . . A tramp? A gypsy? Then why was her tail wagging with excitement?

The bundle stirred. He saw a battered hat. Beneath the hat, round eyes which tilted downwards . . .

'*Gabriel!*'

Horror, awful dread, sent Reuben's stomach plummeting and his heart crashing against his ribs. Then immediately anger flooded his veins like boiling oil was pumping through his body.

'What are *you* doing here?' he yelled. 'You followed me! Didn't you? You followed me!'

Gabriel looked up. His dirty face was tear-stained, pale and creased with anxiety. He shook his head, put his arms round Glory. His mouth hung open; he howled.

'Don't cry! Don't!' Reuben looked around.

Someone might hear. 'Oh, Lord, you've probably never been out of that place before. Shh! How did you get out? How did you follow me?'

Gabriel stopped howling. He snivelled.

Reuben sat down a couple of yards away. Gabriel smelled like a walking cess pit. 'Lord, Gabriel!' Reuben shook his head. 'How did you find me? How did you do it? Were you here all night, on your own? Here by the river?'

'Dog,' said Gabriel.

Glory lay on the grass squeezing herself as close into Gabriel's side as she could. 'Lory.' Gabriel kissed her nose. 'Lory.'

Reuben felt a jarring pain, a blunt blade sawing below his ribs.

'She's pleased to see you,' he said, dully.

'Lory!'

'Did you follow me?'

The boy nodded. 'Mary gone.'

'Yes, Mary has gone,' said Reuben. 'Was she kind to you, this Mary?' If it were true what George had said about her being pregnant by Lord Marley then she'd been kind to her master too. 'Do you miss her, Gabriel? Where's Mary now?' If only I could find her, maybe she'd take you off my hands, he thought.

'Mary gone.'

It was hopeless. The boy could barely speak. He was an idiot. Reuben stood up again. He wanted to move. To go.

'I can't take you with me, Gabriel. I can't. I bet you can hardly walk. I've got miles and miles to go.' Reuben felt like stamping his feet, it was so frustrating. 'I've got to go all the way to Felton. It's a day's travel. I've hardly any food. How can I hide you? People will stare. There'll be trouble . . .'

And Flyte is so close. What to do? What to do?

'Mary gone. Boy gone. R'vens. Watch I.'

'Yes, I know . . .' Reuben clenched his jaw.

'Mary gone. Mary—'

'Very well. I understand. Lord, I can't bear it. What am I to do?'

Reuben got up and paced around. He glanced up the hill towards Wilmot's place. Could he take Gabriel there? No, that wasn't fair. Wilmot had helped him once, he couldn't ask again. Could he run off and leave him? No.

'Come on then, come with me. Come on. We can go together to see the doctor. Doctor Brittlebank is clever and maybe he can help you.'

That was a senseless thing to say, he knew. Nobody could put Gabriel right; he was *so* wrong. He had the sort of wrongness that was never seen. The sort of wrongness that you were born with, not that happened to you because you stared too long at a cow with a crumpled horn or because you were dropped on your head as a baby.

'What *is* wrong with you? If you're coming with me, you must tell me what it is. Is it leprosy? Is it?'

Gabriel shook his head.

'Is it a pox? Some sort of scurvy?'

Gabriel shook his head. 'Fish,' he said.

'What do you mean, *fish*? You always say that! What fish? Why fish?'

The boy began mewing like a kitten. He rubbed at his eyes with his dirty ragcovered hands. He lay down on the earth and tried to bury himself into Glory's fur.

'I'm not taking you with me unless I know. I'm sorry,' said Reuben, 'but I need to know. Please. Show me.' And quickly, he thought. Quickly, please, before Flyte catches up with me.

'*Gabriel!*'

Gabriel jumped.

'Gabriel! I insist.'

Gabriel sat up. He took off his hat and put it very carefully on a stone. He held out his bandaged arms towards Reuben.

'No, you do it. Go on. I don't want to touch.'

Gabriel shuddered. Reuben felt sorry for him then, he regretted his hard words, but he had to see.

He was not going a step further until he did know.

Gabriel sighed. He lifted his right hand to his mouth and pulled at the grey cloth on his hand with his yellow teeth. Very, very slowly, he began to unwind it. Miles of it.

Reuben swallowed and waited.

He had been expecting blood or pus crusting the filthy rags, but there was none.

Reuben's heart began to thump against his ribs; it began to pound and throb up in his throat. He dug his fingers into his palms.

I have no right to do this. This is bad. I am wrong, he told himself. Why did I make him? And all the time he was worrying about Gabriel he was worrying about Flyte too. He looked up at the hillside and along the river and stared at the dark line of trees imagining Flyte was there.

Hurry. Hurry.

The last fragment of linen slipped off. Gabriel held his hand hidden against him.

'Well?'

Suddenly Gabriel stretched forward and placed his naked hand out on the grass as if it were not part of him, something he didn't wish to own.

His hand was horribly deformed. He had no fingers. At least, as Reuben stared and stared, he saw he did have fingers but they were stuck together into a sort of pink paddle shape, like a narrow pointed trowel for digging. The thumb was separate, slightly flattened with a wide, dark nail.

'Fish.'

Gabriel began to unwrap one of his feet.

'No, you don't have to . . . Don't . . .'

But Gabriel did. His feet were even worse. Neither foot had any toes. The feet ended in a sort of frill of flesh and a line of misshapen toenails, grey and flat and sunk into the skin.

'Fish,' said Gabriel. He started to cry.

17

The Knight in the Chapel

'Oh, oh . . .' said Reuben at last. He made a choking sound, as though something was caught in his insides and was trying to get out. 'I've never seen . . .'

He turned away, picked up a handful of gravel from the riverbank and began to hurl the stones one by one into the river. He threw harder and harder until at last a pebble arced right over the water and hit the bank on the other side.

Gabriel was covering himself up again. His paddle hands were surprisingly flexible; he tied knots in the cloth with his teeth.

I wager he's been tormented all his life, Reuben thought. I can imagine that flighty Catherine calling him a fish. And the children living nearby. And worse names too . . .

Reuben's grandmother had helped at many births. He remembered a baby being born with a misshapen, swollen head. Another had a second baby joined on to it. These babies would not survive, so she had quickly helped them out of this world. Better for the mother to think they'd been born dead, than see that, she'd said. But somehow Gabriel had lived. How? Was it Mary who'd kept him alive? Gabriel denied Mary was his mother, but perhaps he didn't know. A girl might deny a monster child, but still look after him and care for him.

'Come on, Gabriel!' Reuben slapped his thigh, encouraging Gabriel the way he would Glory. 'We're walking to Felton. Here, have this bread.'

How much did the boy understand? Was there anything that would get him moving? Now!

'Come on. We must go!'

'Gabe?' said Gabriel. He was still sitting down. He quickly ate the bread.

'Yes. Come with me – with Reuben – and Glory. We must tread careful and hide and look out for . . .' Reuben scratched his head. Lord, this was complicated. 'Gabriel, see, there's a man after me. Wears a black coat and a big wide black hat. Plays a pipe. We must run if he finds us. Run! Understand?'

Reuben looked up towards the path they had to take. They'd been crouching beside the river, partly hidden by the low-hanging willow trees. Now they had to come out into the open. How would they get all the way to Felton and not be seen? He was mad to try, but he had to.

Reuben watched Gabriel struggle to get to his feet. He did not offer to help.

'Come on. Hurry, do! That man, the one that's after me, he's cruel.'

'Rool,' Gabriel repeated.

'Yes. If you hear a whistle, a tin whistle playing a sad tune, then you tell me straight away.'

Gabriel grinned and nodded so violently that Reuben was certain the boy didn't know what he was talking about. He'd probably never seen or heard music in his whole life. How could he?

'Oh, well,' said Reuben, lamely. 'Off we go.'

'Go,' repeated Gabriel. 'Dog. Boy.'

Gabriel had covered most of his face with a long scarf of black satin that Reuben guessed Mary had given to him. On his head was a soft leather hat with a squashed crown. His hands and feet were hidden beneath the strips of cloth.

'You'll do at a distance – but we must keep away from folk,' said Reuben. 'I don't know how. But we must.'

Gabriel hobbled like an old man. It took them a long time to get over the river, cross a couple of fields and make their way up the next hill. There were few good, clear tracks to follow. A soft, fine rain started to fall. A dog began barking in a farmhouse.

'Do try and hurry!' said Reuben. His desperation

was giving him belly-ache. 'Come on! We must get on. Flyte will be after me soon, I know he will. Come on!'

Gabriel looked up at him with his funny goggly eyes and grinned, as if it were a game.

'Com'on!' he mimicked, dribbling. 'Com'on!'

Oh, Lord! What have I gone and lumbered myself with? Reuben turned away. He clenched his teeth grimly. Wish I could shake him off. Leave him. Maybe I'll find a cottage somewhere? A farm where he could stay with some kind person, like my granny was, that would be fine. By the time I reach Felton, the doctor will be on his way back to Lord Marley's!

'Why did you follow me, Gabriel?'

'R'ven. Mary gone. R'ven.'

That was all Gabriel would say.

In the late afternoon, Reuben saw a church spire rising up above the trees. 'A village,' said Reuben. 'I wonder if it's Easton Pacey? We'd best avoid it, too many people. Come on.'

They skirted round the back of the houses, walking along a sheep track on the edge of the trees. The ground sloped away on their right side. The long strips of farming land, differently coloured, brown, yellowy-green and dark green, spread out like bands of cloth. Halfway past the village they came across a little chapel, set apart beneath some tall ash trees. Ancient yew trees guarded the wooden gate.

Gabriel looked up at the chapel tower, where jackdaws hopped in and out of holes in the stonework. The tiles on the roof were dusty pink and covered in moss. He stopped.

'In. In,' he said.

'We don't have time!'

'In!'

'Why would we want to go in there? No.'

'In!'

'Oh, for pity's sake! Don't you understand? We haven't time! I don't want to—'

'In. In.'

'Does it remind you of your old hovel? Does it?' he asked. 'With the tower and the birds? Oh, damn you! Quickly then!'

The church door was ancient. It was made of pale wood that was so weathered it was as soft as silk under Reuben's fingertips. He turned the iron ring handle and they went in.

The air inside was quite different to the air outside. It smelled of mice and old parchment and was heavy and still and full of . . . God perhaps? Peace, anyway. Reuben felt his clenched-up feeling floating away. This was a good place.

The little arched windows set high up in the walls

let in narrow shafts of light. The floor was paved with great stone slabs. Some of them were gravestones and had names and dates engraved on them. Reuben tried not to tread on those.

Gabriel shuffled forward and Reuben and Glory followed.

'Come on, Gabriel. Please,' Reuben hissed. 'You've seen it now. Gabriel!'

But Gabriel was deaf. He crept into every corner; he opened doors and cupboards, fingered the cloth on the altar, picked up a prayer book and leafed through it. It was as if he was looking for something.

'Come on!'

'Com'on!' repeated Gabriel, without looking at Reuben. 'Com'on!' Suddenly he scuttled off. He disappeared into a side chamber set behind railings at the far side of the pews. 'See!' he called.

Reuben followed reluctantly.

Gabriel was looking in a separate private chamber.

A stone knight lay there on top of his stone tomb. His arms rested across his chest, hands pressed together in prayer, pointing heavenward. He looked quietly peaceful, eyes closed, with almost a smile on his face. He was very old. Some of the detail on his armour and the tip of his nose and chin had rubbed away. His stone body was shiny, well rubbed by many hands. He wore flat shoes with long pointing toes, making them look longer than normal. A stone spaniel lay against his feet.

'Lory!' squealed Gabriel. 'Lory.' He stroked the stone dog. He hugged the dog. He kissed her stone head and eyes and nose.

'It does look like her, doesn't it?' Reuben agreed. He glanced down at Glory, who was sniffing along the pews. But the stone dog had a wonderful expression, very intelligent, not like Glory. The stone dog was watchful, waiting and thoughtful. 'She's guarding her knight, Gabriel. Just like in the poem, you know, the one you sang about the ravens. The bit about the knight . . .

'There lies a knight slain under his shield,
With a down.
His hounds they lie down at his feet
So well they do their master keep . . .'

He sang very softly, a little shyly, thinking back to the way his grandmother used to sing it. The words echoed gently and hung like feathers in the enclosed air of the chapel.

'Gabr'el,' said Gabriel, fixing Reuben with his weird eyes. His mouth hung open. 'Gabr'el. Lory.' He stroked the knight's stone leg gently. 'Gabr'el.'

'What d'you mean?' Reuben said. 'What? You mean this is like you? Like you and Glory at your feet and guarding you? I once had a dog that did that. She

156

was called Shadow. She guarded me. She looked after me. Oh, she was a fine dog.'

Reuben watched the way Gabriel stroked the knight's pointed feet and suddenly he realized something else – Gabriel saw his own shape reflected in the stone figure. The fingers closed in prayer were similar to his own paddle hands, and the feet with their pointed toes, they were like his feet. Like fish fins.

'We must leave,' said Reuben, gently. 'We've been here for an age. We don't have time for—'

The door of the chapel burst open, smashing back against the wall. The noise reverberated round the room like thunder. Loose plaster sprinkled the floor.

'What is it?' Reuben hissed, ducking down quickly behind the effigy. 'Hide!' Was it Flyte? A scream stuck in his throat. Flyte here so soon? No! Surely not!

18

Captured

'There!' a man shouted. 'Over there! Get him!'

Not Flyte. Reuben let out his trapped breath. But it was still trouble.

He crawled alongside the tomb and shuffled into a corner behind a carved chest.

Two men were striding down the aisle. Their heavy boots and voices shattered the peace. The air quivered as if outraged.

Where was Gabriel?

There! Not hiding but smoothing the effigy's hands. Oh, Gabriel, you mad doddy-poll! Idiot!

Glory scampered towards the men, wagging her tail, barking with excitement.

The first man was tall with tree-trunk thighs and long blonde hair. He kicked the spaniel out of the way; she yelped. Reuben felt the kick in his own ribs and winced. Glory, Glory, he moaned. You silly dog. You stupid dog. Keep away!

Glory ran to Gabriel and hid behind his legs.

'What's afoot? Who's that? Hey you!' The blonde giant pointed a finger at Gabriel. ''Tis a boy. D'you ken him, Hector?'

'Can't see him plain . . .' said the other man, striding over.

'What are you up to? I said, what are you doing?'

Reuben rubbed his sweaty palms down his jacket. Oh, Lord! Gabriel, you idiot! You fool! Why didn't you hide?

The other man was smaller and older with tiny eyes and a sharp nose like a rat. 'You! Look at us, will yer!' he said.

Both men now stood beside the stone knight. Reuben pressed himself back into the wall, willing them not to see him.

Gabriel curled and shrank into his bandages like a maggot. He tucked his chin to his chest, hunched his shoulders and began to inch away from the men.

The balding, weasel-faced man approached with his chin jutting out. 'Can't see his face. He's only a little 'un. Who are you? We've had thieves here afore,' he said. 'Took stuff—'

'Too'.' Gabriel repeated. 'Too'. Too'.'

Be quiet, be quiet, Reuben urged him.

'What's that? What you be doing?' said the blonde man, 'You mocking us?'

The weasel man grabbed Gabriel. 'My old mother!

He stinks!' He dragged Gabriel into the aisle. 'Why all covered up? What's to hide?'

'No. No!' shrieked Gabriel.

'This is our chapel,' said the blonde man.

'This is our village. Come on, out!'

'He's only a wee lad,' said the blonde man. 'Gentle with him.'

'Aye, and lads can steal like any other, Robert.' The weasel-faced man grabbed Gabriel by the arm and began to drag him to the door. 'Come on, come out into the light and let's see you.'

Gabriel struggled. Glory snapped at the men's ankles and pranced around them, yapping.

Reuben did not move.

Another kick from the blonde man landed on Glory's flanks. The dog let out a high-pitched squeal. That set Gabriel off. He began screaming and crying. He writhed like a snake. The men were so surprised they almost let go of him, but only for a second, then they took hold of him more firmly. Half carrying him, they got him to the door.

Still Reuben didn't move.

They don't know I'm here, he told himself. I'll be safe. I'll get away. I'll be able to run! There's nothing I can do for Gabe, anyway. I'm not clever enough. They'll take him whatever I do.

Reuben crawled out to the pews. His stomach was

churning. He crouched between the oak seats. The door of the chapel was open. He could see trees, green and brown fields stretching out down the hill . . .

Gabriel was crying.

The two men had stopped in the stone porch. Reuben could see them clearly. The rain had ceased. A pale sunshine lit up everything.

'You're a dirty little vagabond,' the weasel-faced man spat at him. 'Church warden'll be pleased we found you before you had chance to steal.'

'Aye,' agreed Robert. 'Hector, take off his toppings. Let's see him.'

Hector smiled, showing broken yellow stumps of teeth. 'My pleasure, Robert.' He yanked off Gabriel's hat and ripped away the satin cloth that Gabriel had so carefully wrapped around his face.

'Ahh!'

They let go of him and he dropped in a heap on the floor.

'What in God's name is that?' said Robert.

'Look at the face!'

'What is it?'

'It's horrible.'

'I've seen some oddmedodds in me time,' said Robert, grimly, 'but nowt as bad as that.'

Gabriel was sobbing loudly. He cowered at their feet like a dog. Slowly he pulled the satin around his face. He squashed his hat over his head.

'Mary,' Gabriel called. 'Mary! Mary gone!'

'He's a monster. He's Devil's spawn,' said Hector. He crossed himself and muttered a prayer.

Robert wiped his big hands down his trouser. 'Ugh, poxy! Is the rest of him bad?' He began to pull off the cloth around one of Gabriel's hands. 'Is he all wrong and—'

'Lord God save us!' Hector stared at Gabriel's hands in horror. 'It's an animal!'

'That's not right.' Robert threw the rags back at Gabriel and took a step back. 'That's not good.'

'We should take him up to Mister Wight,' said Hector. 'He'll know what to do with him. Up! Up!' he added, kicking Gabriel and pushing him to his feet. 'I aren't touching it again!'

They herded Gabriel like a sheep, poking him with sticks. They pushed him off the porch and out on to the path.

Reuben crept out from his hiding place and followed them. He stood in the graveyard behind a tree, watching as they pushed Gabriel through the long grass and meadowsweet. They climbed over a low wall and disappeared amongst the tall ash trees and cottages at the top of the hill.

Reuben looked around for Glory. She had gone.

Glory had gone with Gabriel.

19

Trapped

Reuben leaned against the yew tree until his heart had slowed its mad beating and the lump in his throat had gone. He didn't know if he felt sick mostly because the men took Gabriel or mostly because Glory had left him.

Glory chose Gabriel! She did! She likes him best ... likes Gabriel more than me ... Cheating, faithless cur! All the things I did for you! My God, Glory, when you were a tiny pup, I fed you mushed-up bread and milk. By hand! Damn it! I brushed your coat till it was silky smooth. I saved up my pennies for that collar with real brass studs . . . Reuben ripped at the long stalks of grass. I did all that for you . . .

He looked up the hill towards the village.

Good riddance!

He turned sharply and began to trudge down the hill, down towards the willow trees and the river. Towards Felton. It's just as well, he told himself. I'm better off without them both. I can go fast now.

Faster than Flyte. He looked around nervously. I won't let him catch me!

He passed a single apple tree and roughly pulled an apple off and ate it. Glory liked apples. She'd eat anything. Flighty dog. Spaniels are featherbrained, the doctor even told me so. I should've chosen a Shadow dog, a lurcher, a good faithful creature. Glory's head is more empty than a . . . than a licked-out pudding bowl. Have her then, Gabriel. Take her. You're well matched. Stupid dog. Dim-wit. Mangy mongrel . . .

He stopped by the river. It was shallow, clogged with large mossy stones; the water went by slowly. Reuben knelt and washed his face and drank the cool water. Beside him he noticed a patch of spignel, a few pale white flowers still remaining on the tops of the stalks. He imagined his grandmother's delight: '*Spignel, Reuben dear boy, how lucky! Governed by Mercury, excellent for the gripes and easing childbirth.*'

Might it help Lady Marley? Grandmother had used it for difficult births and colic and wind . . .

Grandmother.

Reuben let his head drop on to the damp grass, his forehead lay in the cool foliage. Dearest Granny, why aren't you here? Why did you have to leave me? We were so content. Now see me here, weeping by the river like a caw-baby. What am I doing? What have I done?

He heard the wind in the trees and the trickle of water and tried to listen beyond it, hoping for a word, something that would tell him what to do. There was silence, no voices. But still, he knew.

He got up slowly. He stared up at the village.

Reuben began to walk slowly towards it.

Halfway up the hill he broke into a run.

Elder trees and brambles and dogwood sped by.

To Gabriel and Glory!

Reuben ran without stopping.

It was a large village. Reuben went by thatched cottages, long barns, dovecotes, gardens full of vegetables and ripe golden fruit. Sheds and tiny cottages clustered together. An abandoned scythe. Hen coops. A pigsty. Stables. A wagon packed with sacks of grain. An alehouse where folk were drinking and chatting. No one paid him any mind.

Where was Gabriel?

Reuben passed down a narrow alley between whitewashed cottages. The blacksmith's doors were open. He was shoeing a fine grey horse. The noise of his hammer on the metal rang out. It was a good solid sound and for a moment Reuben's worries were eased. These people would not hurt a boy.

Opposite the blacksmith's was the village green, a soggy patch of grass with a large duck pond. Two massive twisted oak trees shaded it. The pond water was black. Rotting logs and slimy vegetation lumped around its banks. Grubby ducks paddled in it.

A small crowd was gathering on the opposite side; there were ten or fifteen of them now. He could hear the hum of their voices. Something told him Gabriel was there.

Reuben slipped back between the cottages and circled round until he could get down to the pond and come to the green unseen. He crept up and hid behind the wreck of an old cider mill. The mill's wooden sides had split and its wheels had broken. Reuben crouched behind the mill. It still smelled of apples.

Now Reuben could see clearly. Gabriel was there. How tiny he was beside Robert, the big blonde man from the chapel, who had hold of him. Gabriel was shivering. He was fiddling with his scraps of cloth, covering and re-covering his face and his hands. And Glory, the crazy, stupid dog, sat at his feet.

'I've sent Hector to fetch Mister Wight!' Robert shouted. 'We need Mister Wight to see this.'

'What's wrong with the lad?' a woman asked. 'Why've you brought him here?'

Reuben peeped round to see who was talking.

An ordinary sort of housewife with red cheeks and kind eyes. A mother? She would not hurt the boy, would she?

'He was trying to steal from the chapel,' said Robert. 'We stopped him right enough. But it's not that, Mistress Cowley. Look up, boy!'

Gabriel shook his head and folded his arms over his face.

'You wait. You'll see – his face is out of kilter,' Robert went on. 'And his hands. It's not Godly. He's come straight from Hell, this one. He's not right, not no ways.' Robert pulled the boy's arms down. 'Come on, boy, show them your features there. Show them!' He threw off the hat and tugged off the black satin. 'There now! See!'

The crowd stared at Gabriel's misshapen, bulging head. His flat white face. His big frog-eyes. His gaping mouth. He was dribbling, trying not to cry. The people shrank back like a wave. They blurted out cries of alarm and horror and disgust. They nudged each other. Whispered. Crossed themselves. Then they crept closer. They can't get enough, thought Reuben. He felt sickened by their expressions of disgust and yet such awful interest. He hated them.

Gabriel hugged himself with his little stick-arms and rocked backwards and forwards.

'It's horrible,' someone shouted.

'Not surprised he tries to hide that plate of stew!'

'Disgusting.'

'Aw, he's just a cabbage-head,' said another woman. 'Leave him be.'

'Yeah, let the child alone.'

A large bird passed by overhead. Gabriel glimpsed it and looked upwards. He pointed. 'R'ven. R'ven. R'ven.' Then he returned to rocking and muttering quietly.

Reuben heard a new ripple of whispers in the crowd.

'Devil's child.'

'That raven's his familiar.'

'See that! See him talk to that bird!'

'Evil!'

A thin, pinched-faced woman pushed her way forward. She wore an immaculate white apron over her black dress and the white starched wraps around her hair were pulled skintight. Not a scrap of hair showed.

'I knew it! I knew it!' she said in a low voice. 'You found him at the chapel, didn't you? I was down at the chapel earlier today, sweeping and I *saw* something.' Her voice trembled with emotion, her hands plucked at her stiff apron. 'A man. Dark, all dressed in dark shining clothes with glaring eyes.'

'Now, Mistress Anne,' said Robert, 'your imagination is—'

Mistress Anne spun round at him. Her lips were drawn into a tight line. 'You always doubt me! But you cannot now you've found that thing! I saw the Devil and he's left his child behind to do us ill, drive us wild with his lewd ideas.'

'Mistress Anne . . .'

'She might be right,' said a woman beside her. 'I've seen odd shapes. Last night, looking down the hill . . .'

'And me!' cried another voice.

'My pig's got a black mark on its back. It appeared only this morning,' said a man. 'It's like fingermarks it is, like the Devil put his hand right on the poor pig's back. That's proof for you!'

Gabriel rocked backwards and forwards. He stared at the sky. He looked round at the crowd anxiously, as if he were searching for someone.

'We should tie him up!'

'We should burn him.'

'Wait, wait for Mister Wight,' said Robert. He looked up towards a large house a little way up from the pond. It was set back from the muddy path behind a neat garden. The gates opened. Everyone turned to watch Hector and the tall elegant figure of Mister Wight come towards them.

Reuben's heart sank further.

Mister Wight was a finely dressed gentleman wearing a long grey wig and a green jacket. He picked his way over the muddy ground, trying not to dirty his dainty blue leather shoes with their sky-blue ribbons. He nodded to the villagers as they curtsied and bowed.

'What do we have here?' he said. 'Mistress Anne? Robert Hampton, good day. I hope you haven't disturbed my rest for something frivolous, Robert?'

'Begging your pardon, I don't think so, Mister Wight, sir.' Robert bowed. ''Tis this thing we found. 'T'was in the chapel. It's right odd, sir. Thought you'd better see.'

Reuben did not like Mister Wight's hard blue eyes and girlish hands. He didn't like the way his soft red lips were pursed up in disgust as he came closer to the villagers, or how he held a lace handkerchief to his nose. Reuben scanned the faces of the onlookers. They didn't like Mister Wight either – maybe there was hope.

'Well?' said Mister Wight. 'If it is a vagrant come from another village we'll send him straight back. We shan't be made to keep him. Our coffers aren't deep enough. Or is it a thief? Have you searched his pockets? Where is he? Show him to me!'

Robert stood aside to reveal Gabriel.

'It's just a boy,' said Mister Wight, dabbing at his nose. 'Great heavens! Have you brought me out here to see a boy? A doddy-poll of a boy, at that!'

The crowd sniggered.

Robert pulled Gabriel's hands away from his face and lifted the boy's chin. Reuben winced.

'The Devil has had his hand in this,' Mister Wight agreed. 'Why does he not speak but only stare up into the clouds in that way? What is it that he mutters? Is that dog his familiar?'

Gabriel heard 'dog.' He knelt down and hugged Glory. 'Lory. Lory.'

'Ah, see how he loves it!' said Mistress Anne. 'Hear how he talks to it in strange tongues? These are no ordinary creatures. I told you—'

'And why's he wrapped up like a Christmas pudding?' said Mister Wight.

'Get those things off!'

You can't! Reuben cried silently. Don't.

Gabriel screamed. He kicked Robert. He clutched at his rags.

'Now, boy . . .'

'No! No!'

Hector pulled at the cloths while Robert held Gabriel still.

'Agh! His hands!' someone cried.

'Look at his feet!'

'Monster!'

The crowd shifted and moved, each person trying to get the clearest view.

'Animal!'

Oh, poor Gabriel! thought Reuben. Doesn't anybody care? He scanned the watching faces and saw a flash of sympathy in a mother's face. An embarrassed grimace on another. Help him! Reuben begged them. Why don't you help?

Gabriel's hands hung at his sides like misshapen gloves. He stared at his feet, his awful feet, as if he hated them. He began to wail very quietly, a peculiar mewling sound, so soft that most didn't even hear it.

Reuben did.

'Devil!' screamed Mistress Anne. 'Now! Yes! Now, I recall the man I saw had these hands! Yes, his fingers all joined together just so.'

Then someone said: 'Fish!'

'He's got fins!'

'He's a *fish-boy*!'

Mister Wight was the only person who had gone nearer Gabriel. 'What abomination is this?' he said at last, with a sneer. 'In God's name, what is this creature?'

'Maybe his mother ate a barrel of cod 'afore she had him?' someone said.

'We should lock him up,' said Robert. 'Shouldn't

we, Mister Wight? And let the church men deal with him? They'll know what to do, Reverend Faulkner over at—'

'No.' Mister Wight held up his hand to quieten the crowd. 'I've a better idea. A fish-boy should swim, shouldn't it? Let's see if it can swim!' He clapped his hands together. 'Get it in the water!'

'But Mister Wight, sir—' Robert began, but he was pushed out of the way before he could get any further.

'I don't like to touch him,' said Hector. 'But I will.' Hector met Mister Wight's icy blue eyes. 'I will. Who else?' He turned to the crowd. 'Who'll help me with the fish-boy?'

Robert stood back and shook his head. Plenty of others wanted to help. They came forward rubbing their hands together gleefully, laughing and cheering.

Bravely, the villagers took hold of Gabriel's thin, dirty limbs and held him at ankle and wrist.

Gabriel shouted.

'R'bn! R'bn!'

He twisted and buckled in their hold. He screamed and shouted and fought.

'R'bn! R'bn!'

'Calling for his bird,' an old man said with a chuckle. 'Thinks it'll fly down and carry him off, I'spect!'

People laughed.

An icy coldness flooded over every inch of Reuben's skin. Each hair on his body tingled. He didn't think Gabriel was calling for the bird. It was not the same noise he'd made before. He covered his ears.

Gabriel wriggled like a Devil child. The crowd booed and jeered.

'Look at 'im go!'

'Like an eel!'

'R'ban!' Gabriel screamed, again and again. 'R'ban!'

'Throw him in!'

'Wet his head!'

They lifted Gabriel up and began to swing him backwards and forwards. Higher and higher. Glory barked sharply and skittered up and down the water's edge.

'One.'

'Two!'

'Three!'

Gabriel flew out of their grasp.

Oh, Lord, forgive me. Reuben crossed himself.

Gabriel sailed through the air. He hit the water flatly with a smacking sound and a splash. The ducks flapped and quacked and swam, necks outstretched for the bank. The folk laughed and clapped.

Gabriel disappeared, then his head bobbed up again momentarily and the crowd cheered. He gurgled and yelped. He thrashed around. There was a great flurry of swirling water and waving arms.

'We'll let him live if he swims,' said Mister Wight. 'And if he doesn't . . .'

Reuben jammed his knuckles into his mouth. Gabriel cannot swim, he told them silently. He is not a fish. He is, he is . . . he is Gabriel.

Glory was yapping and whining. She raced nervously up and down beside the pond, this way, that way, barking at the water.

Glory, Glory, hold your noise, thought Reuben. Stop your stupid . . .

Suddenly the spaniel jumped into the pond. Reuben bit his lip. She surely couldn't save the boy! Glory!

Glory set off paddling furiously towards Gabriel. Her brown nose pointed skywards.

Gabriel had seen her. He splashed towards her. He caught her and wrapped his arms round her neck.

'Lory!'

Then they both went under.

20

Locked Up

Reuben ran quickly over the short grass to the pond's muddy edge. His feet sank into its softness. He staggered, arms flailing, as he tried to keep his balance.

'I'm coming!'

Voices shouted behind him. He felt the crowd watching him, maybe even moving forward. He didn't look back. Any moment a hand on his shoulder might grab him. The dirty water lapped around his waist. He lifted his arms clear of it and pushed his way towards the ripples and swirls where the boy and the dog had gone down.

Now the pond water came up to his armpits. It smelled of rotting plants. His feet sank into sludge. Grey stinking mud swirled around him.

Slowly he made his way towards the churning water. He could hear shouting from the bank, but he ignored it. He pushed on, willing his legs to be stronger, willing Gabriel and Glory to stay afloat.

'I'm coming!'

Reuben grabbed Gabriel. He was slippery, muddy, impossible to hold. He yanked Gabriel by his arm and hoisted his head above the water. 'I'm here! Keep still!' he yelled.

Gabriel's eyes were tightly shut. His arms locked in a grip like iron around the lifeless dog.

'Gabe! Gabe! It's me!' Reuben tried to shake Gabriel. He was alive, but he did not respond. He was like a doll in Reuben's hands, hard and unmoving; eyes and lips firmly closed. '*Gabe!*'

Reuben began to drag them both towards the bank. Gabriel was light but his clothes were waterlogged. The dog was like a stone. Reuben turned his back on the crowd and dragged the boy and dog into the shallower water. He stumbled several times, once going right under. His boots slipped and slithered on the weeds. At last he reached the edge. He fell with his load in a heap on the mud. Nobody moved towards them. The crowd was very quiet.

Gabriel opened his mouth and let out a small, animal cry.

'Are you alive, Gabe?' Reuben shook him briefly. 'You *are* alive. All's well. I've got you. Peace now. Peace.'

Gabriel whimpered and coughed. Then he saw the

dog. He fell on her and started rolling backwards and forwards on the earth like something demented. 'Lory, Lory, Lory.'

'Dog's dead,' said someone in the crowd.

'Wish that horrid boy were,' said another.

Glory Be looked dead. Her long fur was black with mud; it stuck darkly to her sides in long strands. Her tail was rat-tail thin. She was so still . . .

'Glory!' Reuben pounded her and rubbed her violently. If I can just get out the water that's in . . . If I can just . . . 'Why did you have to do that? You silly dog, you daft little creature . . . You dim-witted fool . . .'

Glory coughed. Her whole body heaved, she gagged and choked. She staggered up and tottered on shaky legs. She wobbled to Gabriel. She wagged her tail a little, then was sick.

The watching crowd muttered and whispered at them.

'Leave him alone.' Reuben glared at everyone. 'Leave *us* alone.'

Gabriel, coughing softly, crept up beside Reuben. He sat on the earth with his strange hands tucked into his armpits. He folded his strange feet under his bottom and leaned his strange head into Reuben's side.

'That was a spectacle,' said Mister Wight, coldly.

He turned to the villagers. 'Who is this dirty boy?'

'Don't know.'

'Never seen him before.'

An elderly man wearing thick spectacles pushed his way forward. He wore a black coat with a large white collar. His clothes were precise and neat. A Puritan.

'Leave them alone,' he said gruffly. 'Those are but children.'

'It's George Carver,' said Hector, giving the man a courteous nod. Robert Hampton also bid the man a polite hello.

'Leave them alone,' George repeated. 'Children of God, as you all are.'

'Go back home, old man,' said Mister Wight, without looking at him.

'Just a bit of fun,' someone muttered.

'He's the spawn of the Devil,' said Mistress Anne. 'You've no right to stop us! We're doing what's right. He'll kill people. He'll—'

'Go home to your dusting and judging and leave well alone,' said George Carver. 'There is no fun to be had out of teasing children. You shall not hurt them.'

Several women gathered up their skirts and their own children and headed back to their cottages. The old man's disapproval had taken the fun out of it all.

'Please mister,' said Reuben, 'we didn't do

anything. Gabriel can't help the way he is. We didn't do any harm.'

George Carver nodded. 'They'll not hurt you while I'm here.'

'Hector!' Mister Wight shouted, waving his cane. 'Lock the boy and that creature up. Lock them up and we'll decide what to do about them in the morning.'

'Wait,' George Carver said, coldly. 'I am still the village elder, even if I might not be as rich as you Mister Wight or as well-sighted – though sometimes I think my old eyes work much better than your younger ones do . . .'

'Well?'

'Where shall you put them? They are lads. They are cold and wet and no doubt hungry.'

Reuben nodded his head vigorously. He could not stop shivering. He desperately did not want to be stared at.

Mister Wight looked angry. Bright red spots of colour burned on his cheeks. 'That creature doesn't need food. It defies nature by living. No food of mine shall go to it.'

'Then I will provide for *him*.'

'Thank you,' said Reuben. 'We meant no harm. We—'

'Shh. Less said the better,' said George Carver.

'We could lock them up in Mistress Long's cottage, that's empty,' Robert suggested.

'With a fire,' said George. 'They'll need wood for a fire. See how they shiver.'

Mister Wight snorted. 'Very well. See to it, men,' he said. 'Make sure you stay on guard, Robert, all night, mind. Don't let Mister Carver near them. I'll see them tomorrow at midday.' He added quietly to Hector, 'I think there's money to be made from that fish-boy, somehow, and I mean to make it, whatever that dolt Carver says.'

Reuben couldn't stop shaking. Damn you all! he cursed. Damn everything and everyone. I want to be away from here.

Gabriel was huddled on the ground, clinging to Reuben's leg with one arm and Glory with the other. He was covered in mud and weed. Seeing him sent a fresh wave of resentment through Reuben.

It's your fault I'm to be locked up, Gabriel. You and your frog-face and your fish-hands. I wish I'd let you rot in your ruin. I wish I'd never met you or spoken to you. I wish you'd drowned in that bloody pond. No, I don't. No, I swear I don't. But you have spoiled everything for me, Gabriel. Now I'll never find Doctor Brittlebank and get home to Wycke House, never . . .

* * *

Mistress Long's cottage was in a narrow lane behind the alehouse. It consisted of a single, low-ceilinged room. The walls were bare stones, the gaps filled with mud and grass and moss. The floor was made of dry, hardened earth.

'I'll bring you wood to burn,' said George Carver, who had followed and was standing at the doorway. 'I'll come back with my tinder box and a rush-light for you. My wife is ill and needs me at her bedside. But I am not far. Mister Wight and some of these villagers, well . . . they don't like what they don't know.' He nodded gravely and crossed the air in front of him. 'No harm will come to you, I promise. This is the safest place for you for now. Tomorrow I will do all I can to protect you and get you cared for.'

Reuben nodded, too shattered to speak.

Hector came back with some lumps of dark brown bread, very dry and tough, and some bacon and barley cakes. He gave them water in a jug and a basket of logs.

Reuben quickly lit a fire. The dry wood caught and soon the room was filled with the scent of wood smoke. The two boys sat by the flames and ate. Gabriel chewed noisily, letting food drop from his open mouth. Glory picked up the crumbs.

It was dark in the room. The one tiny window at the front of the building let in a glimmer of light through a thick pane of dirty glass and broken shutter. Reuben looked out; the sky was a perfectly smooth sheet of steely grey.

Gabriel lay down. His pale, naked arms looked like bones on the floor. His hands were still bare. Reuben tried not to look at them. He busied himself arranging their wet clothes around the fire. Soon they began to steam, giving off a smell of rotting vegetation.

'Are you all right, Gabe?'

'R'ban. R'ban.'

'Yes. I'm here. We're safe.'

'Mary gone. N'more Mary. Gone. Lory?'

'Yes, Glory's here. Right here.' He pushed the dog over to Gabriel. She tucked herself into the hollow of the boy's curved body, curled into a ball and went to sleep. Gabriel slept too.

Reuben lit the rush-light that George Carver had given them and set it in the tin cylinder and closed the lid. The light seeped out through the tiny holes pierced in the sides of the container. It made a pattern like lace on the pale walls. Reuben stared round at the room and the shadows, seeing no way out.

There was nothing more he could do. Nothing.

Reuben watched Gabriel and Glory breathing deeply and peacefully. Neither of them seemed to be troubled. Gabriel was as much a simple animal as Glory was.

Reuben did not dare shut his eyes; he imagined he could feel the fear and loathing festering in the cottages around him. He heard loud voices from the alehouse. He wondered if they were discussing Gabriel. He imagined the villagers lying awake, fretting, scared the two boys would kill them in their beds.

Reuben sat beside the fire and dozed. Late in the night he was woken by the sound of a tune on a tin whistle.

A melancholy tune.

He felt his insides contracting; his throat went tight, as if clamped by invisible fists; he couldn't swallow, could hardly breathe. He sat up sharply, gasping for breath and skittered over to the window, fast as a rat.

'God be with you!' a man called.

Flyte's voice.

Now I know why Flyte plays that thing, Reuben realized, pressing a hand to his constricted throat. He knows I'll hear it. He knows the effect it has on me. He is telling me he's coming. He is warning me.

Chasing me is but a game for him . . .

21

Flyte is Following

Flyte stood opposite the door of the cottage. His long fingers clasped a purple, velvet-covered Bible against his heart. He stared at Hector and Robert, wrapped in blankets, huddled on the doorstep together.

'What do you want, preacher?' Hector slowly got to his feet. 'This ain't no chapel, you know.'

Robert stood too and peered at the newcomer.

Flyte took off his hat and smoothed back his long grey hair. His shoulders shook as he chuckled soundlessly.

'A boy,' he said, quietly. He fingered the row of black buttons down his long black coat. 'A boy.' He shifted on his feet as if his legs ached. 'And I have heard that one is here. I believe it is my sister's child. He ran away from home due to a little misunderstanding. Nothing more.' Flyte rubbed at his ear. 'You know how children can take things wrong? His name is Reuben. Dark hair, dark eyes. A bad child, I'm sad to report. One lacking in Godliness and morals.'

'Hah!' said Hector. 'Sounds like our boy, don't it, Rob? He said he were called Reuben, didn't he?'

'There's the fish-child, too, preacher,' said Robert. He fumbled with his tinderbox, trying to light the lantern. At last the yellow glow from the flame lit up the stranger's face. They were alarmed at what they saw. The preacher's nose was broken and crooked. Some snag in the flesh below his left eye pulled the lower lid down. White jagged scars crisscrossed his jaw and cheekbone. One ear was torn, almost gone.

But worst were his eyes. They were like stones, cold and without humanity.

'Are you looking for the fish-boy?' asked Hector. 'They're in there together.'

Flyte scowled, then nodded slowly as if he'd suddenly remembered the fish-boy. 'Ah . . . *him*. No, no, you may hold on to your slippery fish-boy, whatever that might be. It is the boy Reuben that I want.'

'Mister Wight,' said Hector, 'he's the one with the power around here, you know. He and Carver say what goes.'

'Do they?' said Flyte, slowly.

'They do.'

'They are to stay locked up in the cottage,' said

Robert. 'For as long as Mister Wight thinks fit, or at least until noon when he will come back and see to them.'

'Are they quite secure in there?' asked Flyte.

'I should say so,' said Robert.

'No means by which they could escape?'

'There's only this door and it is locked, as you can see, with this here padlock and Mister Wight has the key to it. Then there's us here too.'

'So,' said Flyte. He slipped over to the window and peered in. The fire had died down and he could not make out anything through the dirty glass. 'So,' said Flyte again, turning round to them. 'You gentlemen will have a companion for the night.'

'What?'

Flyte smiled. He wrapped his cloak more tightly around his long coat and slithered down on to the doorstep into the place just vacated by the two men.

'What you doing?' Hector gasped. He turned to Robert. 'He can't stay there. You can't do that! That's what we've got to do, isn't it Robert? We've to keep watch, not you! That's our spot.'

'A preacher must follow the Lord's calling,' said Flyte, calmly.

'Well, I'll be!' cried Hector. 'We was all set there, weren't we, Rob? Make him move.'

But Robert only shrugged and moved away. 'Leave

him,' he said, settling down further along the side of the house. 'We'll not leave our post, preacher man, though I suspect that's what you want. We're staying put.'

'As you will,' said Flyte, softly. 'As you will.' He replaced his hat, pulled the brim down over his face and appeared to fall asleep.

Reuben laid more logs on the fire. Sparks flew up brightly in a shower.

No rest now. Not with *that* man outside.

Flyte was there. Flyte was *always* there. How does he always find me? How?

Reuben began to pace up and down the room.

This will never end, he thought. I will run and run and he will follow. And why not? Why not? I deserve it, don't I? I tried to poison him. I'm a worthless thing. I've always been worthless. I should have prevented them from hanging my grandmother. I could have. I could have saved Flyte so he never fell down Cal's Cauldron, could have helped him and then maybe . . .

Reuben stopped and hit the wall. His fist landed beside a spider. The spider dropped to the floor and scuttled away under the wall.

Lucky thing.

I must get out!

Reuben searched the room again for a way out. There was only the one door at the front beside the window. There was a trapdoor in the ceiling, but no way of reaching it and anyway, what good would it do to hide in the roof? Flyte would find them there too.

Suddenly Reuben heard the rumble of cartwheels, the squeak of iron hinges and a loud, cheery voice. He sprang up and raced back to the tiny window.

It was Wilmot! Wilmot the cock-fighter!

Then this village must be Easton Pacey, Reuben realized. Damn! I might as well have taken a lift with Wilmot when he offered it. I'd have got here easy and never got landed with Gabriel either. Or got locked up here. He kicked the wall. Damn! Damn!

Wilmot had stopped his cart and horse beside the cottage. 'Is that you, Rob Hampton?' he called. 'Can't think of another soul with legs as big as your'n!'

'Aye, it's me,' said Robert. 'Wilmot, eh? What brings you here? Lost your cockerel? Come to scupper my prize fighter?'

Wilmot laughed. 'You haven't got a prize fighter.'

Reuben remembered – it was Rob Hampton's bird that had killed Wilmot's cockerel. What was the bird's name? No matter. What mattered was that his friend Wilmot was here.

How can I get a message to him? How can I let him

know I'm here? Reuben's heart began to pound crazily. How could he alert Wilmot? He couldn't bear it if Wilmot went on and never even knew how close he'd come to saving him.

'Can beat you any day,' Robert was saying. 'Beat you before. Beat you again.'

'We'll see about that . . . What are you doing out here, anyways? Who's that with you? Hector is it?'

'Aye.'

'We've got a boy in there.'

'Is that the boy I heard about in Abe's alehouse?' said Wilmot. 'The one with a tail, all covered in scales that swims in the pond?'

'That's him, though sounds like he's changed since I last saw him. And there's another one with him. But he seems right enough.'

'Is there?'

'Says his name is Reuben.'

Wilmot nodded. 'Is that right?'

'*Reuben!*' hissed a voice from the darkness of the doorway. 'Reuben is mine.'

'Is that you again, preacher? Where's your friend, Mister Scarfe? This isn't Lord Marley's property here, I suppose?'

Flyte didn't answer.

'Well, I'm glad I'm not sleeping out in the cold tonight,' said Wilmot.

'Wish I weren't,' said Hector.

'So how's your mangy cockerels faring, Wilmot?' said Robert. 'Think you've got a chance at the mains next for'night?'

'Wish I could stay and discuss it, Robert Hampton,' said Wilmot, smiling tightly. 'But I'm late back as it is. I must be on my way, so I'll bid you all goodnight.'

His eyes did not so much as flicker towards the tiny window where Reuben's face was pressed up against the thick glass. There was nothing Reuben could do. Wilmot flicked the reins and his horse and cart set off with a lurch, squeaking and rattling as it rumbled slowly away.

22

Wilmot's Friends

Wilmot! Don't go! Wilmot!

Reuben crouched on the floor. His heart thudded painfully against his ribs. His mouth was dry. Please. Wilmot, I swear, if you help me, I'll get Hetty to marry you. I will. You'll like her. I do. Oh, Hetty . . . He breathed in deeply, trying to capture her smell – soda, newly baked bread, sun-dried linen. I wish you were here, Hetty.

The night dragged on.

Reuben dozed and fretted and dreamed of shelling peas. *Zlipp, zlipp*, the pea pods burst open and the solid little green balls rattled into the pan.

Reuben woke. The noise of the peas had woken him.

It wasn't peas.

It was a scrabbling noise at the back of the cottage. Rats? No. The scratching was more insistent, more repetitive than rats. Hope burst inside Reuben's chest, like kindling catching fire, and he dashed across the room towards the noise.

'Wilmot?' he whispered to the wall. 'Wilmot?' He stared at the rough whitewashed surface, looking for a crack or a hole, anything.

'Aye. Shh. It's me.'

'Thank the Lord!' Reuben pressed his palms against the stones. 'Thank you, thank you.'

'Shh, shh!' hissed Wilmot. 'No sound. Wait. Be ready.'

'How? What shall I do?' whispered Reuben.

But there was no answer.

Reuben looked around. Where could Wilmot get in? *How* could he get in? There was only the one door and it was well guarded.

Be ready.

Reuben woke Gabriel quickly. He made him put on his damp, smelly clothes, helping him drag them over his stick-like legs and arms. He looked away while Gabriel wound the dry rags round his feet and hands.

Reuben dampened down the fire, spreading out the hot ashes. The room grew a little darker.

They waited.

Reuben went to the window. There was still a light shining in the alehouse. He could hear muffled voices and the clinking of glass and metal.

At last Reuben heard a tiny scuffling sound above

his head. Dust and flakes of white plaster floated down from the ceiling. *Wilmot!*

The hatch in the ceiling creaked open. Wilmot's round, cheerful face appeared in the hatchway. 'Evenin,' Reuben', he whispered. He winked. 'We'll surprise that Rob Hampton, cheat that he is, won't we, by Jove. Come on, then lad. Up you come.'

'I am . . . You can't imagine, but I am so glad to see you,' Reuben whispered back.

'I wager you are. Stir yourselves, then.'

Gabriel was kneeling beside the fire, stroking Glory. He stared open-mouthed at the trapdoor in the ceiling.

'A'gel,' he said.

'Angel? Sort of,' said Reuben. He grinned. 'Here, Gabe, you must hush now. We are going to get out. We're saved.'

Wilmot let down a narrow ladder through the hatchway. The ladder touched the stone floor with just two inches resting against the ceiling. 'There. It fits right enough. A little bird told me where to find it and Mistress Crawley won't miss it from her orchard now, but I must get it back, or I'll be had for a thief. Come on.'

'Com'on!' said Gabriel. He clapped his hands. 'Com'on!'

'Shh!'

'Com'on! Com'on!'

'Will you be quiet, you daft thing!' Reuben snapped, grabbing the boy's arm roughly. The shine faded from Gabriel's eyes. Immediately Reuben was sorry. 'I mean, just be quiet, will you? We must go softly. Like, like . . . like this.' He tiptoed across the floor, exaggerating his quietness. Gabriel's face split into a wide grin.

'Shh!' said Gabriel. He held his stumpy hand to his lips. He copied Reuben and tiptoed to the ladder. Halfway up the ladder, he stopped and turned back. 'Lory!'

'Keep your voice down!' hissed Wilmot. 'And hurry.'

'I've got Glory,' said Reuben. 'Go on, go on, Gabe. Go up and then I'll bring her.'

If Wilmot was shocked by the boy's odd face and awkward movements, he didn't show it. He yanked him up into the roof space beside him without a word. Finally, Reuben slipped through into the dark, warm attic.

'Praise be!' said Wilmot, thumping Reuben happily on the back. They hauled the ladder up quickly.

Reuben heard a shout and burst of laughter from the alehouse. The party was going on late tonight.

He expected darkness as Wilmot closed the

trapdoor. But the place was dimly lit.

Wilmot pointed to the light. 'This way. Come on.'

They scrambled over the wooden beams. The light shone through a gap in the wall where bricks had been removed. The house next door had two storeys more than Mistress Long's, and the opening in the wall led straight into a candle-lit bedchamber.

Wilmot climbed through the hole first, the others followed. They found themselves standing on dark glossy floorboards beside a chest. A fragile-looking man of about thirty was sitting on a large oak bed, watching them. He had a very small nose and blonde hair. He had wrapped himself in thick bed-curtains and he was staring at them with goggle-eyes.

'I watched you by the pond,' he said. He pulled the covers round himself even tighter. 'I saw you.'

'Aye, and didn't do anything to help,' added Wilmot. 'So he's making up for it now, boys. This is Basilly. He's a good fellow, really. Put those bricks back as best you can, Basilly, and you don't know anything about anything.'

Basilly nodded. He slipped off the bed and went to the wall. He wore a long nightgown. His bare white feet were knobbly; the cleanest, whitest feet Reuben had ever seen.

Turning every now and then to stare at Gabriel, Basilly set to work replacing the bricks in the hole.

'He stinks. What ails him?' he asked. 'They say his mother mated with a fish. They say—'

'Has he got a tail? Does he swim?' asked Wilmot, crossly. 'He's no more a fish than you or I.'

'But his hands . . .'

'I can't see his hands and I can't see his feet and I don't want to see any of them,' snapped Wilmot. 'Get on with those bricks, Basilly. You don't want anyone to know you took a part in this, do you? Don't want Mister Wight after you, eh? We must get away.'

'The back door is on the latch,' said Basilly. 'I'll slip down and lock it after you've gone.'

'And you know nothing.'

'And I know nothing,' he repeated.

Basilly placed the bricks back carefully and quickly. There was no rubble or mess; Reuben could tell this had happened many times before.

'Excuse me,' said Basilly. He leaned over Reuben and dragged the small mahogany chest in front of the loose bricks. Once in place, there was no sign of anything amiss.

'Clever,' said Reuben.

Basilly grinned. 'Mistress Long owned that little place next door. She and I, we had an agreement. She'd let me come out through her cottage whenever I wanted. Nobody saw me.'

'But why? Who did you not want to see you?'

Basilly's face fell. 'My wife. I did not get on with her. She wouldn't let me out to the cocking main, nor the races, nor the alehouse.'

'Where is she now?'

The large bed was empty.

'Dead,' said Basilly. He grinned. 'So now I go out of my own front door, whenever I wish.'

'Enough, enough,' said Wilmot. 'We must away.'

Basilly led them down the narrow staircase. 'This way,' he whispered. He took them down a dark stone passageway. It smelled of mildew and sour milk. 'I shan't venture out, if you don't mind,' he said. 'It will only cause suspicion.'

Wilmot eased open the door.

'Wait.'

Wilmot stood very still. A few moments later, the church clock chimed. He grinned at Reuben. 'Listen.'

There was a roar from the alehouse. There was shouting and laughter and the sound of men on the lane, joshing and falling about.

''Tis Theo Worsnop and Laurence Moorhouse,' Wilmot whispered. 'Aye, and Joe Erskine too, by the sounds of it! They said they'd raise a rumpus for me and they HAVE!'

He pulled the big door. The iron hinges squealed. Reuben held his breath. Wilmot chuckled.

'Don't worry. They'll not hear us. Come on!' Wilmot picked up his end of the ladder again. 'This way.'

'Good luck,' Basilly called. 'Here, take this,' he added and thrust some clothes into Reuben's arms. 'It's for the little boy. He'll do better if he's not so smelly.'

'Thank you.'

Reuben heard the bolt slide heavily into place behind them as they crept out into the dark of the lane.

'Here we go, Gabe.' He squeezed Gabriel's fingers around the ladder. 'Hold it. Tight. Do you have it? Come on!'

'Com'on,' said Gabriel. 'Com'on, R'ban!'

'Yes, good. That's right,' said Reuben. 'Here Glory! Stay close. Heel!'

They were in a narrow lane between huddled houses. The merry calls from the alehouse sounded loud in the night air. Reuben and Gabriel followed Wilmot, shadows following shadows, just blacker shapes in the darkness.

Wilmot led them down a smaller track. Trees loomed around them. The leaves rustled gently in a soft breeze.

'Orchard,' hissed Wilmot. 'Mistress Crawley. Ladder.'

They slipped the ladder over the wall. Reuben heard it thud softly on the grass.

'Follow me!'

The clouds slipped away from the moon. There was light enough for Reuben to see they were now creeping along a dark path, past sleeping cottages. At last they went down a track and came to a great barn. Wilmot opened the doors. His horse and cart were stowed inside.

'We're not clear yet, but nearly. I've been all over the place tonight,' Wilmot said. 'Borrowed, bargained and promised. Not all folks is bad. Hah! I got you, young man, didn't I?'

Reuben began to breathe properly again. His heart began to settle.

'You did, Wilmot, thank you,' said Reuben. 'I don't know what I can ever do to repay you. I feared the worst. They were going to do something dreadful to Gabriel. And Flyte . . . Flyte was there!'

'Aye,' said Wilmot. 'Flyte. I wager I've not met such a dark fellow as that in all my life – and I've met a few. I shall take you to Felton myself, young lad, 'tis the only plan. I shall take you and put you there with your doctor so there's no chance of Flyte getting you. Would you find that agreeable?'

Reuben couldn't speak. An enormous weight

lifted from him. He felt something inside him dancing wildly.

'You are the kindest man,' he said. 'The kindest cockerel-master I've ever met.'

'Only one, too, I suspect,' said Wilmot, grinning.

23

To Felton

'Shall we put the little lad up in the back?' said Wilmot, leaning his head towards Gabriel. 'Gabriel, is it?'

'Yes,' said Reuben. 'They were so cruel to him. That Mister Wight . . . Gabe cannot help himself.'

'Poor creature. Where did he come from? You had no travelling companion when you spent the night with me.'

'I found him in a shed with nothing but ravens for company . . .'

A great deal of the grime had washed of Gabriel when he was thrown in the pond, but his clothes were no better for their soaking. He looked like a beggar.

'As soon as we can,' said Reuben, 'we must change him out of those old clothes. The smell will put everyone off.'

'Basilly gave you those clothes?' said Wilmot. 'He's a good fellow. Those were his own child's, I'm thinking. Little Walter died of the fever not two years past.'

They snuggled Gabriel down between the sacks of flour. He smiled as Glory settled into his arms and licked his chin. When Gabriel looked at Reuben his eyes were so sparkling with joy, Reuben could not feel jealous.

'You go to sleep, Gabriel,' Reuben said. 'We're going to find Doctor Brittlebank and then we'll be safe.'

Wilmot swept the blanket off his horse's back and threw it over Gabriel. 'Up you get, Reuben. I'll walk her out.'

Wilmot backed the cart out of the barn and on to the lane. The sky was clear now and the moon shone brightly down on them. From the village they could still hear raucous laughter, shouts and squeals. Reuben hoped that the creaking and squeaking of the old cart, which sounded so loud to him, would not he heard by Flyte and the others.

'Cold?' Wilmot climbed up beside Reuben and took the reins.

'Just a little,' Reuben admitted.

Wilmot leaned against him. 'Keep close. There's another rug there under the seat. Let's put that round our knees, eh?'

Reuben looked back towards the black huddle of

cottages. The only light and noise came from the alehouse.

'I don't think we're missed.'

'They're a load of noodle-brains,' said Wilmot. 'Don't care to imagine what Mister Wight'll say in the morning, mind.'

'Or Flyte,' said Reuben. 'I'm surprised Flyte wasn't more wary . . .'

'Maybe it suited him this way,' said Wilmot.

'How d'you mean?'

'Perhaps he's after us now,' said Wilmot, 'right this instant, because he knew if he had to wait until tomorrow he'd have lost out to Mister Wight. This way, you escape, he follows. He has a better chance of catching you. No competition.'

'Oh.' Reuben pressed himself closer against Wilmot. His mouth was so dry he could barely speak. 'He wanted us to escape?'

'There's some chance of that, I think.'

'Did he have a horse?'

'I don't know. But he'll have one now, I warrant. He won't be walking all the way to Felton on those scrangling legs of his.' Wilmot patted Reuben's knee. 'Don't mind me, I'm not trying to scare you. We need to know what the enemy's up to, that's all.'

They sat without speaking. The horse's hooves thudded on the path. An owl hooted. Reuben imagined Flyte's black-coated figure crouched over his horse's withers as it galloped along behind them, the horse's mane streaking over his hideous face. Horrible.

'I should've killed him. I nearly did, Wilmot,' Reuben said. 'I wanted to kill him and I should have.'

'Well, well,' said Wilmot.

'I fed him deadly nightshade,' said Reuben, 'disguised as cherries.'

He waited to see what Wilmot would say, glancing up at his profile a couple of times.

'Cherries?'

'Yes, the dark purple kind. Very shiny.'

'Shiny?'

'Yes.'

Wilmot crossed himself with his free hand. He laughed out loud. 'You little devil! Don't you try any such witchery on me!'

'Never. It was my only chance to escape.'

'I see that, I do. So, you know all about medicines and herbs then, do you?'

Reuben told Wilmot about his grandmother and how she had taught him to make potions and poultices and medicines.

''Tis dangerous to mess with magic and witchcraft,' said Wilmot.

'She was not a witch . . . She was good. Flyte calls

himself a doctor. He says he knows all about medicines, but it's not true. He's a quack.'

Wilmot nodded. 'He's a bad man, I know . . . What about the lad? You found him in a *shed*, you say?'

'Gabriel. Yes. I came upon him in a ruin on Lord Marley's estate. I think he might have been the maid's child. She's disappeared. Gabe is very strange, Wilmot, with fingers and toes all joined up.'

'I saw his face. I heard the talk in the alehouse. Ah, Reuben, I am putting this and that together . . .'

'How do you mean?'

'Well, my cottage is part of the Marley estate, you know. There's always gossip isn't there, about the rich folk? And I've heard about a child being kept there. Locked up. Was supposed to be a monster, though Gabriel's no monster. And it was said it was the child of Lord and Lady Marley too.'

Reuben gulped. 'No! Do you suggest? You mean . . . ? Gabriel is Lady Marley's child?'

'That's the story. I heard it from Lucy Tucker – that's Mistress Foster's neighbour – and Mistress Foster worked at the Hall once.'

'But Lady Marley cannot know – can she? She so badly wants a child. If she knew . . . She would not keep her own child in a pigsty? What do you think, Wilmot?'

Wilmot shook his head. 'I don't know. The gentry's mighty odd.'

'He's only a little fellow. He would do no harm. He can't do harm.'

'Reminds me of the cockerels, you know?' said Wilmot. 'When a bird's not right, ill or sickening, the others turn on it. 'Tis as if they know something's wrong but they don't know what, just that it niggles them, aggravates so they must peck at it and scratch at it till it's out of their way.'

'No one seems to care for Gabriel,' said Reuben.

'Except you,' said Wilmot, nudging him. 'You're his friend. And I'm your friend so I'm his friend.'

Before the darkness gave way to a cold grey dawn, Reuben slept a little. He was jolted awake by a sudden loud honking noise and woke to see a sleek white goose beside him. He sat up quickly.

Alongside their cart walked a plump girl with curly hair. Beneath each arm she carried a goose. 'Morning!' she called.

Reuben rubbed his eyes. The goose girl was not alone. They passed a fat boy prodding three big pigs along and a man pushing a barrow stuffed full of cabbages, turnips and potatoes. There were lots of people walking into town that morning.

'All going to Felton?' Reuben asked. He stretched

his aching limbs. He turned and peered down the road they'd travelled.

'No sign of Flyte?' asked Wilmot, keeping his eyes firmly on the lane.

'No. But I feel him,' said Reuben. 'I feel him creeping along behind us like a black beetle.'

'Do you then? I hope not. What a crowd!' said Wilmot. 'What a sight! Who'd live in a town, eh? Where you can't grow your own food or chase your own cockerel up a dunghill? Dangerous places, towns.'

They came to the first houses and, although it was still early, there were many people on the street and much noise. Men called to each other and dogs barked. Reuben turned this way and that, his eye caught by a glimpse of a shining buckle, a swirl of ostrich feathers on a cap, a gold belt, a dead cat pecked at by birds.

'Wilmot! Look, look at it! Carriages! Coffee shops! Fine clothes! When I'm a doctor . . .'

'Ah, very grand, aren't we? Doctor, eh?'

Reuben grinned. 'I know. I know I'm not a gentleman or clever or such, but I mean to be a doctor like my cousin . . . He is a real doctor, you know.'

'So you tell me.'

'He's a good doctor too. Very kind . . . Oh, I can't hardly wait to see him!'

A little voice croaked out from the back of the wagon.

'R'ban?'

Gabriel's head emerged from beneath the blanket. Glory poked her nose out and sniffed the air.

'Gabriel? Are you well? Are you? We'll stop soon and get you something to eat – can we, Wilmot?'

Wilmot nodded.

'Gabriel will have to stay hid,' Reuben added in a low voice. 'I mean he'll upset folk. We don't want trouble.'

'I'll stop up there,' said Wilmot, pointing to a painted sign of loaves of bread and pastries dotted with currants. 'I smell fresh bread and cake from here.'

'I can't smell anything else,' said Reuben. 'Though there's much else to smell.' He nodded towards a pile of sewage, and rotting food where a mangy dog and some crows were searching for food.

Wilmot swung himself down from the cart and tied up his horse. He patted Reuben's arm reassuringly, then disappeared into the shop.

Immediately Reuben was scared. He hunched up his shoulders inside his jacket and put his chin down. Without Wilmot he felt as if everyone was staring at him. Maybe amongst the seething masses there was Flyte. Watching. Waiting.

Hurry up, Wilmot!

Hurry.

At last Wilmot appeared. 'Goose pie,' he said waving the pastries at Reuben. 'And a bit of something for Glory too. A bone.' He settled back into his seat and the wagon shifted comfortably beneath his weight. 'And I've located this Mister Cowper's house. A rich man he is, according to them in the shop. Mistress of the pies wanted to know what I was doing calling on the gentry.'

Reuben handed the warm pie to Gabriel. Gabriel immediately offered it to Glory.

'No! No! It's for you!' cried Reuben, pushing it away from the dog.

Gabriel smiled up at him. 'Lory. Eatsup!'

'Here, this is for the dog,' said Wilmot. He passed the bone over.

Gabriel grabbed the bone and began to shred the meat off with his little teeth.

'No, you don't need that.' Reuben pulled the bone from him and threw it for the dog. 'Eat the pie, Gabriel. The pie!'

Gabriel still had the warm pie in his other hand. He seemed amused by it, he laughed at it, but at last began to eat it, nibbling the edges of the piecrust experimentally.

Cowper Priory was the last house in the town. It

backed on to the countryside and was surrounded by walled gardens.

Wilmot stopped his cart at a little iron gate in the wall and peered up at the house, admiring the many windows and the enormous wisteria growing against it.

'I can't go in there,' Wilmot said. 'Not for the likes of me. Nor you, young Reuben. Certainly it ain't for the likes of him.' He stuck his thumb in the direction of Gabriel. 'Are you sure this Cowper fellow will welcome you? Are you certain your doctor is in that house?'

'I am. This Priory is not as grand as Lord Marley's house, in truth it is not,' he told Wilmot. 'Don't fret . . . Let me and Gabriel out and we'll make our own way.'

'I'm shivering all over just looking at that place,' said Wilmot. 'Wouldn't surprise me if they don't eat off silver plates and drink out of proper glass goblets . . . They must have a back door, Reuben, a place for the likes of us, somewheres they keep the chickens and such – do you think they might keep cockerels? You cannot go into that front door, young Reuben, you cannot.'

Wilmot drove to the end of the garden wall and turned along beside it. The countryside seemed to open up around them, golden corn, stripes of brown

211

and green, the trees turning orange and red.

Reuben jigged up and down anxiously. It was taking so long and where was Flyte? How far behind them was he? How much time before he arrived?

Wilmot stopped at a gap in the wall where a path wound up through an orchard to the back of the Priory.

'Thank you!' Reuben shook Wilmot's hand. 'Thank you, thank you from the bottom of my heart.'

Wilmot's hand was firm and calloused, much scarred by cockerels pecking and scratching at it. Reuben hoped he'd have a chance to shake it again. 'I wish I could do something to repay you.'

'Don't need payment,' said Wilmot. 'Nonsense. Had pay already. Had it to know I swiped you from under Hampton's nose. Had it knowing that Flyte was thwarted. Go on now, get inside to your doctor and good luck to you.'

'Goodbye, Wilmot.'

'Aye, farewell, but I'll not be far, Reuben. If you need me, I'm stopping in Felton for the morning. Mister Wethering's farm, out by the Saxon church it is. Remember that.'

'Wethering,' Reuben repeated.

Wilmot nodded, tipped his hat and went on his way.

24

Reuben is Greatly Shocked

Reuben's knees went weak. He sat down on the grassy verge. He needed a moment to gather his thoughts. It was weary-making, being harried and chased. He fixed a makeshift lead of string to Glory and handed her to Gabriel.

Gabriel walked with the dog a little way into the field opposite the wall. There was a scarecrow in the field. Its tattered clothes fluttered in the breeze. Gabriel and the scarecrow were like brothers, only the scarecrow was bigger and better dressed. The idea made Reuben smile.

'We'll put these new clothes on you, shall we? Don't suppose you mind wearing togs that belonged to a dead boy?' said Reuben. 'Some folk are suspicious but I'm not. A good jacket is a good jacket, don't you agree?'

Gabriel walked over to the scarecrow. 'R'ban!'

'What is it?'

'R'ban!'

Reuben got up and crossed the stony ground towards him. Gabriel was staring intently at something hanging on the fence. Reuben went closer. 'What is it there? Is it someone's washing you've found?'

It was five dead ravens hanging by their broken necks along the top of the rickety wooden fence.

Gabriel stumbled up and down alongside the birds.

'R'ven. R'ven. One. Three.'

'Ravens. Yes. Still glossy. Shiny.' Reuben stared at the corpses. Blood oozed from the birds' beaks. Their curled black feet hung suspended like giant spiders. Reuben batted at the flies that swarmed around the birds, but they landed back again immediately. 'Fresh killed. See this bird here – a monster. Three feet long from beak tip to tail end.'

'Mon',' said Gabriel, nodding.

'A beautiful monster,' said Reuben. 'See those great claws, Gabriel, and fine feathers? Hanging them on the fence like this is supposed to keep the other birds off. My grandmother said men did wrong to kill them. She said a pair of ravens stayed together forever and ever, sort of wed, you know? What will happen to this chap's mate now?'

Gabriel stroked the purple-black feathers softly with his stumpy hand. 'N'more,' he said.

Reuben nodded. 'No more sitting in a tree for

them. No more watching over the wounded knight.'

Gabriel looked up and smiled at him. A big, open, dribbly smile.

'Do you understand me, Gabriel? Do you?'

Gabriel's smile faded. 'A'gel,' he said.

'Angel?'

'R'ven.'

And that was it. Not exactly a real conversation, thought Reuben, but almost. If Gabriel had been allowed to live amongst people instead of being locked up in those old ruins, maybe he'd be able to talk properly. It was a cruel thing to have done to him. Even if he was such a strange creature with a strange face, it was cruel and not needed.

'Come on then, Gabriel, we'd better go.' He held out the clothes that Basilly had given to him. 'First you put these on.'

Gabriel did not want to take off his clothes. He clung to the miserable shreds of filthy jerkin and his ripped, holey breeches. At last Reuben stripped them off and got the clean things on to him. Gabriel stroked his new jacket. It had four large wooden buttons down the front and a high collar. He sniffed at the fabric and grinned at what he smelled. There was an old blue undershirt too, much mended, but soft and clean. Gabriel looked much better, and he did not smell so dreadful.

'Those dirty bandages need to go,' said Reuben. 'But I've nothing to replace them with. And your hair needs a wash. I can see the lice crawling from here!'

Gabriel rolled his eyes and scratched his head. He tugged on his old hat.

'Come on, then.'

'C'mon.'

Reuben glanced around quickly before he crossed the lane to the house. Of course Flyte could not be here yet, he thought. Of course he couldn't – but he could not help looking. The man moved so swiftly. It would not surprise me, he thought, if I saw him trudging along right now . . .

They went through the gap in the wall. The grass was long, lush and very green beneath the trees. Between the leafy branches, pears and apples glowed like coloured balls at a fête. Beyond a low yew hedge was a bed of raspberries and gooseberries.

'Doctor Brittlebank might be looking out of his window at the orchard right this moment and see us scuttling around here,' Reuben said. He grinned. 'Think of that, Gabriel. He might spot us down here. He'll be so surprised he'll put down his shaving brush or whatever it is he's doing and say, "Bless my soul!" Then he'll come down and meet us. Wouldn't that be grand?'

Gabriel peered at him. He wiped snot from his nose. 'R'ban?'

'You don't know what on earth I'm saying, do you? It doesn't matter because, anyway, none of what I say is likely.' He stopped and put his hand on Gabriel's shoulder. 'Listen, I think it would be best if you waited here. See, I'll make a little place in this long grass.' He smoothed down the grass at the base of an apple tree. 'Sit there. That's right, with Glory. Do not move, Gabriel,' he told him. 'Sit there and do not move and I will come back for you very soon. I promise.'

Gabriel looked up at him. His drooping eyes were bright. He burbled some odd incoherent words, then clearly said: 'Boy. Dog.'

'Yes, Gabriel stay. With Glory. I'll be back once I've spoken to Doctor Brittlebank. Do you understand? You must stay with Glory.'

'Lory.'

Reuben turned his back on them and set off towards the house.

We don't want another clash with folk like at Easton Pacey, Reuben told himself. He glanced back several times as he trudged towards the house, but Gabriel did not follow him.

Mr Cowper's house looked very fine and big. He wondered if anyone was watching him; but the windows were blanks, reflecting the sky.

Reuben's pace slowed the nearer he got. Wish I was smarter, he thought, rubbing at some dark stains on his blue jacket. At least these woollen breeches are brown and hide the dirt. Gabriel's better dressed than me now.

He went cautiously up the short flight of uneven steps and into the yard.

A skinny, chestnut-haired maid was bending over a giant tub of water. She was rubbing some dark-coloured cloth up and down against a washboard. An elderly manservant was chopping wood nearby.

Reuben approached them warily. 'Morning,' he said.

The maid glanced at him then went back to her work. 'What?' she asked, wearily. 'You a beggar? We don't give to travellers.' Her bare hands and arms were red raw from the water and the front of her dress and apron was stained dark with it.

'No, no,' said Reuben. 'I've come to see Doctor Brittlebank. I believe he's staying here.' He looked up at the blank windows. He peered through the open doorway at the long stone-walled corridor. 'I'm his, he's my . . . We're related. Cousins.'

'Cousin? You don't look like no one's cousin, do he, Simon?'

The manservant dusted off the sawdust from his

front and straightened up, one hand supporting his lower back as if it ached. Carrying the axe, he walked over to Reuben and looked him up and down.

'He's got a dirty face,' he said, 'but it looks an honest face underneath all that earth, Alice. Let's hear more, boy. What do you know of Doctor Brittlebank?'

'I was staying with him at Lord Marley's,' said Reuben.

The two servants exchanged a look of disbelief.

'I was. Honestly. The doctor is my cousin, well my second cousin I think, in truth, but...' He strained to see inside the house again. He willed himself to see right through the walls, to see into the rooms and locate the doctor. But all he saw was walls and closed doors. 'Doctor Brittlebank came here. With Lord Marley . . . Didn't he? But things went wrong for me at Marley Hall . . . I've had to come on all alone with no money or anything, which accounts for why I'm so dirty-looking.'

'What's Lord Marley look like, then?' said Alice, leaning on her washboard and eyeing him coldly.

Reuben described him as best he could.

'You forgot to say that he's as mad as a flea-bitten mongrel,' she added. 'But yes, that's him.'

'I'm surprised you didn't meet with him,' said Simon. 'He's walking in the gardens. He likes to pick his own fruit – for apparently we are trying to poison him.' He raised his eyebrows.

'What a thought!' cried the maid. 'My Mister Cowper, he does bring in some strange types. Scientists and physicals. All sorts. Devilish stuff they does.'

'I didn't see him.' Reuben looked towards the orchard. He thought briefly of Gabriel. A pinprick of worry spiked him. He had to ignore it. 'What about Doctor Brittlebank? Is he awake yet? I want to see him.'

'He may be awake,' said Alice, 'for all I know he *is* awake, but it won't matter to you because he ain't here, anyways.'

'What?' Reuben took a step backwards. He felt as if someone had thumped him in the chest. 'Not here? He must be! Where is he, then? He must be here.'

'Left. Him and Mister Cowper. They had something particular to see up in town.'

'Oh, oh!' Reuben sat down heavily on the edge of a barrel. Then sprung up again. 'This is the worst news . . . I must find Lord Marley then, as soon as I can.'

The world was swinging round, trees, clouds, house, circling and swooping. He sat down again quickly, feeling sick.

'There, there, lad, you've gone green as a leaf under that dirt, ain't he, Simon?'

'He has.' Simon patted his shoulder. 'Don't fret, lad. It can't be that bad.'

'It is. I was counting on Doctor Brittlebank being here,' said Reuben. 'Counting on it. Flyte—' He bit his lip until it hurt. The pain stopped him from feeling sick at least. 'Flyte is after me, you see. He's not dead,' he prattled. 'He's coming to get me.'

'What's he blathering about? There, there,' said Alice. 'If it's Lord Marley you want, you can have him. He's down amongst the cabbages and apples. Maybe he can help you.' She shook her head. 'I doubt it, mind.'

Reuben shivered. He pictured Gabriel beneath the apple tree. '*Apples?*' he gasped.

'Why? Shouldn't his Lordship walk amongst apple trees if it takes his fancy?'

'I—'

A strange, strangled cry from the garden suddenly made all three stop still.

'What was *that?*' said Alice. She dropped her wet cloths back into the tub with a splat and stood with her head cocked on one side, listening.

Simon went still. 'I heard it,' he said.

This time, there was no doubt, as a terrible shriek, a scream of terror, rang out from the orchard.

Gabriel? Reuben felt his own pulse hammering in his ears.

'Oh, my good God,' said Simon. He turned his astonished face to Reuben. ''Tis Lord Marley!' He threw down a chunk of wood and set off down the path with his axe in his hand.

'Come on!' Alice cried. She gathered up her skirt and followed Simon towards the noise.

Another scream rent the air.

Reuben felt the skin all over his back and shoulders tingle and chill. He ran. He zigzagged around the stunted trees, slipping on fallen fruit, turning his ankles on hidden stones and logs. Gabriel!

'Where's his Lordship?' cried Simon.

Another fearful scream set the air shivering around them. Reuben swerved off towards it. Alice and Simon followed close on his heels.

25

Lord Marley Behaves
Very Strangely

Reuben darted down through the grass; careering around the ancient trees, leaping stones and low walls. Fear made his heart crash and bang in his chest, made his legs move faster than ever before. He was the first to reach them. He skidded up to an apple tree and clung to it, panting.

Gabriel did not move or speak. He looked as if he'd been flung forcefully against the apple tree by a tremendous wind. His arms were stretched out around its trunk, his head thrown back. His mouth hung open wetly. He was muttering silently.

Lord Marley was on his knees in the grass. His shrieks and yells had subsided into a gurgling, choking noise like a dying turkey. He was snatching at his throat and tearing at his face as if he wanted to pluck out his eyeballs. Saliva hung in long threads from his open mouth. His wig had slipped off and was caught on the gold braid of his jacket.

Simon joined Reuben, puffing noisily. 'Your

Lordship!' he cried. He took a step towards Lord Marley with his hand extended, but then he stopped as Lord Marley turned his glassy stare on him. His eyes were cold and blank, like pickled eggs. He looked through Reuben and Simon as if they weren't there, and focused instead on Gabriel.

'R'ban,' Gabriel said softly. 'Boy.'

'Gabriel! Stay where you are,' said Reuben. He hoped he sounded calm. 'What happened?'

Alice reached them. 'Lord have mercy!' she said. She held her apron up to her mouth.

Gabriel slithered down on to the grass. He reached for his old hat and quickly pulled it on. He gathered up the bandages that were strewn around and began wrapping them round his bare hand. Then he shrank into himself and went still.

'What's going on?' said Simon, looking from Lord Marley, to Gabriel and then to Reuben. 'What is this child? His hand . . .'

Lord Marley howled quietly.

'What's happening? My lord?' Alice gripped Simon's arm. 'What's going on?'

Simon shook his head.

The three of them stood and watched.

Lord Marley sat back on his heels. His lace was undone and ripped, hanging around his neck like spilled milk. He fingered it nervously. His jacket was half off. His face was terrible; it twitched and snapped in spasms as if minuscule fingers below the skin were pulling it this way and that. His cheeks were scratched and speckled with blood.

Lord Marley began to stand up slowly. He searched around for his wig, but couldn't find it. Reuben could see that Simon was itching to pull the wig off Lord Marley's back where it swung like a dead grey cat, but he dare not approach. Lord Marley staggered on his high-heeled shoes. His arms were jerking as if flicking at invisible flies. He lifted a trembling finger and pointed at Gabriel.

'Kill him!' he spluttered wetly. His mouth was loose and wild. His eyes were goggling, unblinking and dreadful. 'Kill him! You! You guards there! I told you to kill him! He must be killed.'

'Oh, my,' said Alice. She met Reuben's eyes. Her expression seemed to say "I told you so". 'He's gone,' she said. 'Lost his wits.'

'But he's still Lord Marley,' Simon said quietly, 'and our responsibility. Help me, woman! What'll we do?'

Alice raised her eyebrows but bravely took a step towards the lord and tried to smile at him. 'Lord Marley, it's me, Alice. Remember? I brought you your tea this morning, sir?'

But Lord Marley didn't hear her.

'Lord Mar—' Simon tried.

Lord Marley shrank back. A terrible spasm wracked his body so he twisted like an eel on the end of a line. His whole body vibrated, juddering out of control.

'Kill him! Kill him! Kill him!' Spittle was dribbling down his chin. 'He must be dead! Kill!'

'But Lord Marley. Please.' Simon moved towards him.

'Agh! No, not you!' cried Lord Marley. His body jolted upright as if his backbone was struck through with a metal rod. 'Not you too!' he screamed. 'Not you!'

He backed away, tripping over stones and fallen apples. A low apple branch spiked his head and Lord Marley gazed at it with surprise. He took hold of the branch as if it were a lifeline. He swung himself up, feet against the knobbly trunk and climbed quickly through the branches until Reuben could only see patches of his pale blue silk jacket and his stockinged legs and buckled shoes.

'Kill that animal!' Lord Marley shouted. The leaves rustled and shook. An apple was thrown down.

Reuben dodged out of its way.

'Kill it!'

'Sir?'

'No. No. No!'

More apples came showering down, and twigs and leaves. They heard wood tearing and a whole branch, apples and all, fell on to the grass.

'You'd best go to the house, Alice, get help,' Simon said. 'Lord Marley's . . . ill. Broken. He needs a doctor. Get help!'

Alice went scurrying towards the house.

'I'm too old for this,' said Simon. 'I wish I were sitting by the fire with my shoes off.' He sighed. 'Ah, well . . . Is this oddmedodd' – he nodded towards Gabriel – 'yours?'

Gabriel hadn't moved. He was snivelling and rubbing at his eyes.

'Mine? Well . . .' Reuben looked at Gabriel. 'But then I don't know who he does belong to.'

'He is most strange,' said Simon grimly. 'Come.' He sidestepped as Lord Marley lobbed an apple at his head. 'Come, let's move away.'

Reuben felt weak and wasn't sure he could do any more. 'But I have nowhere to move to,' he said, 'now that Doctor Brittlebank isn't here.'

'Come up to the house with me,' said Simon. 'I need to inform the housekeeper. We must send a messenger to get back Mister Cowper from town. Come, and bring the strange child. It appears to be him that is so upsetting my Lord Marley, so we'd best remove him.'

Reuben shot a look at Simon. It was true. Gabriel was the cause of this . . . Was what Wilmot had suggested true, then? Had Lord Marley seen the image of his child again – the too-round eyes, misshapen lips and head, hideous hands – could he see that now in Gabriel?

'Lory?' Gabriel piped. 'Lory?'

'Damn! Where is she?' said Reuben.

Glory was nowhere to be seen.

26

Madness

Simon led them along a gloomy corridor. The floor was covered with a dark narrow leather carpet: the walls were panelled with black wood. At the end of the corridor, they came to a small flight of stairs that led up to the kitchen. The kitchen was as big as a church with people scurrying around the room busily. It smelled of hot meat, onions and gravy. The large fireplace and chimney took up one entire wall and the fire poured out a tremendous heat. Copper and pewter pans hung on the walls. In the middle of the room was a vast table. Lord Marley's two massive greyhounds lay beneath it gnawing on large bones, grizzling and growling when one got too close to the other.

'Reuben, wait here. Don't move an inch. I will come back,' Simon said and went out.

Reuben slipped into a space between a chest and the fire and pulled Gabriel with him. The servants went on with their business, but glanced at them sideways and whispered to each other.

'R'ban!'

'Shh! What?'

Gabriel pointed. Above their heads was a wooden contraption like a double-sided wheel. Inside it was a tiny, wiry black dog. As the dog ran, it turned the wheel. A rope from the wheel was connected to the giant metal spit over the fire, making the spit turn. On the spit was a sheep's carcass.

'Lory,' Gabriel said. His voice cracked. Tears spilled from his eyes. 'Lory.'

Reuben wondered how long the black dog spent running nowhere. Glory, if you only knew how lucky you were!

A small girl with red hair came to the hearth. She stared long and hard at them before turning her attention to her job. Beneath the meat was a metal tray which had collected hot fat and she slid this along on a runner and began to ladle the grease over the turning carcass. The ashes popped and spat as the fat splattered over them.

Reuben swallowed hungrily. Gabriel squashed himself as far behind Reuben as it was possible to go. Around them, the servants went on with their business.

There were three young girls – all with fine white skin and red hair. Sisters, Reuben imagined, and an

230

older, large woman with very red cheeks who was making pastry at the table. He hoped Simon or Alice would come back soon. It was horrible to be stared at like a freak.

A new, wonderful aroma filled the kitchen as one of the girls opened the iron door of the bread oven beside the fire. She slipped a long wooden paddle inside the oven and dragged out four golden loaves of bread.

Reuben followed the bread with his eyes, devouring it as it went from paddle to table. His stomach was aching with hunger. It felt like an age since he'd eaten.

At last the woman sent a girl over with mugs of ale for the two boys and a slice of meat. Reuben took them gratefully.

He noticed the quick, worried look that the girl threw at Gabriel. Everyone must know about him and his strange hands now. They would have to leave this place and get on their way. To where? Anywhere, he told himself, because soon Flyte would be on their tail again.

He glanced up at the little black dog. It couldn't stop running and he knew just how it felt.

Reuben began to think they had been forgotten. Nobody came near them, except the smallest girl who brought them bread and a hardboiled egg.

Reuben peeled the egg and placed it on Gabriel's palm. It looked especially white and pearly on the filthy bandages.

'Eat,' said Reuben. Gabriel ate, nibbling at the egg with his tiny teeth and dropping most of it on the floor.

It was hot and, despite Gabriel's fresh clothes, he smelled. Especially this close. And he kept fiddling with something – what was it?

'Gabe?' Reuben whispered. 'What are you playing with? What have you got there?'

'R'ven.'

Gabriel handed Reuben a small glass bottle with a cork stopper. It was filled with a brilliant green liquid.

Reuben turned it over in his hands. He held it up to the light, trying to remember where he'd seen another bottle just like this . . . Lady Marley. Surely this was her medicine. The green one Lord Marley gave her. How had Gabriel got it? He had fresh clothes on so it hadn't been in his pocket for long . . . He must have picked it up recently, very recently . . . Maybe Lord Marley had dropped it in the orchard. But then why would Lord Marley have it with him, in the morning, in the orchard?

'R'ven,' said Gabriel, nodding when Reuben looked at him. 'R'ven. Man.'

* * *

At last Simon returned. 'Come with me,' he said, and ushered them out of the kitchen and down the hall again. It was much cooler and Reuben felt glad to be out of the hot room.

'What news?' asked Reuben, following him closely.

'His Lordship is settled now,' said Simon. 'The madness has abated somewhat. I'm afraid I had to tell him that the boy had been . . .' he lowered his voice '. . . killed. It seemed the rightest thing.'

Reuben shuddered. He glanced at Gabriel's little face and hoped he did not understand what they said.

'Now, come this way, to Mister Cowper's office. I tried to avoid this, I swear I did, but Alice had already blathered about the boy . . . There are two doctors. They came to see the lord and now they wish to see the little lad with the . . . the hands.'

He'd hoped Alice would not have noticed Gabriel's hands in all the chaos. He tried to walk tall as they entered the room, tried to think clearly. Gabriel clung like a leech to his side.

The two doctors were sitting either side of an elegant mahogany table. Silver candlesticks gleamed. Three glass domes glinted on a carved sideboard; trapped inside them were brilliantly coloured stuffed birds, frozen mid-song on mossy branches, their eyes still bright and lively. Reuben saw Gabriel stare at them in wonder.

Both doctors were dressed in fine black clothes, soft leather shoes and silk stockings.

'I am Doctor Bocking,' said the first doctor. He had very white skin and a gingery beard. His pale wig of tightly curled ringlets looked very strange against his orange beard. His eyes were icy blue.

'And this is Doctor Kissage,' said Simon, pointing to the other man. Doctor Kissage was older, his skin sagged around his nose and mouth. His lips were large and soft. He had the shaggiest eyebrows Reuben had ever seen.

Gabriel inched behind Reuben and burrowed his head into Reuben's back, his hands gripping his jacket tightly.

Reuben bowed and waited.

'Let me see the boy that has caused this terrible indisposition with Lord Marley,' said Doctor Kissage. He pulled at his long eyebrows. 'Surely it's not you!' he pointed a finger at Reuben.

'No, sir.'

These doctors were so cold and distant. What did they want? Reuben reached back and patted Gabriel's arm.

'Behind him, doctor,' said Simon. 'The boy with the hat.'

'That little mite? Step forward!'

'He doesn't understand,' said Reuben. He looked from one doctor to the other. He sensed they were not like *his* doctor. They looked so stern. The lines around their eyes were there from frowning, not smiling. He felt heavy-hearted and a great sadness was threatening to bring tears to his eyes. Glory gone. Doctor Brittlebank gone. I must be strong for Gabriel. I must be strong.

Simon brought Gabriel forward and tried to remove his hat. 'Let go, let go, lad. You must.' But Gabriel held on to it tightly. Simon won in the end. He tossed the hat to Reuben as if to touch it was to contaminate himself. He pulled off Gabriel's scarf.

'Ugh!' Doctor Kissage recoiled. 'This is not pleasant. He is very odd, as the maid did recount correctly. Show me these hands I was told of. Simon, make him do it!'

'Please don't,' said Reuben. 'It upsets him. He is just a boy, that's all…' Reuben stood between Simon and Gabriel. 'Don't.' Simon, not wishing to touch Gabriel if he could help it, leaned back against the wall where he assumed an air of total deafness.

'Where there is disfigurement and obscene changes in personal shape and form, there must be some fault deep within the character,' said Doctor

Bocking, stroking his red beard. 'The boy must have done something to bring about these alterations. In all His Goodness and Greatness, the Lord God would not have made a child like this. This is the work of evil.' He rubbed his hands together. 'Evil.'

'Man was made in *His* own likeness,' said Doctor Kissage. 'This one is not.' Doctor Kissage was twiddling with the long curling hairs of his eyebrows, rolling them into points between thumb and forefinger. He stared ferociously at Reuben. 'Why do you think he had such a dire effect on Lord Marley, eh?'

'I don't know.' Reuben could feel his heart starting to gallop. These two were up to something. He could sense it. They had prearranged this. They knew what they were going to say and do and he was so helpless . . .

'Think, boy, think!'

'I don't know. It's not his fault. I think Lord Marley is insane . . .' The two doctors looked horrified. Reuben wished he had not said the words as soon as they were out of his mouth. He was in no position to speak ill of anyone. The doctors exchanged a look of outrage.

'You are speaking of a lord!' cried Doctor Kissage.

'I beg your pardon,' said Reuben. 'I beg his pardon. I just—'

'I have never seen such a thing,' said Doctor Bocking. 'Have you, Kissage?'

'Never.' Doctor Kissage stood up and refilled his glass of wine. The wine was a deep, mysterious red, like velvet. Reuben saw him whisper something to Doctor Bocking and they nodded, heads close together like children with a secret.

'We are going to keep him,' said Doctor Kissage, turning back to Reuben. 'There, aren't you glad? You told Simon he was not yours. I'm sure you didn't want him, did you? We'll take him off your hands and look after him.'

'You can't!' cried Reuben.

'Be quiet! How dare you raise your voice? Insolent child!'

'He needs a good beating . . .'

'He certainly does,' said Doctor Kissage. 'Now, listen, we have plans to make the boy better. Naturally we will try and do that. We shall mend his ways. I believe surgery . . .'

'I agree,' said Doctor Bocking. 'We can write a paper. The Royal Society . . .'

'And of course there is the damage done to Lord Marley. He is very ill. He might demand compensation. This way we will at least be able to save the boy from the hangman . . .'

At the word 'hangman' Reuben immediately

thought of his grandmother. They – people like these doctors – had hanged his grandmother because they didn't understand her. Now it was the same with Gabriel. They would take him away and destroy him too.

'You shan't touch him!' cried Reuben. 'I will not let you. We've come so far! Listen, please listen . . . I lied. I lied before because I was frightened, but, but Gabriel is my – my brother!'

'What?'

The two doctors leaned towards him. 'What do you say?'

'Yes. And you cannot take him from me. You have no reason. He never did any harm to anyone . . .'

The door behind him clicked opened abruptly, but Reuben went on: 'It is Lord Marley that is deranged, not him.' He heard his voice beginning to crack and falter. He swallowed, tried to breathe. A sob broke out from him like a bird bursting out of a cage. 'When Doctor Brittlebank comes back—'

'Reuben!'

Reuben spun round. Doctor Brittlebank stood in the doorway. Reuben felt something give inside him and he seemed to explode inwards. Tears filled his eyes. He could not speak. He could not move.

Doctor Brittlebank came forward and put his hand on Reuben's shoulders. 'Shh,' he said very quietly. He was smaller than the other two doctors. His clothes were shabbier. His wig had loose curls and bald bits. But he was not afraid.

'Gentlemen, good day,' he went on, softly. 'Mister Cowper and I came back early. I heard Reuben was here . . .' He squeezed Reuben's shoulder and pulled him gently towards his side. 'This is my adopted son, sirs. I heard raised voices,' he continued. 'Reuben is distressed. I can't imagine what could be causing it.' The other two doctors stared at him coldly. 'Is something the matter?' he added, smiling mildly at them.

He did not seem to have noticed Gabriel at all.

'Your little adopted *scallywag* is impeding our work and our wishes.' Doctor Kissage poured more wine. 'He says that boy with the face like a plate is his brother. Therefore . . .'

Doctor Brittlebank looked briefly at Gabriel and then at Reuben. 'Er, yes, absolutely. That is so,' said Doctor Brittlebank with only the slightest hesitation. 'Reuben speaks the truth. I was intending to take them both back to the country today. Did you not know this?'

'This boy is evil!' cried Doctor Kissage, pointing at Gabriel. 'He is marked by the Devil!'

'You speak of my own flesh and blood,' said Doctor Brittlebank coldly. His mouth twitched. 'He is disfigured, that is all. Accidental damage when he was born. I've come to fetch them both home.'

Reuben looked up at the doctor. He felt a smile filling up his chest and spreading over his whole face.

'Accidental—? Damn me, I don't—' began Doctor Bocking.

'Good. All settled,' said Doctor Brittlebank. 'Let us go.' He pushed Reuben out and Gabriel scuttled behind, clinging to Reuben as tightly as a limpet to a rock.

'Damn me!' cried Doctor Bocking as they went out.

Simon followed them and shut the door swiftly behind them.

'Doct—?' Reuben began.

'Shh. Not a word,' said Doctor Brittlebank.

'Aye' agreed Simon, quietly. 'Don't trust them two.' He hurried off down the corridor but called back over his shoulder, 'I'd get out pretty quick if I was you.'

Doctor Brittlebank hurried Reuben and Gabriel upstairs to his bedchamber.

'Those two are rich,' he said, ushering them inside. 'Influential. We need to leave this place.'

'What about Lord Marley? He is not well. He had a sort of fit. They say that Gabriel is mad, but it's not him, it's the lord.'

'Lords are never considered to be insane by those whose bills they pay,' said Doctor Brittlebank. He locked the door behind them. 'A little privacy. Good. Ah, Reuben, never have I been so surprised to see someone as I was to see you – and your friend! Tell me everything that has befallen you! How, for I can still hardly believe it, how did you come to be here, miles from Marley Hall and' – he winked solemnly at Reuben – 'with a *new* member of our family?'

27

Leaving Lord Marley Behind

Gabriel did not like it when the door of Doctor Brittlebank's bedroom closed behind him. He whined. He ran to the window and stared outside. He scratched at the glass.

'Lory. Lory,' he whimpered.

'It's Glory that he's worried about,' Reuben told the doctor. He patted Gabriel's shoulder. 'She'll come back, Gabriel. She will.' He turned to the doctor.

'This is Gabriel,' he said. 'I found him in the ruins at Marley Hall. He followed me. Gabriel? Say hello to the doctor, will you? He's a good doctor. He's our friend.'

But Gabriel was too distracted and stayed beside the window, drumming his hands against the sill.

'Where can Glory have gone?' said Reuben quietly. He stared out across the tangled orchard. 'She was tied up too, Doctor. I don't understand it. Gabriel would never have let her go willingly.'

'She's a clever little dog,' said Doctor Brittlebank. 'I'm sure she'll make her way back to us. We can't wait for her, Reuben. I would not like to say what plans those two doctors are hatching, but they are not to be trusted. We must leave, all of us, and the sooner the better . . .'

He had started packing his belongings and was thrusting things into his trunk and cases as he spoke. He stopped suddenly and held up a paper: 'Mister Newton!' he said. 'He was fascinating. It was a wonderful thing to speak with him, but I wish I had not left you. I should not have left you.'

Gabriel lay down on the Turkish rug and curled up in a ball. He was just like Glory, Reuben thought, the way he could settle anywhere and sleep any time of night or day.

Reuben began to tell the doctor everything that had happened.

When the doctor heard Flyte's name he stopped still. 'Flyte? That devil!' He pulled off his wig and tossed it on the floor. 'So he lives? He did not die at Cal's Cauldron as we thought. God in Heaven, you were right to run, Reuben. Thank goodness you did. From now on you stay close with me.'

'I will, I will! That's all I want to do,' said Reuben.

'We must go straight to Marley Hall,' went on Doctor Brittlebank, smacking a bundle of papers against his leg. 'Tell Lady Marley her husband – what *has* happened to him? Do we know? I am all at sea here!'

'He went mad,' said Reuben. 'He was blathering and dribbling and saying we should kill . . .' he paused. 'I think – kill Gabriel.'

'Good gracious! How strange! Why would he say that? Did poor Gabriel's face so unhinge him? The boy is not *that* odd . . .'

Reuben swallowed. 'I think I know.'

'You do?'

'It was Wilmot who told me. He said it was rumoured there was a child, a monster child, shut up in the ruins at Marley Hall. Catherine, the maid, she knew of him. I saw her take him food. She's the sort that would spread such stories. Stories that he's the child of Lord and Lady Marley . . .'

The doctor stared at the little boy lying on the floor. 'Well, well. Gabriel *Marley*.' He sighed. 'I am certain Lady Marley does not know he is alive.'

'Will we tell her?'

The doctor shook his head. 'It is not for us to interfere. But, we do need to visit Marley Hall. We need to see if Gabriel is missed. Then we shall return to Wycke House. And, after a good pie of Hetty's and a few pints of mead, I plan to not move again. Not for a long time.'

'What about Gabriel?'

'I don't know.' The doctor scratched his head. 'He is not ours to simply take. If possible we will bring him back home with us. Do you think he will scrub up clean? Could we rid him of that awful smell?'

Reuben grinned. 'I think so, yes.' Reuben softened his voice to a whisper. 'Under the bandages, Doctor, his feet and hands are webbed like a toad's. He cannot really talk. He doesn't know anything. He scares people.'

'Webbed?' Doctor Brittlebank's eyebrows shot up. 'I've seen that once in a newborn but the child never so much as took a breath ... The sooner we get distance between him and those two so-called physicians downstairs the better . . . Now, I do not want to disturb our host, Mister Cowper, or let him see how desperate we are . . . How shall we go? What transport . . . ? This cock-master you've told me about, this Wilmot – where did he say he was staying? Let us send a boy with a message and see if he will come and collect us in his wagon and take us home.'

Home. Hetty. Reuben smelled fresh linen, waxed furniture and lavender. He saw the uneven oak floorboards that led to his room, the top stair which was trodden into a smooth soft shine. His own curtained bed.

'Yes please,' he said.

'I shall tell Mister Cowper that I'm indisposed and need to return,' said Doctor Brittlebank. 'You and the boy must remain in this room with the door locked. Promise me! I do not know what those interfering doctors are capable of. I do not know how far away Flyte might be. Lock the door . . .'

'Wilmot said he was going to Wethering Farm . . . It is near a Saxon church . . . He told me most particular – as if he guessed I'd need him. I do hope he is still there. The day is nearly gone,' Reuben added, glancing out of the window. The sky was grey and gloomy. 'I would like you to meet Wilmot, he is a good man.'

'Then we will find him,' said Doctor Brittlebank. He stuck his head out of the door and yelled for a servant. A small girl with big brown eyes appeared after a moment.

'Yes, sir?'

Reuben could see her trying to peer round the doctor and snatch a look at Gabriel.

'I need a boy to go on an errand. Does Mister Cowper have such a boy?'

'Yes, sir. That would be Bartholomew. He's out in the stable. What is the errand, sir? I could tell him.'

'Do you know a farm beside a Saxon church? A farm called Wethering Farm?'

'I don't know nothing about no Saxton church,'

said the maid, 'but I knows Farmer Wethering. He's my sister's husband's cousin. Least I think that's what he is.'

Doctor Brittlebank grinned. 'Could you send the boy, this Bartholomew, to the farm? There is a man called Wilmot there. A cock-master by trade . . .'

'I knows Wilmot!' shrieked the little maid. 'He's my auntie's brother's best mate, he is. Fancy!'

'Well. Good. What a close neighbourhood this is. Can you send Bartholomew?'

'I will.' She spun round eagerly then back again. 'Oh, Doctor, I done gone and forgot what I had to tell our Bart to do.'

Doctor Brittlebank smiled. 'Tell this Mister Wilmot to come here,' he said. 'As soon as he possibly can. To help Reuben. Have you got that? It's for Reuben.'

The maid nodded, gathered up her skirts and clattered off down the corridor.

'There,' said Doctor Brittlebank. 'Let's hope your friend has not left for home just yet.'

'I do hope not,' agreed Reuben. 'Wilmot is the sort of man who makes you feel safe. It will be good to travel with him.'

The doctor went to make his apologies to his host. He told Reuben, when he came back, that Mister Cowper had promised to care for Lord Marley.

'That Doctor Bocking and Doctor Kissage are in charge of my lord,' he said. 'Dear God, I fear for my lord's soul, but it is not up to me . . . And good news, the boy Bartholomew is back – with Wilmot!'

Reuben ran downstairs. The front door was open. Wilmot was standing on the top step. He was peering into the interior of the house shyly, his eyes as round as saucers.

'Wilmot!'

'Reuben, lad!'

'I'm so glad you could come. Here is my dear Doctor Brittlebank! I know you'll like each other. And here's little Gabriel too, but he's in low spirits I fear. Glory has gone.'

'Gone?'

'Run away. And we don't know where or how.'

The doctor shook hands with Wilmot. 'I am forever in your debt, Mister Wilmot,' said Doctor Brittlebank, quietly. 'We both are.'

Wilmot rubbed his red cheeks. 'I was glad to help Reuben before and I'm glad to help now. 'Tis only my journey homewards and a bit besides to reach Marley Hall. 'Tis nothing. Though we need to get going, mind. It's late enough.'

'True,' said Doctor Brittlebank. 'We will have to stay the night somewhere.'

'There's an inn on the way,' said Wilmot, 'The

Bear. It keeps good company. Ah, Reuben, I should never have left you,' he added. 'I knew this place wasn't for the likes of us. I said so.'

'You were right,' said Reuben.

'But no sign of that bad preacher fellow?'

'No.'

'Well that's good to hear, young lad. I see him round every corner, I confess. I hear his voice when I'm in a crowd. He has got right into my – my bones!'

The doctor's boxes of papers and trunks of clothes had already been stowed in the waiting wagon. They were ready to go.

'Beg your pardon, 'tis not a carriage like what you're used to, I expect,' said Wilmot. He helped Doctor Brittlebank up on to the seat at the front. 'There's no springs on this cart, no cushions neither . . .'

'Wilmot, it is perfect,' the doctor assured him. 'The boys can climb up in the back amongst the – amongst the what, I am not sure?'

''Tis the feed for the cockerels,' said Wilmot. 'Don't ask me to divulge exactly as it's secret lotions and mixtures. I follow ancient recipes to get them cockerels fit – and they do work.'

'How are they managing without you?' Reuben asked. He climbed up into the back of the wagon and settled down amongst the soft bags and sacks with Gabriel.

'My neighbour, Jack Sowerby, comes by when I'm off for more than a night. He sees to them. I do the same for Jack when he's got to leave his lambs. Don't worry on that score.'

28

Back to Marley Hall

The early evening air was cool; Reuben snuggled down beneath a blanket. A gentle breeze pulled streams of red and golden leaves down from the trees and sent them floating across the lane. The countryside rustled around them.

Reuben felt so very different to how he had felt on the journey towards Felton. He did not need to look back all the time to see if Flyte was on his heels. He did not fret about Flyte at all. If he thought about him for one moment he had only to look up at Doctor Brittlebank and Wilmot and his worries faded. Flyte would never dare come near when I have those two to protect me, he thought. Flyte is probably still in Easton Pacey, looking for us. Mister Wight and the others must have been astonished to find Mistress Long's cottage empty! Would that I could have seen their faces!

But Glory. Where was she? His lap felt empty without her. His hands, so used to stroking her and rubbing the long curling hair on her ears, were strangely idle.

'Lory?' Gabriel was missing her too. He leaned out of the wagon and peered out over the passing fields. 'Lory?' he called.

'Where is she, Gabe?' Reuben asked. He'd asked many times and had no answer that he could understand. 'What happened? You were the last to see her. Where's she gone?'

Gabriel shook his head. 'Gone. Lory gone. Mary gone. Mon.' He chewed the words around in his mouth as if trying to make them come out differently. 'R'ven. Mon.' He rested his forehead on the side of the wagon. His cupid lips turned down at the edges. Tears rolled down his cheeks. 'R'ven,' Gabriel repeated. 'R'ven!'

'Raven-man? Or do you mean a man and a raven?' Or was it *mon* like in *monster* he was trying to say? Was he remembering what Reuben had said about the dead bird? 'A monster raven?' Reuben suggested.

Gabriel stamped his feet in frustration. He shook his head and banged his fists against the sacks of corn. 'Gone. Boy, boy, boy!' He spoke rapidly. He spat and dribbled. It was as if he were trying to explain something to a fool. 'R'ven!' he said earnestly. 'Mon. Gone!'

Reuben shuddered. 'All right. All right.' It must

have been a man, he thought. A dog stealer. Dog stealers took dogs for bear baiting. Or they used them in dog fights. Glory could not fight. She could not defend herself at all. Or they skinned dogs and used their hides to make fine coats for gentlemen. Please, please, not any of that, thought Reuben. Let her have been found by a kindly person who will love her, or please let her be on her way home right now, walking back to Wycke House all by herself.

They spent the night at The Bear Inn. It was a quiet old tavern. The rooms were clean, the pewter dishes well polished. There were few guests that night so they got the big bedchamber all to themselves. They took dinner in their room too, so that Gabriel could be kept hidden.

'Come sit by me, Gabriel,' said Doctor Brittlebank when dinner was served and they sat down at the table.

But Gabriel crept away into a corner.

'I don't think he's used to dining at a table,' said Reuben, 'or with other folk.'

'When he is more used to me I shall look at his hands and his feet and see if I can help him at all,' said Doctor Brittlebank. 'But I would not like to distress him now.'

Gabriel wandered around the chamber patting the walls, opening and closing the wardrobe doors, scratching at the window. He ate only a few of the scraps that Reuben handed to him. At last Reuben enticed him to lie down on one of the mattresses and he lay down beside him.

'I was hoping we might clean him a little,' said Doctor Brittlebank, as he covered the little boy over with a blanket. 'But I see that will not be possible.'

Gabriel curled up in a ball in the centre of his mattress and pulled his hat over his face.

'I'll try in the morning,' said Reuben. 'There. Go to sleep, Gabriel. Don't worry about Glory, now.'

Gabriel turned watery eyes to Reuben and peered at him intently. 'Mary gone. Mary.'

'Hush. Go to sleep.'

The doctor and Wilmot shared a pipe beside the fire and a glass or two of rum before settling down.

'I cannot sleep beside a gentleman such as the doctor,' Wilmot whispered to Reuben as they prepared to bed down too. 'I am embarrassed. And I snore like a pig.'

'You have no choice,' said Reuben. He grinned. 'And to tell the truth, you don't only snore like a pig, but more like a pig with a cold in his nose and three pints of ale inside it.'

'Reuben! You cheeky young scallywag!'

* * *

Reuben wondered if Gabriel would recognize Marley Hall, but as the wagon rolled down the drive towards the house the following morning, the little boy didn't even look around. He was distracted, making little mewling cries and calling all the time for Glory.

In his mind, Reuben had designed a new life for Glory. She had been found and taken in by an old widow not unlike his grandmother. The widow had been very lonely, now she was happy. Glory would sit by her and enjoy being fed tidbits. If I never see her again, that is how I will always imagine her, Reuben thought.

At last they arrived at Marley Hall.

'So this is my landlord's little place, is it?' said Wilmot, with a chuckle. 'Think of the cockerels he could keep if he had a mind to, eh? What a place!'

'I'm afraid he was not inclined towards cock fighting – pheasant shooting, yes, but not cockerels,' said Doctor Brittlebank.

'I told you it was grand,' said Reuben.

'Aye, you did. Look at the windows on it. Think of the glass. Think of the expense . . . Think of them farms and cottages that pays him rent so he can have his fine windows,' he added. 'Like me.'

'It's the aristocracy,' said Doctor Brittlebank. 'It's England's way.'

'Aye,' said Wilmot. 'It is.'

Marley Hall brought a rush of mixed feelings for Reuben. Doctor Brittlebank had laughed when Reuben had told him about Lady Marley's offer to adopt him. He'd said if Reuben didn't behave himself and work hard at his studies he would agree to the adoption and good riddance. Reuben knew he was safe. But he had abused Lady Marley's kindness and he did feel bad now, and dreaded meeting her again.

Wilmot brought his old wagon to a standstill outside the front porch. Reuben covered Gabriel up with the blanket before jumping down and stretching his legs. It was very important that nobody saw Gabriel with them.

George came out to greet them.

'Doctor Brittlebank, it is good to see you again,' he said. He swayed over to them. Reuben noticed a strong smell of ale about him. George helped the doctor down. 'Lady Marley is in her library. She is much distressed to hear of her husband's illness and indisposition, of course she is. Aren't we all, indeed, we are. We heard yesterday.' He grinned suddenly, then quickly tried to cover his smile with his hand. 'Excuse me. You!' He jabbed a finger at Wilmot. 'You can feed and water the horse round thataway.'

'Thank you, George,' said Doctor Brittlebank.

'We do not plan to stay long. Please will you bring down the bags we left behind in our room? Are they ready to collect?'

'They are, Doctor. We got them packed up when little Reuben left. I'll get old Smithy to bring them down.'

'I'll see to everything, don't you worry,' said Wilmot, nodding towards the back of the wagon where Gabriel was hidden. 'Walk on!' he called and his horse ambled slowly off towards the stables.

Lady Marley was sitting in her favourite chair beside a roaring fire. She wore a dress of bright green silk. Her hair was full of bows and ribbons. She did not appear to be pining for her husband at all.

Reuben came in half hidden behind the doctor. I hope she's forgotten all that passed between us, he thought. She'll have too much on her mind, surely, worrying about her husband, to worry about adopting me.

'Doctor Brittlebank,' she said in her soft voice. 'How pleasant to see you. What news of my husband? A messenger came yesterday with word of his illness. I was not surprised to hear of it. Although he would never admit it, my lord's disposition was unsettled and so airy I sometimes believed he would float away with his fancies and ideas . . . They've locked him up in Bedlam. I hope they won't make a spectacle of him? Do you think they will, Doctor? Or will they lock him away where no one will ever see him?'

'I'm sure he will make a full recovery, Lady Marley,' said Doctor Brittlebank. 'He—'

'In any case,' went on Lady Marley, 'I manage very well without his Lordship's company. Look, doctor, do you see these?' She pointed to three small bottles of green medicine on the table beside her. 'I am not taking it. I do not know what is in the mixture but it does me no good at all. I even,' she dropped her voice slightly 'I even think, I believe, I might be with child.'

'My congratulations to you,' said Doctor Brittlebank. 'But it's very soon . . .'

'Very soon. But I am listening to my body, Doctor Brittlebank. I heed it's warnings. And if I am with child, I will require you to be my physician. Do you promise you will?'

'Well, your ladyship, I—'

'Yes. You will. My dear husband had it quite wrong. The green medicine stopped me from conceiving, quite the reverse of what it was intended for. I wonder at the skill of his apothecary; my lord said he was good and not cheap either. He needs another.'

'I do hope you are right in your predictions, Lady Marley, it is only a matter of a few days . . .'

'That's all that's needed for me to know. Look at me, Doctor, look! Do I not look different?'

Reuben thought she did. Her cheeks seemed plumper and pinker. Her eyes shone. Even her thin hair looked thicker and more lustrous. Was it possible? Certainly her bright clothes made her look more cheerful.

'I remember clearly how I felt the first time,' she said. 'But this babe will stay and live and be strong. And it will be a beautiful little *girl*.'

'I pray you are correct,' said Doctor Brittlebank.

'And so I won't need Reuben,' she added. 'It will be a great disappointment for him, I am sure . . .' she nodded at Reuben. 'Did the boy tell you about the preacher? Did he tell you what happened when you had gone?'

Doctor Brittlebank shook his head. 'I—' he began.

But Lady Marley interrupted him. She wanted to describe how the preacher had been taken ill. 'He had a talisman, Doctor Brittlebank, something in a little leather bag around his neck. I don't know what it was . . . a toad's leg? A newt with no eyes? Whatever it was, he held on to it night and day. I saw no prayers. I heard no conversations with God. No. He was a strange preacher . . . He insisted on getting up as soon as the fever had abated. It did not last long. It was not scarlet fever after all . . .'

'I am glad. It would have been terrible to bring the illness into Marley Hall.'

'As soon as he could stand, he borrowed a horse and one of my men to accompany him. I gave him Scarfe. I do not like Scarfe. He was so worried about you, Reuben. He called you his little lost lamb . . .'

Doctor Brittlebank and Reuben exchanged a look. The doctor had planned on telling Lady Marley the truth about her 'preacher', but now they both saw it would be impossible to do so.

While Lady Marley continued with her tale, Reuben looked out of the window towards the distant woods and thought about home.

He saw the old servant, Smithy, wander by with a dead rabbit slung over his shoulder and then another figure came into view. Goodness, it was Gabriel. He'd escaped from Wilmot.

'Excuse me,' Reuben said hastily. 'I must go.'

Lady Marley frowned. 'That boy rushes about far too much, Doctor Brittlebank. He's like a spinning top. You need to control him.'

'Yes, my lady.' The doctor sat down and took Lady Marley's hand. 'Do go on, Lady Marley,' he said. 'I have all the time in the world.' He winked at Reuben.

Reuben ran.

Gabriel was hunched on the damp grass beside an

urn of faded yellow flowers. He was covering his ears with his bandaged hands, rocking backwards and forwards and whining.

'What is it? What's the matter, Gabe?' He *does* remember this place! thought Reuben. It must be too dreadful for him! He hates it. Reuben crouched down beside the little boy and tried to move his hands away from his head. 'What is it? Tell me. What is the matter?'

Gabriel shook Reuben off and threw himself face down in the grass, whining.

Reuben heard a dog bark. He froze. That bark sounded like Glory. But it couldn't be ... He felt himself lighten. It seemed as if he was swelling up with the idea: Glory was alive. Oh, let it be true!

'Gabriel, listen! Gabriel!' He shook him. 'Listen! It's Glory!'

But Gabriel didn't seem to want to hear. He muttered and chattered; a string of meaningless half-words. Tears rolled down his cheeks.

'Don't you want to hear her?'

Suddenly Reuben thought he understood. It was because half of him didn't want to hear her. In case he was wrong. In case it wasn't her. 'You heard it already, did you?' he said. 'You heard it and ran out here, but didn't dare believe it? Is that it? But it *is* Glory. She's here. I recognize her bark too!'

Gabriel wiped his eyes. He stared up at Reuben hopefully.

'Lory?'

'It is her! I swear it is. I don't understand how. It's not possible, but it is her.'

Reuben turned to where he'd heard the bark. He concentrated. There was no sound at the moment. He stood very still and listened intently.

Then they both heard it at the same instant: a volley of barking from near the ruins. They looked at each other and grinned. Gabriel got up and reached for Reuben's hand and pulled him towards the sound. 'Dog. Boy. Go!'

29

The Secret of the Ruins

'Glory! Glory!' Reuben called as they crossed the meadow. She was barking but she did not come. Reuben stared ahead towards the copse of trees. You could see nothing of the old chapel and ruins. No one would know that it existed unless they followed the path down to the stone bridge and crossed the stream.

Gabriel gabbled softly to himself, half-words and broken sounds which Reuben could not understand.

They were midway across the meadow, nearing the tall trees that surrounded the ruins, when the dog suddenly stopped barking. Now it was strangely silent. The sky was grey and heavy and a sudden breeze chilled the air. 'It was her. I'm sure it was her,' Reuben said.

He was walking as fast as he could, but Gabriel was lagging behind. Reuben took hold of Gabriel's hand. 'We want to find her, don't we? Come on, Gabe.' Reuben felt the lumpy fingers beneath the bandages.

He tried to ignore the sensation. He tried to not remember those awful, unnatural shapes. Gabriel cannot help it, he told himself. He must live with those hands – and if he can live with them, I can too.

'Glory must have followed us,' Reuben said. 'She must have made her own way back, all the way here to Marley Hall.'

'Lory! Com'on, Lory.' Gabriel patted his thigh the way he had seen Reuben call the dog.

Fancy Glory coming back here, to the ruins, Reuben thought. Not to Wycke House, not to me. It hurts. But then she's daft. Let it be.

'She loves you, Gabriel, and no mistake. She's come back to your place, Gabe. What did you do to make her love you so much?' He smiled at Gabriel. The boy flashed his tiny teeth at him in a wide grin, as if he understood. 'That was certainly her barking, wasn't it? We couldn't both think it was her if it wasn't.'

Gabriel was stumbling and tripping over the uneven ground so Reuben slowed down. He wondered if Gabriel's feet hurt. He never complained and yet they probably did pain him. He had never walked anywhere much, Reuben supposed, except to follow him and Glory.

'There we go, Gabe. It's all right. She'll wait for us, I reckon. And all the time I was dreaming Glory was with that old lady . . . Still, that doesn't matter.'

They did not hear Glory bark again.

They neared the ruins. Reuben's legs grew heavy. It was a horrid place. An eerie place. He felt the hairs prickle on his neck and a shiver run down his back. It was colder here. The tall trees and the crumbling tower leaned over them and blocked out what little light there was. There was no birdsong. There were no bees. Few flowers.

They went over the bridge. Even the water gurgling and trickling beneath them sounded melancholy. The air was damp, misty and heavy.

They came to the ruins.

Gabriel stopped dead.

'It's all right,' said Reuben. 'Don't be afraid.' I wager you do recognize this old place, don't you? he thought.

Gabriel suddenly started to shake. His teeth rattled like dried peas in a pot. He clutched a fistful of Reuben's jacket tightly and clung to him.

'What is it? Do you think I'm taking you back there? To put you back in that horrid pigsty?' said Reuben.

Gabriel nodded his head in sudden, quick jerks. His eyes were round and full of tears.

'I wouldn't do that! I would never do that, Gabe.'

Gabriel clutched at him tighter, as if trying to

burrow into Reuben's jacket. His jaw worked but no words came out.

'Come. You're my friend.'

Gabriel looked up at him as if understanding what he said for the first time.

'I won't lock you up. We're going to see Glory.'

Gabriel nodded slowly. He relaxed his hold a little.

Reuben called out as loudly as he could: 'Glory! Glory!'

Silence.

'What's she playing at, Gabe?' He patted his hand. 'Silly little dog. She was always such a dim-witted spaniel...'

Reuben tried to pull Gabriel gently towards the shed.

'No, no, no.' Gabriel squealed. He dug his heels into the ground and would not move. 'No!'

'Oh, Gabe,' Reuben put his arm around the boy's tiny shoulders. 'I wish I could explain . . .' He could feel Gabriel trembling. 'Don't fret. Peace, peace! I won't force you . . .'

What could he do? The doctor would fret if they were too long . . . They heard a raven's *kronk kronk* call from the distance. It sent shivers right through him, making him shudder. Then there was a sudden noise from the back of the buildings; the sound of rubble shifting gently. Something fell with a dull thud on to the soft ground. They both jumped.

'Hear that? She must be round the back there.' But how was he to move with Gabriel holding him like this? 'Come on,' he urged. 'Look, we'll go right round the yard, along the wall and avoid . . . *that*. That place you called home.'

Gabriel whimpered. Without letting go of Reuben's hand, he followed Reuben around the yard. There was a narrow gap between the wall of Gabriel's shed and the yard wall. They squeezed through and under the branches of a sycamore sapling, over bracken and weeds.

The old building was much bigger than Reuben had first imagined; the crumbling mass of stones reached out into the tangle of shrubs and trees beyond. Ivy stems twisted and curled through the arched windows like thick brown veins. Dark greenery cascaded over the fallen stones and sagging roof like a shroud.

They pushed their way through the nettles and shrubs to a small wooden door, framed with elaborate stonework. Despite its age, the wood was still mostly intact. The iron hinges and handle were weathered and cobwebby.

'Let's try this,' said Reuben. 'Maybe she's got inside somehow. I surely heard something.'

Reuben listened at the door. He wished she'd bark

again. He thought he heard a whine but it might have been the creaking of the trees as they swayed and leaned against each other.

Gabriel looked up with hopeful, expectant eyes.

Reuben pushed the door. It grated noisily over crumbs of masonry scattered on the stone floor. They stepped inside over a heap of fallen twigs and leaves and grit. Above them, through the shattered roof, the broken tower rose up to the grey sky. Reuben could see the raven's nest balancing on a high stone buttress.

Something buzzed; a large black fly circled his head.

'Smells bad,' Reuben said. 'Really bad. There's something died in here.'

Reuben put his hand over his nose. The foul smell did not upset Gabriel. Perhaps, Reuben thought, he'd lived with such a stench for long enough not to care.

Gabriel seemed excited inside the ruined chapel. His teeth clattered. He barked and crowed. He tugged at Reuben's jacket, chanting, 'Boy. Boy.'

The floor was littered with rotting leaves and branches torn from the trees. Slates from the roof had fallen. They lay crashed into pieces against the stone slab floor, and crunched noisily under their feet. Great wooden timbers had fallen from the ceiling and lay at awkward angles over the pews. Mould, like pale wet fingers, sprouted from the rotting wood. Large cockroaches scuttled off as the boys kicked through the debris.

The damp seeped into the very core of Reuben's limbs.

'It's hateful in here.' Reuben shivered. '*Glory!*' he called. 'Where are you?' But the place was still and quiet.

'Com'on.' Gabriel pulled him forward.

'What is it?'

'Com'on. Boy. Com'on.' Gabriel guided Reuben to the far side of the chapel. The roof was intact here and beneath it was an arched alcove cut into the wall. A silvery stone knight lay sleeping. His smooth limbs gleamed.

They went up close to the effigy. It reminded Reuben of the stone knight in the little chapel in Easton Pacey. The knight lay on his back with his head resting against a stone pillow. He wore chain mail. His hands were pointed in prayer. His legs were crossed and his feet were encased in pointed shoes. Beneath his feet lay some sort of animal, so smoothed and worn down that it was almost as featureless as the stone pillow.

Above him was a plaque: *Here lyeth the body of Nicholas Marrlaye who departed this life and slept with his Fathers ye 23rd day of May, anno 1552.* There was more writing but it was worn away and impossible to read.

Gabriel touched the knight gently on his forehead. He lifted a twig from where it had fallen on to the knight's breast. The stone figure was the only thing in the chapel that was not covered in moss or leaves or cobwebs, as if it had been cleaned . . .

'It was you that did it, wasn't it, Gabriel?' said Reuben. 'You must have got in somehow, and kept him neat and tidy. You did it because the knight's got odd-looking hands and feet? Is that it?'

'Com'on,' said Gabriel. He tugged urgently again at Reuben's hand. He squeaked and chattered.

'What now? What is it?'

He allowed Gabriel to lead him to a darker corner of the chapel. Here, beneath the low timbers of the roof were four wide stone steps leading down to an enclosed area.

Reuben felt uncomfortable. He felt the hairs prickle on his neck.

As they approached, the smell – a fearful stench of rotting meat – grew stronger. Reuben gagged. He held his nose and scrunched up his face. He blinked and swatted at the flies that swarmed around and bounced against his cheeks.

'It's nasty.' He shuddered. 'I don't want to go

nearer, Gabe, it's not wholesome in here. I don't like it.' He licked his dry lips.

But Gabriel held him tightly and pushed and pulled at him.

Now Reuben heard a low buzzing noise; it grew stronger as they got further into the dark corner. He saw at last what it was, a mass of flies: so many, they looked like one dark shifting shape. They swarmed over something . . . something laid out on a stone slab . . .

'Oh, my God!' he whispered.

He saw red-gold hair.

'Glory?' Reuben could not get his cotton-dry mouth to form words. 'Is it Glory?'

He forced himself to edge nearer.

It was not his dog. He saw the unmistakable shape of a human profile.

The flies rose in a dark buzzing, whining cloud and before the flies sank back again, Reuben saw a woman's body.

Her long red hair lay in a fan around her head. Her grey face was awful; she had no eyes. Her skin was like candle wax tinged with green. The veins in her neck and temples showed clearly like brown and purple roots twisting beneath the skin. She wore a grubby yellow dress. Her little feet were shoeless, dirty white stockinged toes flopped sideways.

Her apron – stained red-brown with blood – had been untied from her waist and laid out across her body like a sheet. There were dark stains on her dress too and on the stone.

'Who is it? Do you know this woman?' Reuben managed to ask. His words came out broken and choked. 'She's been dead a week, maybe ten days . . .'

'Mary,' said Gabriel. 'Mary n' more.'

'*Mary!*' Reuben was stunned. She was here, had been here all along. Dead.

Suddenly Gabriel reached out and yanked the apron off her body.

Reuben jumped back as the flies swarmed, spinning and droning angrily.

Beneath the apron was a gaping hole. Mary's belly had been cut open. She was empty except for a seething mass of maggots, flies and beetles.

'Gone,' said Gabriel. He turned his moon-face up to Reuben. He looked neither sad nor angry; he looked bemused. 'Gone.'

Reuben pressed a hand to hold down the awful upward heaves in his stomach; he was going to be sick. He needed fresh air. He turned to Gabriel and was amazed at the blankness of his stare. Gabriel does not understand. How could he? Reuben realized. What can he know about life and death and . . . murder?

Reuben stumbled a few paces up the steps and vomited.

'Got to get out,' he said. 'Out!'

Gabriel took his arm and guided him through the pews and down the aisle to the far end of the chapel where there was a large hole in the wall. Gabriel pushed him through.

Reuben felt straw under his feet. He smelled a different but still unpleasant smell. He had just enough wit to notice that he was inside Gabriel's shed, and then they were pushing their way out of the door and into the yard.

Reuben fell on to the cobbles and was sick again.

Oh, God, oh God, he thought. That poor girl! Poor Mary! Who killed her? Who did that? Poor woman. Please God you didn't see this happen, Gabe . . .

Gabriel was watching Reuben closely. His mouth hung open. He wiped his snotty nose on his bandaged hand.

'R'ven,' he said firmly, with a hint of frustration. Then again, with a touch of fear: 'R'ven.'

Then he ran.

30

The Trick

R'ven.

Reuben heard the word. He had the impression that a great black bird came swooping down from above. *R'ven.* Instead of feathers, he felt something solid crash against his head. Pain screamed at him. Dots of light spun in a deep darkness. A high-pitched whine blew through his ears.

Reuben wanted to move but he felt too ill. His head throbbed. His stomach heaved painfully. The ground beneath him was dipping and tilting. He kept his eyes closed. He dreamed that a great bird came down and its wings blocked the sun. Then little dark mice scampered over his body and nibbled at his hands and his feet. He opened his eyes. He saw the cobbles, grass poking up between the stones, a dried-out bone, a brown apple core and a small red beetle. He rolled over and stared at the sky. When he tried to sit up, he couldn't. His hands and feet were tied.

'Gabe!' he croaked. He stared at the cord around

his wrists. 'Gabe?' His heart began to pound. He felt suddenly very, very cold.

Something was swinging just out of his line of vision. Something was dangling from a tree. Dreading what he would see, he twisted slowly round until he could see it properly.

It was a long rope shaped into a noose.

'Oh, no, no!'

Grandmother. *Swish, swish,* he heard the noise of her skirts rustling as she swayed. *Creak, creak,* went the wood of the gallows.

'No!' he yelled. 'No!' What was happening? Why was there a noose?

He tried to get to his feet but could only make it to his knees. The cobbles dug into him.

He heard nothing and saw nothing, but a second later a hand clamped him on the shoulder and long, hard fingers dug into his flesh and tightened on his bones.

'Reuben.'

'Flyte!'

'Correct.'

Flyte stared down at him. His piercing eyes burned through him.

Reuben thought in a sudden rush: this man is dead. He has no soul. God has abandoned him. No hope for him.

There is no hope for me . . .

'I've been waiting some while, Reuben. I might have taken a chill. That has angered me. I do not like to wait. I am feeling dangerous,' said Flyte. 'Coldly dangerous and full of devilment.'

He seemed to grow taller and more menacing as Reuben looked up at him. 'Our little game is over. Hide and seek, wasn't it? It's done.'

Flyte tossed his hat across the yard. He still wore the long black preacher's coat buttoned tightly up from hem to neck. His hands were encased in black leather gloves; they were poised at his sides, curved like a raven's claws. He flexed his fingers eagerly. 'Done.'

'What?' said Reuben. Or maybe he didn't say anything. He wasn't sure. He tried to speak but his mouth was so dry and his head so full of wild and disjointed words and images, he didn't know. He could not prevent himself from glancing over to the swaying noose. 'What?'

Flyte grinned. 'That's for you, Reuben.' He cocked his head on one side and winked. 'Like your dear old granny, eh? See, I could have killed you plenty of times, Reuben. A dagger ripping through your guts, a blow to the head . . . even a potion, a brew . . . but no, that would have been too quick. I wanted you to suffer, Reuben, in the ways I have suffered.'

Reuben's eyes darted over the scars on Flyte's face
'Yes, yes, take a good look. Scars made by you! So,
Reuben, I deliberated and I considered and I decided
on hanging. That, I said to myself, that, was the worst
possible way for you to go. Your grandmother was
hanged. Hanged by the neck until she was dead. You
wanted to make it easier for her, didn't you?
Remember? *Remember?*'

Reuben's heart was beating crazily. He tried to
concentrate. He tried to keep himself there,
with Flyte, there, right now, but his mind was
slipping back to the moment of his grandmother's
hanging. He could see the folds of her skirts
billowing slightly, her striped petticoat, the scorch
mark on the hem from brushing too close to the
hearth one cold evening . . . then the feel of the
rough cotton between his fingers as he wrapped his
arms round her skirt, her thin legs like chicken legs
beneath it. Then he pulled on her, dragged on her, the
way she'd asked him to, so that she would die quicker.
Yes, he remembered.

Reuben heard Glory bark. He started. He was
confused. He'd forgotten the dog and Gabriel. He
looked round the yard. Where were they? Gabriel,
run and get help, he urged silently. Go and find the
doctor. Get Wilmot. Where are you, Gabe?

'Hush your noise, cur!' Flyte shouted over his

shoulder. 'Don't you wonder at that dog being here, Reuben?' Flyte said as he pulled Reuben to his feet. 'Didn't you wonder where she had gone?'

Reuben shook his head. He stared ahead, willing help to appear. This could not happen. He could not die like this.

'I snatched the dog from that idiot child in Cowper's orchard. Did you not guess, you toad?'

Reuben shook his head again.

Flyte took hold of Reuben's collar. He pulled him over towards the dangling noose.

'No! Help!' Reuben yelped. 'You can't!' He tried to kick, but his legs were tied. He writhed like a worm until Flyte dealt him such a blow on his ear that he stopped. 'Let go! Let me go!'

Reuben dug his heels into the ground: he made himself limp and heavy.

'I will tell you, Reuben – pick up your feet! – I want you to know what I've done. It would be a shame for you to die without appreciating my skill. I want you to know it all . . . I am my lady's preacher and Lord Marley's mystery apothecary . . . Ha! I felt you jump at that! Yes, yes, dear Reuben, it was I that provided that emerald concoction for his rat-faced, washed-up, barren wife. Quack, you once called me. I am no quack! She had no child did she? That was what his Lordship wanted. And murderer, yes! I'm that too!'

He laughed and yanked Reuben hard, making him choke and cough.

Reuben struggled. Suddenly he jerked his head back with all his force, whacking Flyte in the stomach. He heard Flyte gasp. He tried to run, but immediately Flyte hit him again. He was too strong. He dragged Reuben under the tree. Beneath the rope.

'If you try once more to harm me, or escape, I will cut off your nose,' said Flyte, giving him a shake. 'With a blunt knife. Now keep still!'

Reuben kept still.

'You must have thought yourself so clever, toad, the way you ran and hid. When that airs-and-graces Mister Wight locked you up in that hovel, I thought I'd lost you. You were safe from me in there. But you did me a favour getting free. If you hadn't, Mister Wight would've bagged you and the fish-boy and I'd've lost you. Then, 'twas so good of you to fly to Mister Cowper's, Reuben. See, I had to take medicine to Lord Marley – the green concoction. We'd arranged to meet in the orchard . . . And then, ain't this lucky,' he paused for greater effect, 'I recognized that ugly little dog.'

Flyte had twisted the collar of Reuben's jacket so tightly that Reuben could barely breathe. He looked up. The noose was swinging directly above him.

'The maid, the pretty little red-haired maid,' went

on Flyte. 'I liked her . . . What was her name? What was her name, Reuben? You do know it!'

'Mary . . .' croaked Reuben miserably.

'Mary, that's the girl. She was expecting Marley's child, you understand. He needed to know – did it have four legs? Six eyes? His wife had made him a hellish creature before.' He paused. He pushed his face close to Reuben's. 'Hellish.' He nodded to the pigsty home of Gabriel. 'Do you know, that moon-faced boy is his offspring? He didn't want another of those, but he daren't kill it. Odd eh? Wouldn't let me do away with it . . . Mind I think I will, now, 'cos it's your friend, ain't it? If you care for it, I'll snap its head off!' He laughed. 'If the maid's child were healthy, my lord would take it as a good omen. Fool. Rich fool.' He shook Reuben. 'He wasn't having any bastard child take over his estate . . . though Mary's child would've been so pretty . . .'

Flyte released his hold a little while he reached for the circle of the noose.

'Oh, God!' cried Reuben. He coughed. 'You are mad! You and my Lord Marley are both crazed!' he spluttered. 'You killed her! Doctor Brittlebank will find you and—'

'Hold your gulsh! Course I killed her. Enjoyed it too. She was such a pretty thing, creamy skin, red hair . . . Now, I am going to kill you too,' said Flyte, pulling the noose alongside Reuben's face. 'You'll die slowly. Knowing I did it. Knowing I had my revenge. You will curse me and die with foul words on your lips and go to Hell!'

'I hate you,'spluttered Reuben. 'Evil—'

Flyte chuckled. 'That's the way! I believe I am evil,' he said. 'I truly believe – thanks to my maker, whoever that might be – that I am.'

Reuben wriggled and kicked. He tried to throw himself at Flyte, but Flyte was too strong and held him. Flyte slipped the noose over Reuben's head. Reuben felt it lying over his collarbone like a lead weight.

'Let me go!' Reuben shrieked. 'Doctor Brittlebank. Doctor! Help! Help!'

'Quiet!' said Flyte. 'Though you can scream and shout all you like, no one will hear you.'

'I hate you! I hate you!' Reuben screamed, twisting about. 'I should have killed you before! I wish I had!' He did not want to cry but he felt wetness on his cheeks. His voice was no more than a croak: 'I wish I'd done for you, Flyte!'

'I dare say you do, little maggot.' Flyte stepped back.

'Please! Please! I beg you!' Reuben heard himself and loathed himself for pleading but couldn't stop. 'Help me! Please! Flyte, please don't!'

Flyte laughed.

'Your words fall like autumn leaves about my ears,' he said.

Slowly Flyte began to haul up the rope. Reuben felt it below his chin, scratching his bare skin, rubbing against his ears.

'Oh!' Flyte stopped and let the rope slacken. He pushed his face close to Reuben's. 'One last thing. What magic did you do to me, witch's boy? What curse did you use to harm me at Marley Hall?'

Reuben shook his head.

'Now Reuben, you must tell me.'

Deadly nightshade. He wouldn't tell.

'I put a curse on you,' Reuben lied. 'It will make you die. Whatever you do. You'll die. Soon. Horribly. Much, much worse than this!' He could barely speak; the rope held his chin up awkwardly, his toes were brushing the ground. 'Much worse!'

Flyte laughed. He stroked his amulet at his neck. 'I won't die yet. You know it will not happen. I have my toadstone to protect—'

'It's nothing! There's no such thing!' Reuben shouted. 'I know there isn't. There's no stone in a toad's head! It's a lie!'

Flyte pulled the rope tighter. He twisted it round the gatepost to take the strain. Reuben was on his tiptoes, trying to go up with the rope, to take the pressure off. Flyte suddenly jerked the noose. Reuben's chin snapped up, his head flew back and his feet left the ground. His tied hands flew up, desperate to loosen it. His fingers picked and pulled at it.

'*You're* lying. Now *you'll* die,' said Flyte.

Reuben screamed but no sound came out. He kicked and felt space beneath him. He twitched like an eel on a line. The rope tightened more. Keep still, be still, said a voice inside him, and he tried to keep still because moving made it worse, but he couldn't stop his limbs from jerking about wildly. They would not rest.

My head! It will burst!

He spun round when he twisted. Through his half-open eyes he saw the wall and trees go past in a blur. For an instant, the old shed appeared and Reuben saw an angel above it. A white face. Kind eyes. Then it was gone. Now he knew he would die. Was nearly dead.

Grandmother!

His body flipped and flapped like a fish on a hook.

His ears ached. Blood poured into his brain, boiling-hot blood that squeezed behind his eyes, pulsed crazily through his temples. His eyes burned, gold and bronze and crimson. Something popped and banged deep inside his skull.

He couldn't breathe. He sucked and sucked and

tried to get air into his lungs but the rope was too tight. He couldn't swallow. His tongue was too big for his mouth. He spat, he wheezed, he choked.

He heard a ghastly rasping croak, but didn't know that it was he who made it as he tried to grab, to bite at the air. He tried . . . *Plahp. Plahp.* His lips plopped together feebly, like a trout out of water.

He could not breathe; it was as if his nose and mouth were stuffed with sawdust. *Plahp, plahp* . . .

A creeping dark, a black numbness seeped through him; he felt it travelling up the veins in his legs and arms and oozing, like tar, into his lungs. Blackness wormed its way along invisible tracks into his head. The dark was complete. His ears were blocked with it. His mouth. His eyes.

Silence lapped around.

He stopped kicking.

He swung. He was a toy on a string, swaying, back and forth.

He was going to die.

31

Hanging

Flyte laughed. He stepped back from the swaying body and leaned against the wall of the dilapidated shed. He took the toadstone – a small mottled pebble, shaped like a toad – from the leather purse where he kept it. He set it on his palm and wrapped his fingers tightly round it.

Glory shot out from the bushes, as if from a spring. Her lead trailed behind her. She galloped to Reuben.

'You're next,' said Flyte, winking at her. 'And I've half a mind to skin you and eat you. For amusement!'

Glory jumped up. She yapped at Reuben's spinning toes.

'Shut up! Hold your gulsh, you fleabag! Mongrel! Cur!'

Flyte did not notice that there was someone on the roof behind him. He did not hear the soft slithering sounds the small figure made as it crawled over the broken tiles of the shed towards him.

Gabriel crept up to the very edge where the stone copings were loose and peered over. He muttered to himself as he looked back and forward from Flyte to Reuben. Dribble trailed from his mouth.

Flyte watched Reuben. 'Neck's not broke,' he said under his breath. 'I didn't jolt you enough, you little piece of scum. Maggot. Toad's arse. It'll take longer now . . . Do you hear me, Reuben?' he roared. 'You'll take an age to die. May it pain you!'

Flyte's shouting blocked out the noises above him.

By the time Flyte did hear something, it was too late. He glanced up in surprise, sensing something was there, wondering if perhaps there was a cat on the roof. It was not a cat. It was the idiot boy, staring down at him.

'Wha—?' he cried.

Gabriel lurched and pushed against the old stone coping. The stones were held together by dry dust and weeds. They burst apart. A great ball of stones and grit and roof tiles flew down.

Flyte did not have time to move. He fell. The toadstone flew from his fingers.

Gabriel had propelled himself against the loose stones with such force that he couldn't stop; his momentum threw him forward. He somersaulted through the air, a whirr of flaying arms, and legs that ran in air. He landed on the cobbles amidst fallen tiles and stones.

The fall would have killed some.

Gabriel opened his eyes. Something, some deep, desperate need, forced him to move. He had to get up. 'R'ban. R'ban.' He looked at the swinging body.

Gabriel whimpered as he stood. He pushed his hand hard against his belly, as if he feared his insides were coming out. He winced. There was blood trickling from his nose and mouth.

Flyte groaned. Gabriel ignored him. He limped over to Reuben.

Reuben hung from the tree like a dead bird, head on one side. Slack and silent. Swinging gently.

Gabriel stared at Reuben. He stuck his own tongue out, the way Reuben stuck out his.

'R'ban?' He reached up for Reuben's dangling legs. He wrapped his arms round his shins. 'R'ban? Com'on!'

He pulled on him with all his might.

32

Wilmot Remembers the Lambs

Wilmot had been searching for Gabriel. He heard Glory's crazed barking and he ran as fast as he could. It did not take him long to reach them.

'Dear God!' He saw Flyte lying all twisted and broken-looking; his eyes staring sightlessly up at the clouds. He saw Reuben. He leaped towards him. 'Let go, Gabriel!' he roared at him. 'Let go!'

Gabriel clung even tighter. Glory bounced in a circle round them, yipping.

Quickly, Wilmot untied the rope from the gatepost. Reuben slipped to the ground. Gabriel fell too, still wrapped around his legs. He rubbed his blood-smeared face into Reuben's clothes.

'Leave him, Gabriel!'

Glory danced about, trying to lick Reuben's face. Wilmot swatted at her. 'Oh, my God! My God!' he said.

'R'ban, R'ban, R'ban . . .' Gabriel chanted, holding on tightly. 'Gone, gone.'

Wilmot frantically loosened the noose from Reuben's neck. His fingers were as unwieldy as a fistful of sausages. Tenderly he stretched Reuben out flat. 'Reuben, poor boy . . .'

Reuben's skin was tinged with blue. His lips were swollen and purple. The whites of his eyes peeped through his open lids.

'No, lad, no! I won't have this!' cried Wilmot. 'You're not to be dead, I won't have it! Reuben, no! I'm saying no!'

He shook Reuben's limp and lifeless body.

'That devil! Flyte did this!' Wilmot said to no one. He quickly untied Reuben's hands and legs. 'Thank the Lord that scoundrel's dead or I should be forced to do it, wring his blithering neck like a cockerel's. No more Flyte.'

'N'more,' echoed Gabriel.

'Reuben!' Wilmot shook Reuben roughly. 'Come back to us!' He put his face close to Reuben's. 'Come back, d'you hear?'

Time stood still. Reuben did not move.

'Oh, dear God, what'll I do?' Wilmot looked around the yard for inspiration. In an instant he remembered. A young lamb of Jack Sowerby's had been left out in a deep frost and froze. Jack had rubbed it all over, like Wilmot was rubbing Reuben's lifeless limbs now, then he'd blown down the lamb's nostrils. He'd done its breathing for it. And it had lived.

'Don't tell no one I did this!' he warned Gabriel. 'I could just as easy kill him, I'm thinking, as save him. Damn me, I wish you were here now, Jack Sowerby, my friend. I don't know what to do, but he's near dead and … God damn that Flyte!'

He quickly slipped his arm under Reuben's head. He lifted Reuben's chin and placed his own mouth over Reuben's lips and nose. He blew gently. Beneath him he felt Reuben's chest rise as his breath inflated him. 'Take it easy, Wilmot, take care!' he told himself. 'You'll break them little ribs if you blows too hard. Take care, you big oaf.' He blew more gently this time, then again and again, feeling Reuben's chest rising and falling. He gazed at Reuben's face. 'Look, look there, Gabriel! It's not so blue! See his lips is pink now!'

'Com'on,' said Gabriel.

Wilmot shook Reuben gently. 'That's it. Hear your friend? Come on, come on!' He rubbed Reuben and chaffed his cheeks. 'You're coming back! You are! You will come back!'

Reuben suddenly twitched. His face twisted in a sort of spasm. His limbs flayed around as if he were fighting some invisible force; he beat his heels on the ground. He shuddered from head to toe. Then every sinew and muscle went rigid. His arms and legs shot out so that for a moment he was like a wooden doll. Wilmot held on to him tightly.

'Stop! Calm down. Oh, Reuben . . .'

Suddenly Reuben opened his mouth. He gulped in air. He breathed.

'That's it! He will do, he will, you know!' cried Wilmot. 'Thank God!' He rubbed Reuben's chest. He pulled his clothes straight. 'Oh, Reuben!' He picked him up and made for the gate. 'Come on, young fellow. Follow me, Gabriel. Come.'

Gabriel stopped beside Flyte. 'R'ven?' he said. 'R'ven man.'

'What do you say? Don't worry about him. The man is dead at last. Come on. As quick as you can now.'

Wilmot raced along the meadow path, his sturdy short legs buckling every now and then beneath Reuben's weight.

'There, there, young fellow,' Wilmot muttered. 'There, there. Soon be home. Soon be back. Hold on there. Doctor'll set you right. Doctor'll mend you.'

Gabriel trailed along behind him. His twisted feet snagged in the tussocks of dry grass. He stumbled and tripped. Each time he jarred himself he winced and pressed his fist to his belly. Blood seeped from his nose.

Glory trotted beside them, trailing her lead.

Wilmot almost wept with relief and joy when he saw Doctor Brittlebank coming towards him. 'Hello!' he yelled. 'I've got him! Reuben's all right!'

Reuben was put to bed to recover – the same bed he had slept in before – though he didn't know it. He was too ill to care.

Doctor Brittlebank spun a story to Lady Marley. Reuben had a fever, he told her and must be isolated. Lady Marley was only too pleased to keep away. She had her unborn baby to consider.

Reuben spent two days in a dreamy haze. He woke enough to take broth and to sip the doctor's potions, but little else. But on the third day, he was much recovered.

He opened his eyes.

Sitting beside him, he saw a small man with his grey wig pushed to the back of his bald head. His spectacles were balanced on the end of his nose. His lips were moving as he read silently. Reuben looked at what he was reading: *Observations & Experiments made on the Blood & Blood Vessels of Animals* . . .

'Doctor, dear Doctor . . .' Reuben's voice came out as a croak.

'Hello,' said Doctor Brittlebank. He put down his pamphlet and patted Reuben's hand. 'There,

there. Don't weep. You are safe now.'

Reuben nodded. He put his hands up to his throat and felt around tenderly. 'Sore,' he whispered.

'I wager it is,' said Doctor Brittlebank. 'I'm glad to hear your voice. So glad to see you awake.' He brushed Reuben's hair from his damp forehead. 'Do you remember what happened?'

Reuben shook his head. 'I remember Glory barking and—' he sat up with a groan. 'Gabriel, where is he? Oh, poor Mary!' His voice cracked. He sank back again, feeling giddy.

The doctor smoothed the bed covers. 'Hush now. It's all right.'

'What happened?' Reuben croaked. 'I don't understand? Am I ill?'

Doctor Brittlebank smiled at him. 'You have been ill. I'm glad you don't remember . . . Flyte is dead.'

Reuben gasped. 'Dead? Truly?' Just the mention of Flyte's name had set his heart hammering.

The doctor had hold of Reuben's wrist and felt his pulse flare. 'Now, now, I shall not tell you a thing if you take on so,' he said. 'Settle down.'

'I promise,' said Reuben, sinking back on the pillows. 'I am wearing your nightshirt. I am sorry . . .'

'You've sweated your way through two already.'

'I'm sorry. So sorry . . . Oh, but I am so glad to

hear about Flyte. It's terrible, but I am glad. How did he die?'

'Some of the old building at the ruins fell on him. It was most fortuitous. If they hadn't, you would not be here now.'

'Oh,' said Reuben.

'He tried to kill you, Reuben, by hanging you from a tree . . .'

'I remember a hanging . . . I thought I saw my grandmother . . .'

'You were very, very lucky. Your neck did not break. You nearly suffocated, but Wilmot reached you just in time.'

'Wilmot?' Reuben peered round the bedchamber. Through the window he glanced a pale grey sky and the tops of distant trees. Candles burned. Bunches of herbs by the fire filled the air with pungent smells. But no Wilmot.

'We'd never have managed without Wilmot. I have sent him back to his cockerels. He wanted to stay but I knew he needed to get home. He has promised to come and visit us at Wycke House. Now, where was I? Yes, Flyte is dead. And so is Mary Beasley, the maid who'd gone missing.'

'I remember. Her belly . . .' said Reuben. He flexed his neck muscles and rubbed at his aching jaw. 'Her baby's gone. I can recall some things Flyte told me . . . He did work for Lord Marley.'

The doctor nodded. 'We found signed papers that prove my lord's involvement. Flyte made the green potion.'

Reuben nodded weakly. He knew.

'When we brought little Gabriel in, George was mighty alarmed. "Don't let her Ladyship see him," he said. "Keep him hid!" So he knew too,' said Doctor Brittlebank. He sighed. 'I have spoken to an old woman living in the gatehouse. A Mistress Foster – George took me to her. She was midwife. She looked after Gabriel till Mary had charge of him.'

'Poor Gabriel.'

'I surmise that Lord Marley took one look at the baby and said "Get rid of it!" Mistress Foster didn't hold with that. She kept the baby alive somehow. Mistress Foster passed the job to Mary.'

'She lives at the gatehouse, you say?' Reuben suddenly remembered the sour-faced old lady at the gatehouse window when they had first arrived at Marley Hall. 'And then Mary became pregnant . . . You cannot hide such things in a big house like this, not from the staff anyway, though you can hide unwanted heirs from the Lady of the Manor, it appears. Lady Marley sent Mary away . . . She may have suspected who the father was . . .'

There was a knock on the door and Catherine the

maid put her head around. She smiled at Reuben.

'Awake, young lad? How's the fever?'

'Diminishing,' said Doctor Brittlebank. 'He's on the mend.'

'I won't come in, case it be contagious,' said Catherine, 'but her Ladyship wants a word.'

'Very well,' said the doctor.

'Remember my tale,' said Doctor Brittlebank. 'You were taken ill. Covered in spots. Fever.'

Lady Marley came to the door. She held a sprig of herbs to her nose and a lace handkerchief to her lips.

'I wanted to see the boy with my own eyes,' said her Ladyship. 'He is alive? He is getting better?'

'See for yourself. But don't come near,' said Doctor Brittlebank. 'I would never forgive myself if—'

'Yes. Nor would I,' said Lady Marley. She stroked her belly. 'I know this child is well. It is beautiful.'

'I am so pleased,' croaked Reuben.

'The boy sounds very ill.' Lady Marley backed out. 'I will pray for him.' She disappeared.

Reuben lay back against the pillows. His head hurt. His throat hurt. 'Can we go back to Wycke House? I do want to go home.'

'As soon as you are strong enough.'

They sat in silence for a while. Doctor Brittlebank read his pamphlet. After a while, Reuben said, 'Why is Gabriel the way he is?'

The doctor shook his head. 'I cannot say. It's God's mysterious will.'

'What about Lord Marley?' said Reuben. 'Where is he?'

Doctor Brittlebank shrugged. 'Lord Marley's fine doctors have taken him to Bedlam Hospital to be cured. Hah! I fear he might not recover in there! The cures are wickedly cruel in my opinion. Indeed I rather hope that he does not get cured, but that is very unChristian of me.' He smiled at Reuben. 'There, now, you look weary, shall I go?'

'I will never forgive you if you do.'

Doctor Brittlebank grinned. 'Lord Marley believed it was Lady Marley's fault the child was born as it was. When I see such madness in a man, I wonder if it can be so. Even though the child grows inside the woman, might there not be something in the man's blood or spirit that makes a child so unnatural?'

'Or the Devil?'

'Perhaps. But then why are not *all* mad people, robbers and heathens ugly and deformed?'

Reuben shook his head. 'Why did Lord Marley want Flyte to kill Mary?'

'Who knows?' Doctor Brittlebank shook his head. 'Maybe Mary threatened him? Maybe he was impatient to see the child?'

'Lord Marley became deranged when he saw Gabriel,' Reuben said. 'No one could understand why . . .'

Doctor Brittlebank nodded. 'It must have been a hideous shock. Imagine! Like seeing a ghost!'

'Lady Marley has a son,' said Reuben quietly. 'We should tell her.'

Doctor Brittlebank shook his head. 'I don't think so. I don't think she would find it easy to love him, do you? She is happy now. And . . .'

Doctor Brittlebank had gone very still.

'What?' Reuben tensed. 'Is it Gabriel? What is it?' Reuben asked. He sat up and grabbed the doctor's hand. 'There's more, isn't there? What are you hiding from me?'

'Gabriel,' said Doctor Brittlebank. 'He is not well.'

'What's the matter with him?'

The doctor shook his head. 'I do not know. He won't or can't tell me. He won't let me near. Are you able to walk?'

'Yes.'

'Come on then.'

Reuben got out of bed slowly. His legs were as soft as jelly. He almost fell and had to sit back on the bed to gather his strength.

'You are not well, either,' said Doctor Brittlebank. He helped Reuben to his feet. 'You need to rest.'

'I am well enough. Please take me to see him, please. I might be able to get him to talk. I can understand him. We are friends but he will be fearful of you . . .'

'Come, then.'

33

Gabriel

The doctor helped Reuben into the adjoining room. 'We've kept Gabriel hidden,' he said. 'It has not been too difficult. Lady Marley keeps to her room. Truth does not interest her. Catherine and George have been surprisingly loyal . . .'

In a small side chamber, Gabriel lay on a narrow white bed, very still, very quiet. Candles flickered around the room. The curtains were drawn. It was gloomy and the room smelled of sickness despite bowls of lavender.

Gabriel looked different. His skin was clean. His thin hair was washed and fluffed around his face like a dandelion clock. There were no bandages on his hands; they looked very pink against the white linen. They were very ugly. Reuben knew that the doctor was right: Lady Marley would not have loved this boy.

Gabriel lay on his back with his hands pressed together as if in prayer. At his feet, Glory lay curled in a tight ball. She uncurled and thumped her tail when she saw Reuben, then after a pause, got off the bed to greet him.

Reuben patted her gently. 'Good girl. Good dog. Are you looking after Gabe?'

Glory wagged her tail, gave him a lick, and jumped back on to the end of the bed.

The doctor shook his head. 'If only I knew what had happened! He is loathe to let me touch him. He speaks of the ravens and Mary, but that is all I understand. He has a fever most of the time. He is bleeding inside, I am certain, but from what I have no clue. His belly is swollen and painful. I don't know, but I suspect Flyte did this. It is serious, Reuben.'

Reuben slithered down to his knees beside Gabriel. Gabriel turned his flat, white face to his. He smiled.

'R'ven man. Gone,' said Gabriel.

'He talks a lot about the raven-man,' said Doctor Brittlebank. 'It's time for his medicine.' He poured some powder out of a square of paper and mixed it with water in a glass. 'This will ease the pain.'

Reuben helped Gabriel to sip the drink.

'Who is it? Is it Flyte that's the raven-man? Flyte snatched Glory from him, Doctor. Gabe might even have seen him kill Mary . . . Drink up,' Reuben added. 'Come on.'

Gabriel smiled. 'Com'on,' he said. 'Com'on, R'ban.' His voice was weak and small.

Reuben thought Gabriel had shrunk since he'd last seen him. Now he was so very thin, the blue veins showed clearly in the translucent skin at his temple. His eyes looked bigger than ever; stranger than ever.

'Yes, here I am, Gabe.' Reuben could barely speak. Tears clogged his throat. 'Here I am.' He smoothed out the sheets and stroked Gabriel's arm. 'I don't think he cares he's ill, Doctor. I think he's happy. He's smiling. Always that smile.'

Gabriel lay very still. He kept his hands together, pointing heavenwards.

'Do you know why he insists on lying like that?' asked Doctor Brittlebank, quietly. 'It is very strange.'

'The knight. The knight looked like him,' said Reuben. 'Oh, Doctor, he means to die, and to die like a knight. He's even got his dog at his feet . . . Is there nothing we can do?'

Doctor Brittlebank shook his head. 'Even if I knew what was wrong with him,' he said, 'I don't think we could save him. It's his insides. Something is broken or punctured. He is sinking and he doesn't seem to mind. I've given him powdered valerian to help him sleep and a salix and betonica infusion for the pain.'

Reuben shook Gabriel gently. 'Oh, Gabriel! Come on, Gabe. Surely we can do something? Tell me what happened. Tell me how we can help you.'

Gabriel smiled secretively. 'Mary gone,' he whispered. 'R'ven man. Come. Com'on, Lory.' He patted the sheet until Glory responded and inched her way up to him. She lay full length beside him with her snout pressed into his neck. She whined and snuffled against him. Gabriel stroked her head. 'Lory. Lory. R'ban.'

'Glory will stay with you. I'll stay with you.'

The doctor patted Reuben on the shoulder. 'You must go back to your bed,' he said. 'You're not strong, either. I see you're shivering.'

'No, I can't go. I must be with him,' said Reuben. 'He likes me here, I know. See how he smiles at me? I don't want him to think I've left him – like Mary did. Please, let's take his bed into my room. I need to be with him.'

Doctor Brittlebank sighed and nodded. He got up. 'I'll call George to help me move the mattress.'

'What happened, Gabe? If you could tell us, then the doctor could help. Doctor Brittlebank is good. He's kind. Can't you say what the matter is? Was it Flyte? Did he hurt you? Did you eat some bad berries?'

Gabriel closed his eyes and turned his face into

Glory's fur. He breathed in deeply. 'Com'on,' he said very softly.

'Come on what? Who?'

'Angel.'

'Oh Gabriel, I wish I understood you better. I wish, I hope . . .' He couldn't say his thoughts out loud.

Gabriel wants to die, that was what he thought. He's letting go. Giving up and dying. Poor, poor little thing . . .

Doctor Brittlebank came back in quietly. He put his hand on Reuben's shoulder. 'He has not had a happy life,' he said, 'but you know, Reuben, I think you made it a little better.'

'Folk we met were cruel to him. Catherine was not kind. No one can just love him. Not even me . . . because . . . because he is so different.'

'Poor child,' said the doctor. 'It should not be so.'

They moved Gabriel into Reuben's chamber. They built up the fire. Doctor Brittlebank gave him more medicine. He took the boy's pulse and laid a cool, damp cloth on his forehead.

Reuben got into his own bed. He still felt weak and his throat pained him greatly when he swallowed. He lay and watched Gabriel. He tried to stay awake, but he slept.

In the middle of the night, he was woken by Glory

whimpering and scratching at the floor beside Gabriel's bed. As if she was trying to dig there. Reuben jerked awake, his nerves tingling. A terrible coldness crept through his limbs.

'Glory! What is it? Hush!'

He slipped out of bed, pulled a cover over his shoulders and went to Gabriel's bedside.

'Gabe?'

Gabriel's skin was a startling white. A soft pearly sheen covered his skin. His big eyes were open. His breathing was quick and rasping. His weird cupid mouth turned in a smile when he saw Reuben.

'Hello, Gabe. It's me. May I get you something?'

'Out,' Gabriel said in a tiny voice. 'Gone out. I gone. Out.'

'Oh, Gabe . . . I should have been kinder. Done more . . . I wish I could have made you better. I swear when I'm a doctor I'll make babies better, and children. Everyone. Gabe. Don't go.'

'Gone.'

Gabriel closed his eyes. His breathing grew very rapid. His chest heaved and fell with a dreadful dry sound, like a saw sawing hard, dry wood. Then it stopped. It just stopped.

Glory whimpered.

Reuben rested his forehead against the edge of the mattress. 'Goodbye, boy,' he whispered.

Gabriel had died. Reuben looked for a spirit flying up to Heaven. For a sign. But there was nothing that he could see. Where was the difference? he wondered. Why was there a difference? What happened to Gabriel's heart? Why? It was no longer beating. Blood no longer pulsed through his veins. His lungs didn't inflate. His eyes didn't see.

Reuben stared and stared. Gabriel was so still. His lips and skin were grey . . . His arms crossed over his chest, those hands . . . So like the stone effigies in the church.

Except for his smile, thought Reuben, which is the sweetest smile that I have ever seen.

'Peace, peace,' whispered Reuben. 'Goodbye.'

In the early morning, long before Lady Marley was awake, George and old Smithy and Doctor Brittlebank carried Gabriel's body out of the house. Reuben followed them out to the family plot behind the Hall.

'We should have a preacher,' muttered old Smithy. He sucked on his blackened pipe. 'We should have a Bible reading and prayers and the like. 'Tisn't proper like this.'

'I agree,' said Doctor Brittlebank, 'but I am afraid we must keep this incident a secret.'

'I know, I know. I said I would, didn't I?' grumbled

the old man. 'But I never was employed to dig graves. 'Tis not work for a man like me—'

'Hush your complaining,' said George. He handed him a small bottle. 'Take a swig of this. This'll sort you.'

Old Smithy glugged from the bottle gratefully.

The old man had lifted the Marley gravestone. There was no grave beneath it, so he had had to dig a hole. They lay Gabriel's body down on the grass beside it. It was wrapped in white linen. It looked very small.

Doctor Brittlebank read a short prayer from the Bible he had brought and then they gently slipped Gabriel's body into the ground.

Reuben shut his eyes while they replaced the earth. He listened to the sound of the soil pattering down on the linen. He hoped Gabriel couldn't feel it. Far away he heard a raven call. *One for sorrow*. What a short, unhappy life Gabriel had had.

'Could we put his name on it now?' he said.

Doctor Brittlebank shook his head. 'I wish we could. No, he must remain a secret. The child that never was.'

Here lies the remains of an infant child born and died August 21 1674.

'In a way he has come home,' said Reuben. 'He will truly lie here, where he should be. At last.'

* * *

Wycke House was bathed in October sunlight; its walls were tinted a pale golden-yellow, the glass in the windows glinted. There were still some roses falling around the porch. The tall pale pink and purple hollyhocks were looking ragged, their leaves were full of holes, but Reuben still thought they were the best flowers in the world. Just as he thought Wycke House was the best house in the world and Hetty was the best maid.

Reuben was leaning on the garden gate, watching the lane. Waiting. Glory was not allowed out of the garden because she yipped at any passing horses and she chased the geese. She had pushed her nose through the bars of the gate. She was waiting too.

At last they heard a wagon. Reuben went still as he concentrated. He heard a great deal of wood and leather creaking. A wobbling wheel. A large horse plodding. It could be anyone at all . . .

Reuben opened the gate and rushed into the lane. Glory followed him, yapping with excitement.

'Wilmot!'

It *was* Wilmot. Reuben recognized his faded blue wagon, and big brown-and-white horse.

Reuben ran towards them, waving his arms above his head and calling. Slowly the wagon ambled up to him. Wilmot put out his arm and swung Reuben up beside him.

'Young lad! Young fellow! It's good to see you!' he said. 'And you're looking mighty fit and well, that's good! How are you? How's the good doctor? How's everything?'

'It's all wonderful, Wilmot. How are your cockerels? How did Blackie do at the fight? Did he win?'

'Aye, he did win,' said Wilmot. He laughed shortly. 'He beat Rob Hampton's cockerel – Mister Crow, he called it – and it did crow, poor blighter, when Blackie got it. Mind, I don't like to see a cockerel worked over so bad, but it was gratifying, it truly were, that my Blackie won. And they none of them had a clue about me and you and little Gabriel escaping that night, you know. They're still talking in Easton Pacey about the fish-boy and his friend that flew up the chimney and disappeared!' He laughed and slapped his knee. ''Twas a good trick!'

'Here we are!' cried Reuben as the wagon drew level with Wycke House. 'Stop!'

Wilmot steered the cart into the yard behind the house. Reuben went with him into the stable and showed him where everything was. They made the horse comfortable with hay and water. Reuben could hear noises from the kitchen. He thought he saw Hetty's skirt flash past the open door.

He wished that Hetty would come out, but he knew she'd be shy.

'Do hurry, Wilmot. Please. Doctor Brittlebank will be so pleased to see you.'

At last Wilmot was ready. Reuben dragged him across the yard to the kitchen. It was deserted. A big copper pan bubbled and steamed on the fire. There was the warm, comforting scent of newly baked bread.

'She's not here. She *was* here. She's so lovely, Wilmot . . . Oh, well. I'll go and get the doctor.'

'I'll sit here and wait, then,' said Wilmot.

'But you must come into the house. The doctor will be in his study!'

'I'll sit here, if you don't mind.' Wilmot sat down in the Windsor chair by the fire. The tabby cat leaped into his lap. 'See, cat knows. This is where I does belong.'

Reuben went to find the doctor. 'I won't be a moment!' he called. Glory raced along at his heels. Oh, I'm so glad he's here, thought Reuben. Now if only I can get Hetty to like him. I must, somehow! They really would make such a fine pair.

It took longer than he liked to find the doctor – he was right down the end of the garden talking to the bees. When Reuben came back with him, Hetty was in the kitchen, sitting at the scrubbed table, cutting up potatoes. The room was still and quiet. Almost as if, thought Reuben, Hetty and Wilmot had just stopped an animated talk.

He looked from one to the other. They did look strange.

'Here's Wilmot!' Reuben said.

Doctor Brittlebank shook Wilmot's hand warmly. 'So good of you to visit. Splendid. We will go into Stonebridge on the morrow. There's a man selling cockerels you might be interested to meet. And we could go fishing in the afternoon, what do you say?'

'If Mistress Hetty would fancy cooking fish for our supper? Do you think she would? I love fish myself,' said Wilmot.

Hetty's face was hidden below folds of white linen.

'Sorry, Wilmot. Hetty doesn't like fish,' said Reuben. 'She says they're smelly.'

'Hush your nonsense,' said Hetty. 'A trout is a tasty fish, you know I think it. I love a fish all baked with tarragon. What are you thinking about Reuben, lad?'

'Nothing,' said Reuben.

Except how strange you grown-ups are.

Reuben went to wish Doctor Brittlebank a goodnight. The doctor was in his study. He was looking at some complicated diagrams and some writing from a fellow at the Royal Society.

'Goodnight, my boy,' said the doctor. 'We really must start you on some studies soon, you know. I think I should send you to school. What do you think?'

Reuben swallowed hard. 'Perhaps,' he said. 'Though I think I would rather stay here and study with you. You make a fine teacher, I think.'

He looked up at the shelves where the doctor kept his specimens, glass phials, bottles and powders. He was going to try and impress the doctor by naming something.

He saw a pearly-skinned fish in a bottle. Without warning, he was transported back to Lord Marley's chamber of horrors. In a flash, he saw the lord's collection of preserved animals and body parts. The baby pigs. Baby hedgehogs.

The pale *human* baby . . . The baby that wasn't ready to be born.

'Oh! Oh!'

'What is it, Reuben?' The doctor got up in alarm. 'Are you ill?'

'No, but that baby! That baby in the jar at Lord Marley's . . . Do you suppose it was Mary's baby? I am sure it was! Remember how proud he was? How he relished it so?'

Doctor Brittlebank's face furrowed with concern as he considered what Reuben was saying.

'I think you are right, by God. He preserved his own infant, had it there in a bottle to gaze upon whenever he wished. He could see his own child every day and be certain that this baby, at least, was normal . . . Was it normal, Reuben?'

Reuben shrugged. 'I really cannot say. I didn't stare at it. I was upset. It was sad even then, not knowing what I know now, to see such a baby . . .'

They stared at each other.

'I hope Lord Marley never gets out of Bedlam!' said Doctor Brittlebank.

'And I hope Lady Marley has a beautiful baby with all its necessary parts and pieces,' said Reuben.

Doctor Brittlebank patted Reuben's shoulder. 'Well, she should have had you, lad, then, shouldn't she? You have all your bits and pieces, plus extras! I even offered her money to take you off my hands, but—'

'Doctor!'

'Ah, Reuben. Don't fret. I'm teasing. Run along to bed. There is nothing for you to worry about now – except Latin and mathematics.'

Reuben ran upstairs to his tiny bedchamber with Glory scampering along beside him, her nails click-clacking on the oak floorboards.

Reuben patted the smooth worn-down top step on the flight of stairs. He ran for his bed. As he flung back the bed curtains, lavender and beeswax scents filled the air. Glorious smells.

He lay in his bed with Glory at his side. From the kitchen below he could hear the murmur of voices. He knew it was Wilmot and Hetty. He smiled. Glory licked his chin.

Reuben and Glory both fell asleep dreaming about Gabriel.